The Compass Rose

Books by Ursula K. Le Guin

Novels

The Beginning Place
Malafrena
Very Far Away from Anywhere Else
The Word for World Is Forest
The Dispossessed
The Lathe of Heaven
The Farthest Shore
The Tombs of Atuan
A Wizard of Earthsea
The Left Hand of Darkness
City of Illusions
Planet of Exile
Rocannon's World

Short Stories

The Compass Rose
Orsinian Tales
The Wind's Twelve Quarters

For Children

Leese Webster

Poetry and Criticism

Hard Words
The Language of the Night
From Elfland to Poughkeepsie
Wild Angels

The Compass Rose

Short Stories by
Ursula K. Le Guin

HARPER & ROW, PUBLISHERS, New York

Cambridge, Philadelphia, San Francisco,

1817 London, Mexico City, São Paulo, Sydney

FIRST EDITION

Designed by Robin Malkin

Library of Congress Cataloging in Publication Data

Le Guin, Ursula K., date
    The compass rose.

    I. Title.
PS3562.E42C6   1982   813'.54   81–48158
ISBN 0–06–014988–4   AACR2

---

82 83 84 85 86 10 9 8 7 6 5 4 3 2 1

Contents

Preface

BY CALLING this book *The Compass Rose* I hoped to suggest that some pattern or coherence may be perceived in it, while indicating that the stories it contains tend to go off each in its own direction. They take place all over the map, including the margins. It is not even clear to me what the map is a map of. A mind, no doubt; presumably the author's. But I expect there is more to it than that. One's mind is never simply one's own, even at birth, and ever less so as one lives, learns, loses, etc.

The four directions, NESW, of the Rose of the Winds, our magnetic compass, converge into or arise out of an unspoken fifth direction, the center, the corolla of the rose.

Many of the American peoples who were dispossessed by the compass-guided invaders from the East structured their world upon the four wind directions (or half-directions) and two more, Above and Below, also radial to the center/self/here and now, which may sacramentally contain the other six, and thus the Universe. This is the compass in four dimensions, spatial and temporal, material and spiritual, the Rose of the New World.

As a guide to sailors this book is not to be trusted. Perhaps it is too sensitive to local magnetic fields.

Within it, various circling motions may be perceived, as between the first and last stories, and the fourth and seventeenth. It gives rise to apparent excursions outward which are in fact incursions inward, such as the eleventh story; while the only piece describing a place whose objective reality may be confirmed on a present-day map of present-day Earth, the seventh, is perhaps the most subjective one of the lot.

As for the reasons why a particular story is assigned to a particular direction, they are not very serious. Nadir may be down underground, for instance, or in the depths, or simply downhearted. The organising principle may be historical, or poetical, or literal. Surely one of the means of learning to know the world as alive with symbol and meaning is to cultivate the art of taking things literally?

The title of an earlier collection of my stories was *The Wind's Twelve Quarters,* a compass borrowed from A. E. Housman. To this one, let me set as motto a French poem of Rainer Maria Rilke, from the group *Les Roses.*

> *Est-ce en exemple que tu te proposes?*
> *Peut-on se remplir comme les roses,*
> *en multipliant sa subtile matière*
> *qu'on avait fait pour ne rien faire?*
>
> *Car ce n'est pas travailler que d'être*
> *une rose, dirait-on.*
> *Dieu, en regardant par la fenêtre,*
> *fait la maison.*

In English, Rilke asks the rose something like this:

> *Is it as a model you propose*
> *yourself? Can one be filled up like a rose*
> *by multiplying one's subtle stuff?*
> *Is make-work enough?*
>
> *For really, you can't call it work,*
> *to be a rose.*
> *God, while looking out the window,*
> *keeps the house.*

Ursula K. Le Guin

The Compass Rose

Nadir

The Author of the Acacia Seeds

And Other Extracts from the *Journal of the Association of Therolinguistics*

MS. FOUND IN AN ANTHILL

THE MESSAGES were found written in touch-gland exudation on degerminated acacia seeds laid in rows at the end of a narrow, erratic tunnel leading off from one of the deeper levels of the colony. It was the orderly arrangement of the seeds that first drew the investigator's attention.

The messages are fragmentary, and the translation approximate and highly interpretative; but the text seems worthy of interest if only for its striking lack of resemblance to any other Ant texts known to us.

Seeds 1–13

[I will] not touch feelers. [I will] not stroke. [I will] spend on dry seeds [my] soul's sweetness. It may be found when [I am] dead. Touch this dry wood! [I] call! [I am] here!

Alternatively, this passage may be read:

[Do] not touch feelers. [Do] not stroke. Spend on dry seeds [your] soul's sweetness. [Others] may find it when [you are] dead. Touch this dry wood! Call: [I am] here!

No known dialect of Ant employs any verbal person except the third person singular and plural and the first person plural. In this text, only the root forms of the verbs are used; so there is no way to decide whether the passage was intended to be an autobiography or a manifesto.

Seeds 14–22

Long are the tunnels. Longer is the untunneled. No tunnel reaches the end of the untunneled. The untunneled goes on farther than we can go in ten days [*i.e.,* forever]. Praise!

The mark translated "Praise!" is half of the customary salutation "Praise the Queen!" or "Long live the Queen!" or "Huzza for the Queen!" — but the word/mark signifying "Queen" has been omitted.

Seeds 23–29

As the ant among foreign-enemy ants is killed, so the ant without ants dies, but being without ants is as sweet as honeydew.

An ant intruding in a colony not its own is usually killed. Isolated from other ants, it invariably dies within a day or so. The difficulty in this passage is the word/mark "without ants," which we take to mean "alone" — a concept for which no word/mark exists in Ant.

Seeds 30–31

Eat the eggs! Up with the Queen!

There has already been considerable dispute over the interpretation of the phrase on Seed 31. It is an important question, since all the preceding seeds can be fully understood only in the light cast by this ultimate exhortation. Dr. Rosbone ingeniously argues that the author, a wingless neuter-female worker, yearns hopelessly to be a winged male, and to found a new colony, flying upward in the nuptial flight with a new Queen. Though the text certainly permits such a reading, our conviction is that nothing in the text *supports* it — least of all the text of the immediately preceding seed, No. 30: "Eat the eggs!" This reading, though shocking, is beyond disputation.

We venture to suggest that the confusion over Seed 31 may result from an ethnocentric interpretation of the word "up." To us, "up" is a "good" direction. Not so, or not necessarily so, to an ant. "Up" is where the food comes from, to be sure; but "down" is where security, peace, and home are to be found. "Up" is the scorching sun; the freezing night; no shelter in the beloved tunnels; exile; death. Therefore we suggest that this strange author, in the solitude of her lonely tunnel, sought with what means she had to express the ultimate blasphemy conceivable to an ant, and that the correct reading of Seeds 30–31, in human terms, is:

Eat the eggs! Down with the Queen!

The desiccated body of a small worker was found beside Seed 31 when the manuscript was discovered. The head had been severed from the thorax, probably by the jaws of a soldier of the colony. The seeds, carefully arranged in a pattern resembling a musical stave, had not been disturbed. (Ants of the soldier caste are illiterate; thus the soldier was presumably not interested in the collection of useless seeds from which the edible germs had been removed.) No living ants were left in the colony, which was destroyed in a war with a neighboring anthill at some time subsequent to the death of the Author of the Acacia Seeds.

— G. D'Arbay, T. R. Bardol

ANNOUNCEMENT OF AN EXPEDITION

The extreme difficulty of reading Penguin has been very much lessened by the use of the underwater motion-picture camera. On film it is at least possible to repeat, and to slow down, the fluid sequences of the script, to the point where, by constant repetition and patient study, many elements of this most elegant and lively literature may be grasped, though the nuances, and perhaps the essence, must forever elude us.

It was Professor Duby who, by pointing out the remote affiliation of the script with Low Greylag, made possible the first tentative glossary of Penguin. The analogies with Dolphin which had been employed up to that time never proved very useful, and were often quite misleading.

Indeed it seemed strange that a script written almost entirely in wings, neck, and air should prove the key to the poetry of short-necked, flipper-winged water-writers. But we should not have found it so strange if we had kept in mind the fact that penguins are, despite all evidence to the contrary, birds.

Because their script resembles Dolphin in *form*, we should never have assumed that it must resemble Dolphin in *content*. And indeed it does not. There is, of course, the same extraordinary wit, the flashes of crazy humor, the inventiveness, and the inimitable grace. In all the thousands of literatures of the Fish stock, only a few show any humor at all, and that usually of a rather simple, primitive sort; and the superb gracefulness of Shark or Tarpon is utterly different from the joyous vigor of all Cetacean scripts. The joy, the vigor, and the humor are all shared by Penguin authors; and, indeed, by many of the finer Seal *auteurs*. The temperature of the blood is a bond. But the construction of the brain, and of the womb, makes a barrier! Dolphins do not lay eggs. A world of difference lies in that simple fact.

Only when Professor Duby reminded us that penguins are birds, that they do not swim but *fly in water*, only then could the therolinguist begin to approach the sea literature of the penguin with understanding; only then could the miles of recordings already on film be restudied and, finally, appreciated.

But the difficulty of translation is still with us.

A satisfying degree of promise has already been made in Adélie. The difficulties of recording a group kinetic performance in a stormy ocean as thick as pea soup with plankton at a temperature of 31° Fahrenheit are considerable; but the perseverance of the Ross Ice Barrier Literary Circle has been fully rewarded with such passages as "Under the Iceberg," from the *Autumn Song* — a passage now world famous in the rendition by Anna Serebryakova of the Leningrad Ballet. No verbal rendering can approach the felicity of Miss Serebryakova's version. For, quite simply, there is no way to reproduce in writing the all-important *multiplicity* of the original text, so beautifully rendered by the full chorus of the Leningrad Ballet company.

Indeed, what we call "translations" from the Adélie — or from any group kinetic text — are, to put it bluntly, mere notes — libretto without the opera. The ballet version is the true translation. Nothing in words can be complete.

I therefore suggest, though the suggestion may well be greeted with frowns of anger or with hoots of laughter, that *for the therolinguist* — as opposed to the artist and the amateur — the kinetic sea writings of Penguin are the *least* promising field of study: and, further, that Adélie, for all its charm and relative simplicity, is a less promising field of study than is Emperor.

Emperor! — I anticipate my colleagues' response to this suggestion. Emperor! The most difficult, the most remote, of all the dialects of Penguin! The language of which Professor Duby himself remarked, "The literature of the emperor penguin is as forbidding, as inaccessible, as the frozen heart of Antarctica itself. Its beauties may be unearthly, but they are not for us."

Maybe. I do not underestimate the difficulties: not least of which is the imperial temperament, so much more reserved and aloof than that of any other penguin. But, paradoxically, it is just in this reserve that I place my hope. The emperor is not a solitary, but a social bird, and while on land for the breeding season dwells in colonies, as does the adélie; but these colonies

are very much smaller and very much quieter than those of the
adélie. The bonds between the members of an emperor colony
are rather personal than social. The emperor is an individualist.
Therefore I think it almost certain that the literature of the emperor will prove to be composed by single authors, instead of
chorally; and therefore it will be translatable into human speech.
It will be a kinetic literature, but how different from the spatially extensive, rapid, multiplex choruses of sea writing! Close
analysis, and genuine transcription, will at last be possible.

What! say my critics — Should we pack up and go to
Cape Crozier, to the dark, to the blizzards, to the −60° cold, in
the mere hope of recording the problematic poetry of a few
strange birds who sit there, in the mid-winter dark, in the blizzards, in the −60° cold, on the eternal ice, with an egg on their
feet?

And my reply is, Yes. For, like Professor Duby, my instinct
tells me that the beauty of that poetry is as unearthly as anything we shall ever find on earth.

To those of my colleagues in whom the spirit of scientific
curiosity and aesthetic risk is strong, I say, Imagine it: the ice,
the scouring snow, the darkness, the ceaseless whine and scream
of wind. In that black desolation a little band of poets crouches.
They are starving; they will not eat for weeks. On the feet of
each one, under the warm belly feathers, rests one large egg,
thus preserved from the mortal touch of the ice. The poets cannot hear each other; they cannot see each other. They can only
feel the other's *warmth*. That is their poetry, that is their art.
Like all kinetic literatures, it is silent; unlike other kinetic literatures, it is all but immobile, ineffably subtle. The ruffling of a
feather; the shifting of a wing; the touch, the slight, faint, warm
touch of the one beside you. In unutterable, miserable, black
solitude, the affirmation. In absence, presence. In death, life.

I have obtained a sizable grant from UNESCO and have
stocked an expedition. There are still four places open. We leave

for Antarctica on Thursday. If anyone wants to come along, welcome!

— D. Petri

EDITORIAL. BY THE PRESIDENT OF THE THEROLINGUISTICS ASSOCIATION

What is Language?

This question, central to the science of therolinguistics, has been answered — heuristically — by the very existence of the science. Language is communication. That is the axiom on which all our theory and research rest, and from which all our discoveries derive; and the success of the discoveries testifies to the validity of the axiom. But to the related, yet not identical question, What is Art? we have not yet given a satisfactory answer.

Tolstoy, in the book whose title is that very question, answered it firmly and clearly: Art, too, is communication. This answer has, I believe, been accepted without examination or criticism by therolinguistics. For example: Why do therolinguists study only animals?

Why, because plants do not communicate.

Plants do not communicate; that is a fact. Therefore plants have no language; very well; that follows from our basic axiom. Therefore, also, plants have no art. But stay! That does *not* follow from the basic axiom, but only from the unexamined Tolstoyan corollary.

What if art is not communicative?

Or, what if some art is communicative, and some art is not?

Ourselves animals, active, predators, we look (naturally enough) for an active, predatory, communicative art; and when we find it, we recognise it. The development of this power of recognition and the skills of appreciation is a recent and glorious achievement.

But I submit that, for all the tremendous advances made by therolinguistics during the last decades, we are only at the beginning of our age of discovery. We must not become slaves to our own axioms. We have not yet lifted our eyes to the vaster horizons before us. We have not faced the almost terrifying challenge of the Plant.

If a non-communicative, vegetative art exists, we must rethink the very elements of our science, and learn a whole new set of techniques.

For it is simply not possible to bring the critical and technical skills appropriate to the study of Weasel murder mysteries, or Batrachian erotica, or the tunnel sagas of the earthworm, to bear on the art of the redwood or the zucchini.

This is proved conclusively by the failure — a noble failure — of the efforts of Dr. Srivas, in Calcutta, using time-lapse photography, to produce a lexicon of Sunflower. His attempt was daring, but doomed to failure. For his approach was kinetic — a method appropriate to the *communicative* arts of the tortoise, the oyster, and the sloth. He saw the extreme slowness of the kinesis of plants, and only that, as the problem to be solved.

But the problem was far greater. The art he sought, if it exists, is a non-communicative art: and probably a non-kinetic one. It is possible that Time, the essential element, matrix, and measure of all known animal art, does not enter into vegetable art at all. The plants may use the meter of eternity. We do not know.

We do not know. All we can guess is that the putative Art of the Plant is *entirely different* from the Art of the Animal. What it is, we cannot say; we have not yet discovered it. Yet I predict with some certainty that it exists, and that when it is found it will prove to be, not an action, but a reaction: not a communication, but a reception. It will be exactly the opposite of the art we know and recognise. It will be the first *passive* art known to us.

Can we in fact know it? Can we ever understand it?

It will be immensely difficult. That is clear. But we should not despair. Remember that so late as the mid-twentieth century, most scientists, and many artists, did not believe that even Dolphin would ever be comprehensible to the human brain — or worth comprehending! Let another century pass, and we may seem equally laughable. "Do you realise," the phytolinguist will say to the aesthetic critic, "that they couldn't even read Eggplant?" And they will smile at our ignorance, as they pick up their rucksacks and hike on up to read the newly deciphered lyrics of the lichen on the north face of Pike's Peak.

And with them, or after them, may there not come that even bolder adventurer — the first geolinguist, who, ignoring the delicate, transient lyrics of the lichen, will read beneath it the still less communicative, still more passive, wholly atemporal, cold, volcanic poetry of the rocks: each one a word spoken, how long ago, by the earth itself, in the immense solitude, the immenser community, of space.

The New Atlantis

COMING BACK from my Wilderness Week I sat by an odd sort of man in the bus. For a long time we didn't talk; I was mending stockings, and he was reading. Then the bus broke down a few miles outside Gresham. Boiler trouble, the way it generally is when the driver insists on trying to go over thirty. It was a Supersonic Superscenic Deluxe Long Distance coal-burner, with Home Comfort, that means a toilet, and the seats were pretty comfortable, at least those that hadn't yet worked loose on their bolts, so everybody waited inside the bus; besides, it was raining. We began talking, the way people do when there's a breakdown and a wait. He held up his pamphlet and tapped it — he was a dry-looking man with a schoolteacherish way of using his hands — and said, "This is interesting. I've been reading that a new continent is rising from the depths of the sea."

The blue stockings were hopeless. You have to have something besides holes to darn onto. "Which sea?"

"They're not sure yet. Most specialists think the Atlantic. But there's evidence it may be happening in the Pacific too."

"Won't the oceans get a little crowded?" I said, not taking

it seriously. I was a bit snappish, because of the breakdown, and because those blue stockings had been good warm ones.

He tapped the pamphlet again and shook his head, quite serious. "No," he said. "The old continents are sinking, to make room for the new. You can see that that is happening."

You certainly can. Manhattan Island is now under eleven feet of water at low tide, and there are oyster beds in Ghirardelli Square.

"I thought that was because the oceans are rising from polar melt."

He shook his head again. "That is a factor. Due to the greenhouse effect of pollution, indeed Antarctica may become inhabitable. But climatic factors will not explain the emergence of the new — or, possibly, very old — continents in the Atlantic and Pacific." He went on explaining about continental drift, but I liked the idea of inhabiting Antarctica, and daydreamed about it for a while. I thought of it as very empty, very quiet, all white and blue, with a faint golden glow northward from the unrising sun behind the long peak of Mount Erebus. There were a few people there; they were very quiet, too, and wore white tie and tails. Some of them carried oboes and violas. Southward the white land went up in a long silence towards the pole.

Just the opposite, in fact, of the Mount Hood Wilderness Area. It had been a tiresome vacation. The other women in the dormitory were all right, but it was macaroni for breakfast, and there were so many organised sports. I had looked forward to the hike up to the National Forest Preserve, the largest forest left in the United States, but the trees didn't look at all the way they do in the postcards and brochures and Federal Beautification Bureau advertisements. They were spindly, and they all had little signs on, saying which union they had been planted by. There were actually a lot more green picnic tables and cement Men's and Women's than there were trees. There was an electrified fence all around the forest to keep out unauthorised persons. The Forest Ranger talked about mountain jays, "bold little

robbers," he said, "who will come and snatch the sandwich from
your very hand," but I didn't see any. Perhaps because it was
the weekly Watch Those Surplus Calories! Day for all the wom-
en, and so we didn't have any sandwiches. If I'd seen a mountain
jay I might have snatched the sandwich from his very hand, who
knows. Anyhow it was an exhausting week, and I wished I'd
stayed home and practised, even though I'd have lost a week's
pay because staying home and practising the viola doesn't count
as planned implementation of recreational leisure as defined by
the Federal Union of Unions.

When I came back from my Antarctic expedition the man
was reading again, and I got a look at his pamphlet; and that
was the odd part of it. The pamphlet was called "Increasing
Efficiency in Public Accountant Training Schools," and I could
see from the one paragraph I got a glance at that there was
nothing about new continents emerging from the ocean depths
in it — nothing at all.

Then we had to get out and walk on into Gresham, because
they had decided that the best thing for us all to do was get onto
the Greater Portland Area Rapid Public Transit Lines, since
there had been so many breakdowns that the charter bus company didn't have any more busses to send out to pick us up. The
walk was wet, and rather dull, except when we passed the Cold
Mountain Commune. They have a wall around it to keep out
unauthorised persons, and a big neon sign out front saying
"Cold Mountain Commune," and there were some people in authentic jeans and ponchos by the highway selling macrame belts
and sand-cast candles and soybean bread to the tourists. In
Gresham, I took the 4:40 GPARTL Superjet Flyer train to
Burnside and East 230th, and then walked to 217th and got the
bus to the Goldschmidt Overpass, and transferred to the shuttle-
bus, but it had boiler trouble too, so I didn't reach the downtown
transfer point until 8:10, and the busses go on a once-an-hour
schedule at eight, so I got a meatless hamburger at the Long-
horn Inch-Thick Steak House Dinerette and caught the nine

o'clock bus and got home about ten. When I let myself into the apartment I turned on the lights, but there still weren't any. There had been a power outage in West Portland for three weeks. So I went feeling about for the candles in the dark, and it was a minute or so before I noticed that somebody was lying on my bed.

I panicked, and tried again to turn the lights on.

It was a man, lying there in a long thin heap. I thought a burglar had got in somehow while I was away, and died. I opened the door so I could get out quick or at least my yells could be heard, and then I managed not to shake long enough to strike a match, and lighted the candle, and came a little closer to the bed.

The light disturbed him. He made a sort of snoring in his throat, and turned his head. I saw it was a stranger, but I knew his eyebrows, then the breadth of his closed eyelids, then I saw my husband.

He woke up while I was standing there over him with the candle in my hand. He laughed and said still half asleep, "Ah, Psyche! from the regions which are holy land."

Neither of us made much fuss. It was unexpected, but it did seem so natural for him to be there, after all, much more natural than for him not to be there; and he was too tired to be very emotional. We lay there together in the dark, and he explained that they had released him from the Rehabilitation Camp early because he had injured his back in an accident in the gravel quarry, and they were afraid it might get worse. If he died there it wouldn't be good publicity abroad, since there have been some nasty rumors about deaths from illness in the Rehabilitation Camps and the Federal Medical Association Hospitals; and there are scientists abroad who have heard of Simon, since somebody published his proof of Goldbach's Hypothesis in Peking. So they let him out early, with eight dollars in his pocket, which is what he had in his pocket when they arrested him, which made it, of course, fair. He had walked and hitched home from Coeur D'Alene, Idaho, with a couple of days in jail in Walla Walla for being caught hitchhiking. He almost fell asleep telling me this, and when he had told me, he did fall asleep. He needed a change of clothes and a bath but I didn't want to wake him. Besides, I was tired too. We lay side by side and his head was on my arm. I don't suppose that I have ever been so happy. No; was it happiness? Something wider and darker, more like knowledge, more like the night: joy.

It was dark for so long, so very long. We were all blind. And there was the cold, a vast, unmoving, heavy cold. We could not move at all. We did not move. We did not speak. Our mouths were closed, pressed shut by the cold and by the weight. Our eyes were pressed shut. Our limbs were held still. Our minds were held still. For how long? There was no length of time; how long is death? And is one dead only after living, or before life as well? Certainly we thought, if we thought anything, that we were dead; but if we had ever been alive, we had forgotten it.

There was a change. It must have been the pressure that changed first, although we did not know it. The eyelids are sensitive to touch. They must have been weary of being shut. When the pressure upon them weakened a little, they opened. But there was no way for us to know that. It was too cold for us to feel anything. There was nothing to be seen. There was black.

But then — "then," for the event created time, created before and after, near and far, now and then — "then" there was the light. One light. One small, strange light that passed slowly, at what distance we could not tell. A small, greenish-white, slightly blurred point of radiance, passing.

Our eyes were certainly open, "then," for we saw it. We saw the moment. The moment is a point of light. Whether in darkness or in the field of all light, the moment is small, and moves, but not quickly. And "then" it is gone.

It did not occur to us that there might be another moment. There was no reason to assume that there might be more than one. One was marvel enough: that in all the field of the dark, in the cold, heavy, dense, moveless, timeless, placeless, boundless black, there should have occurred, once, a small, slightly blurred, moving light! Time need be created only once, we thought.

But we were mistaken. The difference between one and more-than-one is all the difference in the world. Indeed, that difference is the world.

The light returned.

The same light, or another one? There was no telling.

But, "this time," we wondered about the light: was it small and near to us, or large and far away? Again there was no telling; but there was something about the way it moved, a trace of hesitation, a tentative quality, that did not seem proper to anything large and remote. The stars, for instance. We began to remember the stars.

The stars had never hesitated.

Perhaps the noble certainty of their gait had been a mere effect of distance. Perhaps in fact they had hurtled wildly, enormous furnace fragments of a primal bomb thrown through the cosmic dark; but time and distance soften all agony. If the universe, as seems likely, began with an act of destruction, the stars we had used to see told no tales of it. They had been implacably serene.

The planets, however. . . . We began to remember the planets. They had suffered certain changes of appearance and course. At certain times of the year Mars would reverse its direction and go backwards through the stars. Venus had been brighter and less bright as she went through her phases of crescent, full, and wane. Mercury had shuddered like a skidding drop of rain on the sky flushed with daybreak. The light we now watched had that erratic, trembling quality. We saw it, unmistakably, change direction and go backwards. It then grew smaller and fainter; blinked

— an eclipse? — and slowly disappeared.

Slowly, but not slowly enough for a planet.

Then — the third "then"! — arrived the indubitable and positive Wonder of the World, the Magic Trick, watch now, watch, you will not believe your eyes, mama, mama, look what I can do —

Seven lights in a row, proceeding fairly rapidly, with a darting movement, from left to right. Proceeding less rapidly from right to left, two dimmer, greenish lights. Two-lights halt, blink, reverse course, proceed hastily and in a wavering manner from left to right. Seven-lights increase speed, and catch up. Two-lights flash desperately, flicker, and are gone.

Seven-lights hang still for some while, then merge gradually into one streak, veering away, and little by little vanish into the immensity of the dark.

But in the dark now are growing other lights, many of them: lamps, dots, rows, scintillations: some near at hand, some far. Like the stars, yes, but not stars. It is not the great Existences we are seeing, but only the little lives.

In the morning Simon told me something about the Camp, but not until after he had had me check the apartment for bugs. I thought at first he had been given behavior mod and gone paranoid. We never had been infested. And I'd been living alone for a year and a half; surely they didn't want to hear me talking to myself? But he said, "They may have been expecting me to come here."

"But they let you go free!"

He just lay there and laughed at me. So I checked everywhere we could think of. I didn't find any bugs, but it did look as if somebody had gone through the bureau drawers while I was away in the Wilderness. Simon's papers were all at Max's, so that didn't matter. I made tea on the Primus, and washed and shaved Simon with the extra hot water in the kettle — he had a thick beard and wanted to get rid of it because of the lice he had

brought from Camp — and while we were doing that he told
me about the Camp. In fact he told me very little, but not much
was necessary.

He had lost about twenty pounds. As he only weighed 140
to start with, this left little to go on with. His knees and wrist
bones stuck out like rocks under the skin. His feet were all swollen and chewed-looking from the Camp boots; he hadn't dared
take the boots off, the last three days of walking, because he was
afraid he wouldn't be able to get them back on. When he had to
move or sit up so I could wash him, he shut his eyes.

"Am I really here?" he asked. "Am I here?"

"Yes," I said. "You are here. What I don't understand is
how you got here."

"Oh, it wasn't bad so long as I kept moving. All you need is
to know where you're going — to have some place to go. You
know, some of the people in Camp, if they'd let them go, they
wouldn't have had that. They couldn't have gone anywhere.
Keeping moving was the main thing. It's just that my back's
seized up, now."

When he had to get up to go to the bathroom he moved
liked a ninety-year-old. He couldn't stand straight, but was all
bent out of shape, and shuffled. I helped him put on clean
clothes. When he lay down on the bed again a sound of pain
came out of him, like tearing thick paper. I went around the
room putting things away. He asked me to come sit by him, and
said I was going to drown him if I went on crying. "You'll sub-
merge the entire North American continent," he said. I can't
remember what else he said, but he made me laugh finally. It is
hard to remember things Simon says, and hard not to laugh
when he says them. This is not merely the partiality of affection:
he makes everybody laugh. I doubt that he intends to. It is just
that a mathematician's mind works differently from other people's. Then when they laugh, that pleases him.

It was strange, and it is strange, to be thinking about
"him," the man I have known for ten years, the same man,

while "he" lay there changed out of recognition, a different
man. It is enough to make you understand why most languages
have a word like "soul." There are various degrees of death, and
time spares us none of them. Yet something endures, for which
a word is needed.

I said what I had not been able to say for a year and a half:
"I was afraid they'd brainwash you."

He said, "Behavior mod is expensive. Even just with drugs.
They save it mostly for the V.I.P.s. But I'm afraid they got a
notion I might be important after all. I got questioned a lot the
last couple of months. About my 'foreign contacts.'" He snort-
ed. "The stuff that got published abroad, I suppose. So I want to
be careful and make sure it's just a Camp again next time, and
not a Federal Hospital."

"Simon, were they . . . are they cruel, or just righteous?"

He did not answer for a while. He did not want to answer.
He knew what I was asking. He knew what thread hangs hope,
the sword, above our heads.

"Some of them . . ." he said at last, mumbling.

Some of them had been cruel. Some of them had enjoyed
their work. You cannot blame everything on society.

"Prisoners, as well as guards," he said.

You cannot blame everything on the enemy.

"Some of them, Belle," he said with energy, touching my
hand — "some of them, there were men like gold there —"

The thread is tough; you cannot cut it with one stroke.

"What have you been playing?" he asked.

"Forrest, Schubert."

"With the quartet?"

"Trio, now. Janet went to Oakland with a new lover."

"Ah, poor Max."

"It's just as well, really. She isn't a good pianist."

I make Simon laugh, too, though I don't intend to. We
talked until it was past time for me to go to work. My shift since
the Full Employment Act last year is ten to two. I am an inspec-

tor in a recycled paper bag factory. I have never rejected a bag
yet; the electronic inspector catches all the defective ones first.
It is a rather depressing job. But it's only four hours a day, and
it takes more time than that to go through all the lines and
physical and mental examinations, and fill out all the forms, and
talk to all the welfare counsellors and inspectors every week in
order to qualify as Unemployed, and then line up every day for
the ration stamps and the dole. Simon thought I ought to go to
work as usual. I tried to, but I couldn't. He had felt very hot to
the touch when I kissed him goodbye. I went instead and got a
black-market doctor. A girl at the factory had recommended
her, for an abortion, if I ever wanted one without going through
the regulation two years of sex-depressant drugs the fed-meds
make you take after they give you an abortion. She was a jeweler's assistant in a shop on Alder Street, and the girl said she was
convenient because if you didn't have enough cash you could
leave something in pawn at the jeweler's as payment. Nobody
ever does have enough cash, and of course credit cards aren't
worth much on the black market.

The doctor was willing to come at once, so we rode home on
the bus together. She gathered very soon that Simon and I were
married, and it was funny to see her look at us and smile like a
cat. Some people love illegality for its own sake. Men, more
often than women. It's men who make laws, and enforce them,
and break them, and think the whole performance is wonderful.
Most women would rather just ignore them. You could see that
this woman, like a man, actually enjoyed breaking them. That
may have been what put her into an illegal business in the first
place, a preference for the shady side. But there was more to it
than that. No doubt she'd wanted to be a doctor, too; and the
Federal Medical Association doesn't admit women into the medical schools. She probably got her training as some other doctor's private pupil, under the counter. Very much as Simon
learned mathematics, since the universities don't teach much but
Business Administration and Advertising and Media Skills any

more. However she learned it, she seemed to know her stuff. She fixed up a kind of homemade traction device for Simon very handily, and informed him that if he did much more walking for two months he'd be crippled the rest of his life, but if he behaved himself he'd just be more or less lame. It isn't the kind of thing you'd expect to be grateful for being told, but we both were. Leaving, she gave me a bottle of about two hundred plain white pills, unlabelled. "Aspirin," she said. "He'll be in a good deal of pain off and on for weeks."

I looked at the bottle. I had never seen aspirin before, only the Super-Buffered Pane-Gon and the Triple Power N-L-G-Zic and the Extra Strength Apansprin with the miracle ingredient more doctors recommend, which the fed-meds always give you prescriptions for, to be filled at your FMA-approved private-enterprise friendly drugstore at the low, low prices established by the Pure Food and Drug Administration in order to inspire competitive research.

"Aspirin," the doctor repeated. "The miracle ingredient more doctors recommend." She cat-grinned again. I think she liked us because we were living in sin. That bottle of black-market aspirin was probably worth more than the old Navajo bracelet I pawned for her fee.

I went out again to register Simon as temporarily domiciled at my address, and to apply for Temporary Unemployment Compensation ration stamps for him. They only give them to you for two weeks and you have to come every day; but to register him as Temporarily Disabled meant getting the signatures of two fed-meds, and I thought I'd rather put that off for a while. It took three hours to go through the lines and get the forms he would have to fill out, and to answer the crats' questions about why he wasn't there in person. They smelled something fishy. Of course it's hard for them to prove that two people are married, if you move now and then, and your friends help out by sometimes registering one of you as living at their address; but they had all the back files on both of us and it was obvious that we had been around each other for a suspiciously long time. The State really does make things awfully hard for itself. It must have been simpler to enforce the laws, back when marriage was legal and adultery was what got you into trouble. They only had to catch you once. But I'll bet people broke the law just as often then as they do now.

The lantern creatures came close enough at last that we could see not only their light, but their bodies in the illumination of the light. They were not pretty. They were dark-colored, most often a dark red, and they were all mouth. They ate one another whole. Light swallowed light all swallowed together in the vaster mouth of the darkness. They moved slowly, for nothing, however small and hungry, could move fast under that weight, in that cold. Their eyes, round with fear, were never closed. Their bodies were tiny and bony, behind the gaping jaws. They wore queer, ugly decorations on their lips and skulls: fringes, serrated wattles, featherlike fronds, gauds, bangles, lures. Poor little sheep of the deep pastures! Poor ragged, hunch-jawed dwarfs squeezed to the bone by the weight of the darkness, chilled to the bone by the cold of the darkness, tiny monsters burning with bright hunger, who brought us back to life!

Occasionally, in the wan, sparse illumination of one of the lantern creatures, we caught a momentary glimpse of other large, unmoving shapes: the barest suggestion, off in the distance, not of a wall, nothing so solid and certain as a wall, but of a surface, an angle. . . . Was it there?

Or something would glitter, faint, far off, far down. There was no use trying to make out what it might be. Probably it was only a fleck of sediment, mud or mica, disturbed by a struggle between the lantern creatures, flickering like a bit of diamond dust as it rose and settled slowly. In any case, we could not move to go see what it was. We had not even the cold, narrow freedom of the lantern creatures. We were immobilised, borne down, still shadows among the half-guessed shadow walls. Were we there?

The lantern creatures showed no awareness of us. They passed before us, among us, perhaps even through us — it was impossible to be sure. They were not afraid, or curious.

Once something a little larger than a hand came crawling near, and for a moment we saw quite distinctly the clean angle where the foot of a wall rose from the pavement, in the glow cast by the crawling creature, which was covered with a foliage of plumes, each plume dotted with many tiny, bluish points of light. We saw the pavement beneath the creature and the wall beside it, heartbreaking in its exact, clear linearity, its opposition to all that was fluid, random, vast, and void. We saw the creature's claws, slowly reaching out and retracting like small stiff fingers, touch the wall. Its plumage of light quivering, it dragged itself along and vanished behind the corner.

So we knew that the wall was there; and that it was an outer wall, a housefront, perhaps, or the side of one of the towers of the city.

We remembered the towers. We remembered the city. We had forgotten it. We had forgotten who we were; but we remembered the city, now.

When I got home, the FBI had already been there. The computer at the police precinct where I registered Simon's address must have flashed it right over to the computer at the FBI building. They had questioned Simon for about an hour, mostly about what he had been doing during the twelve days it took him to get from the Camp to Portland. I suppose they thought he had flown to Peking or something. Having a police record in Walla Walla for hitchhiking helped him establish his story. He told me that one of them had gone to the bathroom. Sure enough I found a bug stuck on the top of the bathroom doorframe. I left it, as we figured it's really better to leave it when you know you have one, than to take it off and then never be sure they haven't planted another one you don't know about. As Simon said, if we felt we had to say something unpatriotic we could always flush the toilet at the same time.

I have a battery radio — there are so many stoppages because of power failures, and days the water has to be boiled, and so on, that you really have to have a radio to save wasting time and dying of typhoid — and he turned it on while I was making supper on the Primus. The six-o'clock All American Broadcasting Company news announcer announced that peace was at hand in Uruguay, the President's confidential aide having been seen to smile at a passing blonde as he left the 613th day of the secret negotiations in a villa outside Katmandu. The war in Liberia was going well; the enemy said they had shot down 17 American planes but the Pentagon said we had shot down 22 enemy planes, and the capital city — I forget its name, but it hasn't been inhabitable for seven years anyway — was on the verge of being recaptured by the forces of freedom. The police action in Arizona was also succesful. The Neo-Birch insurgents in Phoenix could not hold out much longer against the massed might of the American Army and Air Force, since their underground supply of small tactical nukes from the Weatherpeople in Los Angeles had been cut off. Then there was an advertisement for Fed-Cred cards, and a commercial for the Supreme Court — "Take your legal troubles to the Nine Wise Men!" Then there was something about why tariffs had gone up, and a report from the stock market which had just closed at over 2000, and a commercial for U.S. Government canned water, with a catchy little tune: "Don't be sorry when you drink — It's not as healthy as you think — Don't you think you really ought to — Drink coo-ool, puu-uure U.S.G. Water?" — with three sopranos in close harmony on the last line. Then, just as the battery began to give out and his voice was dying away into a faraway tiny whisper, the announcer seemed to be saying something about a new continent emerging.

"What was that?"

"I didn't hear," Simon said, lying with his eyes shut and his face pale and sweaty. I gave him two aspirins before we ate. He ate little, and fell asleep while I was washing the dishes in the bathroom. I had been going to practise, but a viola is fairly wakeful in a one-room apartment. I read for a while instead. It was a bestseller Janet had given me when she left. She thought it was very good, but then she likes Franz Liszt too. I don't read much since the libraries were closed down, it's too hard to get books; all you can buy is bestsellers. I don't remember the title of this one, the cover just said Ninety Million Copies in Print!!! It was about small-town sex life in the last century, the dear old 1970s when there weren't any problems and life was so simple and nostalgic. The author squeezed all the naughty thrills he could out of the fact that all the main characters were married. I looked at the end and saw that all the married couples shot each other after all their children became schizophrenic hookers, except for one brave pair that divorced and then leapt into bed together with a clear-eyed pair of Government-employed lovers for eight pages of healthy group sex as a brighter future dawned. I went to bed then, too. Simon was hot, but sleeping quietly. His breathing was like the sound of soft waves far away, and I went out to the dark sea on the sound of them.

I used to go out to the dark sea, often, as a child, falling asleep. I had almost forgotten it with my waking mind. As a child all I had to do was stretch out and think, "the dark sea . . . the dark sea . . ." and soon enough I'd be there, in the great depths, rocking. But after I grew up it only happened rarely, as a great gift. To know the abyss of the darkness and not to fear it, to entrust oneself to it and whatever may arise from it — what greater gift?

We watched the tiny lights come and go around us, and doing so, we gained a sense of space and of direction — near and far, at least, and higher and lower. It was that sense of space that allowed us to become aware of the currents. Space was no longer entirely still around us, suppressed by the enormous pressure of its own weight. Very dimly we were aware that the cold darkness moved, slowly, softly, pressing against us a little for a long time, then ceasing, in a vast oscillation. The empty darkness flowed slowly along our unmoving unseen bodies; along them, past them; perhaps through them; we could not tell.

Where did they come from, those dim, slow, vast tides? What pressure or attraction stirred the deeps to these slow drifting movements? We could not understand that; we could only feel their touch against us, but in straining our sense to guess their origin or end, we became aware of something else: something out there in the darkness of the great currents: sounds. We listened. We heard.

So our sense of space sharpened and localised to a sense of place. For sound is local, as sight is not. Sound is delimited by silence; and it does not rise out of the silence unless it is fairly close, both in space and in time. Though we stand where once the singer stood we cannot hear the voice singing; the years have carried it off on their tides, submerged it. Sound is a fragile thing, a tremor, as delicate as life itself. We may see the stars, but we cannot hear them. Even were the hollowness of outer space an atmosphere, an ether that transmitted the waves of sound, we could not hear the stars; they are too far away. At most if we listened we might hear our own sun, all the mighty roiling, exploding storm of its burning, as a whisper at the edge of hearing.

A sea wave laps one's feet: it is the shock wave of a volcanic eruption on the far side of the world. But one hears nothing.

A red light flickers on the horizon: it is the reflection in smoke of a city on the distant mainland, burning. But one hears nothing.

Only on the slopes of the volcano, in the suburbs of the city, does one begin to hear the deep thunder, and the high voices crying.

Thus, when we became aware that we were hearing,

we were sure that the sounds we heard were fairly close to us. And yet we may have been quite wrong. For we were in a strange place, a deep place. Sound travels fast and far in the deep places, and the silence there is perfect, letting the least noise be heard for hundreds of miles.

And these were not small noises. The lights were tiny, but the sounds were vast: not loud, but very large. Often they were below the range of hearing, long slow vibrations rather than sounds. The first we heard seemed to us to rise up through the currents from beneath us: immense groans, sighs felt along the bone, a rumbling, a deep uneasy whispering.

Later, certain sounds came down to us from above, or borne along the endless levels of the darkness, and these were stranger yet, for they were music. A huge, calling, yearning music from far away in the darkness, calling not to us. *Where are you? I am here.*

Not to us.

They were the voices of the great souls, the great lives, the lonely ones, the voyagers. Calling. Not often answered. *Where are you? Where have you gone?*

But the bones, the keels and girders of white bones on icy isles of the South, the shores of bones did not reply.

Nor could we reply. But we listened, and the tears rose in our eyes, salt, not so salt as the oceans, the world-girdling deep bereaved currents, the abandoned roadways of the great lives; not so salt, but warmer.

I am here. Where have you gone?

No answer.

Only the whispering thunder from below.

But we knew now, though we could not answer, we knew because we heard, because we felt, because we wept, we knew that we were; and we remembered other voices.

Max came the next night. I sat on the toilet lid to practise, with the bathroom door shut. The FBI men on the other end of the bug got a solid half hour of scales and double stops, and then a quite good performance of the Hindemith unaccompanied viola sonata. The bathroom being very small and all hard surfaces, the noise I made was really tremendous. Not a good sound, far too much echo, but the sheer volume was contagious, and I played louder as I went on. The man up above knocked on the floor once; but if I have to listen to the weekly All-American Olympic Games at full blast every Sunday morning from his TV set, then he has to accept Paul Hindemith coming up out of his toilet now and then.

When I got tired I put a big wad of cotton over the bug, and came out of the bathroom half deaf. Simon and Max were on fire. Burning, unconsumed. Simon was scribbling formulae in traction, and Max was pumping his elbows up and down the way he does, like a boxer, and saying, "The e-lec-tron emission . . ." through his nose, with his eyes narrowed, and his mind evidently going light-years per second faster than his tongue, because he kept beginning over and saying, "The e-lec-tron emis-sion . . ." and pumping his elbows.

Intellectuals at work are very strange to look at. As strange as artists. I never could understand how an audience can sit there and *look* at a fiddler rolling his eyes and biting his tongue, or a horn player collecting spit, or a pianist like a black cat strapped to an electrified bench, as if what they *saw* had anything to do with the music.

I damped the fires with a quart of black-market beer — the legal kind is better, but I never have enough ration stamps for beer, I'm not thirsty enough to go without eating — and gradually Max and Simon cooled down. Max would have stayed talking all night, but I drove him out, because Simon was looking tired.

I put a new battery in the radio and left it playing in the bathroom, and blew out the candle and lay and talked with Simon; he was too excited to sleep. He said that Max had solved the problems that were bothering them before Simon was sent to

Camp, and had fitted Simon's equations to (as Simon put it) the bare facts: which means they have achieved "direct energy conversion." Ten or twelve people have worked on it at different times since Simon published the theoretical part of it when he was twenty-two. The physicist Ann Jones had pointed out right away that the simplest practical application of the theory would be to build a "sun tap," a device for collecting and storing solar energy, only much cheaper and better than the U.S.G. Sola-Heetas that some rich people have on their houses. And it would have been simple only they kept hitting the same snag. Now Max has got around the snag.

I said that Simon published the theory, but that is inaccurate. Of course he's never been able to publish any of his papers, in print; he's not a Federal employee and doesn't have a Government clearance. But it did get circulated in what the scientists and poets call Sammy's-dot, that is, just handwritten or hectographed. It's an old joke that the FBI arrests everybody with purple fingers, because they have either been hectographing Sammy's-dots, or they have impetigo.

Anyhow, Simon was on top of the mountain that night. His true joy is in the pure math; but he had been working with Clara and Max and the others in this effort to materialise the theory for ten years, and a taste of material victory is a good thing, once in a lifetime.

I asked him to explain what the sun tap would mean to the masses, with me as a representative mass. He explained that it means we can tap solar energy for power, using a device that's easier to build than a jar battery. The efficiency and storage capacity are such that about ten minutes of sunlight will power an apartment complex like ours, heat and lights and elevators and all, for twenty-four hours; and no pollution, particulate or thermal or radioactive. "There isn't any danger of using up the sun?" I asked. He took it soberly — it was a stupid question, but after all not so long ago people thought there wasn't any danger of using up the earth — and said no, because we wouldn't be pulling out energy, as we did when we mined and forested and split atoms, but just using the energy that comes to us anyhow: as the plants, the trees and grass and rosebushes, always have done. "You could call it Flower Power," he said. He was high, high up on the mountain, ski jumping in the sunlight.

"The State owns us," he said, "because the corporative State has a monopoly on power sources, and there's not enough power to go round. But now, anybody could build a generator on their roof that would furnish enough power to light a city."

I looked out the window at the dark city.

"We could completely decentralise industry and agriculture. Technology could serve life instead of serving capital. We could each run our own life. Power is power! ... The State is a machine. We could unplug the machine, now. Power corrupts; absolute power corrupts absolutely. But that's true only when there's a price on power. When groups can keep the power to themselves; when they can use physical power-to in order to exert spiritual power-over; when might makes right. But if power is free? If everybody is equally mighty? Then everybody's got to find a better way of showing that he's right. ...."

"That's what Mr. Nobel thought when he invented dynamite," I said. "Peace on earth."

He slid down the sunlit slope a couple of thousand feet and stopped beside me in a spray of snow, smiling. "Skull at the banquet," he said, "finger writing on the wall. Be still! Look, don't you see the sun shining on the Pentagon, all the roofs are off, the sun shines at last into the corridors of power. ... And they shrivel up, they wither away. The green grass grows through the carpets of the Oval Room, the Hotline is disconnected for non-payment of the bill. The first thing we'll do is build an electrified fence outside the electrified fence around the White House. The inner one prevents unauthorised persons from getting in. The outer one will prevent authorised persons from getting out. ...."

Of course he was bitter. Not many people come out of prison sweet.

But it was cruel, to be shown this great hope, and to know that there was no hope for it. He did know that. He knew it right along. He knew that there was no mountain, that he was skiing on the wind.

The tiny lights of the lantern creatures died out one by one, sank away. The distant lonely voices were silent. The cold, slow currents flowed, vacant, only shaken from time to time by a shifting in the abyss.

It was dark again, and no voice spoke. All dark, dumb, cold.

Then the sun rose.

It was not like the dawns we had begun to remember: the change, manifold and subtle, in the smell and touch of the air; the hush that, instead of sleeping, wakes, holds still, and waits; the appearance of objects, looking grey, vague, and new, as if just created — distant mountains against the eastern sky, one's own hands, the hoary grass full of dew and shadow, the fold in the edge of a curtain hanging by the window — and then, before one is quite sure that one is indeed seeing again, that the light has returned, that day is breaking, the first abrupt, sweet stammer of a waking bird. And after that the chorus, voice by voice: This is my nest, this is my tree, this is my egg, this is my day, this is my life, here I am, here I am, hurray for me! I'm here! — No, it wasn't like that at all, this dawn. It was completely silent, and it was blue.

In the dawns that we had begun to remember, one did not become aware of the light itself, but of the separate objects touched by the light, the things, the world. They were there, visible again, as if visibility were their own property, not a gift from the rising sun.

In this dawn, there was nothing but the light itself.

Indeed there was not even light, we would have said, but only color: blue.

There was no compass bearing to it. It was not brighter in the east. There was no east or west. There was only up and down, below and above. Below was dark. The blue light came from above. Brightness fell. Beneath, where the shaking thunder had stilled, the brightness died away through violet into blindness.

We, arising, watched light fall.

In a way it was more like an ethereal snowfall than like a sunrise. The light seemed to be in discrete particles, infinitesimal flecks, slowly descending, faint, fainter than flakes of fine snow on a dark night, and tinier; but blue. A soft, penetrating blue tending to the violet, the color of the shadows in an iceberg, the color of a streak of sky between grey clouds on a winter afternoon before snow: faint in intensity but vivid in hue: the color of the remote, the color of the cold, the color farthest from the sun.

On Saturday night they held a scientific congress in our room. Clara and Max came, of course, and the engineer Phil Drum, and three others who had worked on the sun tap. Phil Drum was very pleased with himself because he had actually built one of the things, a solar cell, and brought it along. I don't think it had occurred to either Max or Simon to build one. Once they knew it could be done, they were satisfied and wanted to get on with something else. But Phil unwrapped his baby with a lot of flourish, and people made remarks like, "Mr. Watson, will you come here a minute," and "Hey, Wilbur, you're off the ground!" and "I say, nasty mould you've got there, Alec, why don't you throw it out?" and "Ugh, ugh, burns, burns, wow, ow," the latter from Max, who does look a little Pre-Mousterian. Phil explained that he had exposed the cell for one minute at four in the afternoon up in Washington Park during a light rain. The lights were back on on the West Side since Thursday, so we could test it without being conspicuous.

We turned off the lights, after Phil had wired the table-lamp cord to the cell. He turned on the lamp switch. The bulb came on, about twice as bright as before, at its full 40 watts — city power of course was never full strength. We all looked at it. It was a dime-store table lamp with a metallised gold base and a white plasticloth shade.

"Brighter than a thousand suns," Simon murmured from the bed.

"Could it be," said Clara Edmonds, "that we physicists have known sin — and have come out the other side?"

"It really wouldn't be any good at all for making bombs with," Max said dreamily.

"Bombs," Phil Drum said with scorn. "Bombs are obsolete. Don't you realise that we could move a mountain with this kind of power? I mean pick up Mount Hood, move it, and set it down. We could thaw Antarctica, we could freeze the Congo. We could sink a continent. 'Give me a fulcrum and I'll move the world.' Well, Archimedes, you've got your fulcrum. The sun."

"Christ," Simon said, "the radio, Belle!"

The bathroom door was shut and I had put cotton over the bug, but he was right; if they were going to go ahead at this rate there had better be some added static. And though I liked watching their faces in the clear light of the lamp — they all had good, interesting faces, well worn, like the handles of wooden tools or the rocks in a running stream — I did not much want to listen to them talk tonight. Not because I wasn't a scientist; that made no difference. And not because I disagreed or disapproved or disbelieved anything they said. Only because it grieved me terribly, their talking. Because they couldn't rejoice aloud over a job done and a discovery made, but had to hide there and whisper about it. Because they couldn't go out into the sun.

I went into the bathroom with my viola and sat on the toilet lid and did a long set of sautillé exercises. Then I tried to work at the Forrest trio, but it was too assertive. I played the solo part from *Harold in Italy,* which is beautiful, but wasn't quite the right mood either. They were still going strong in the other room. I began to improvise.

After a few minutes in E minor the light over the shaving mirror began to flicker and dim; then it died. Another outage. The table lamp in the other room did not go out, being connected with the sun, not with the twenty-three atomic fission plants that power the Greater Portland Area. Within two seconds somebody had switched it off too, so that we shouldn't be the only window in the West Hills left alight; and I could hear them rooting for candles and rattling matches. I went on improvising in the dark. Without light, when you couldn't see all the hard shiny surfaces of things, the sound seemed softer and less muddled. I went on, and it began to shape up. All the laws of harmonics sang together when the bow came down. The strings of the viola were the cords of my own voice, tightened by sorrow, tuned to the pitch of joy. The melody created itself out of air and energy; it raised up the valleys, and the mountains and hills were made low, and the crooked straight, and the rough places plain. And the music went out to the dark sea and sang in the darkness, over the abyss.

When I came out they were all sitting there and none of them was talking. Max had been crying. I could see little candle flames in the tears around his eyes. Simon lay flat on the bed in the shadows, his eyes closed. Phil Drum sat hunched over, holding the solar cell in his hands.

I loosened the pegs, and put the bow and the viola in the case, and cleared my throat. It was embarrassing. I finally said, "I'm sorry."

One of the women spoke: Rose Abramski, a private student of Simon's, a big shy woman who could hardly speak at all unless it was in mathematical symbols. "I saw it," she said. "I saw it. I saw the white towers, and the water streaming down their sides, and running back down to the sea. And the sunlight shining in the streets, after ten thousand years of darkness."

"I heard them," Simon said, very low, from the shadow. "I heard their voices."

"Oh, Christ! Stop it!" Max cried out, and got up and went blundering out into the unlit hall, without his coat. We heard him running down the stairs.

"Phil," said Simon, lying there, "could we raise up the white towers, with our lever and our fulcrum?"

After a long silence Phil Drum answered, "We have the power to do it."

"What else do we need?" Simon said. "What else do we need, besides power?"

Nobody answered him.

The blue changed. It became brighter, lighter, and at the same time thicker: impure. The ethereal luminosity of blue-violet turned to turquoise, intense and opaque. Still we could not have said that everything was now turquoise-colored, for there were still no things. There was nothing, except the color of turquoise.

The change continued. The opacity became veined and thinned. The dense, solid color began to appear translucent, transparent. Then it seemed as if we were in the heart of a sacred jade, or the brilliant crystal of a sapphire or an emerald.

As at the inner structure of a crystal, there was no motion. But there was something, now, to see. It was as if we saw the motionless, elegant inward structure of the molecules of a precious stone. Planes and angles appeared about us, shadowless and clear in that even, glowing, blue-green light.

These were the walls and towers of the city, the streets, the windows, the gates.

We knew them, but we did not recognise them. We did not dare to recognise them. It had been so long. And it was

so strange. We had used to dream, when we lived in this
city. We had lain down, nights, in the rooms behind the
windows, and slept, and dreamed. We had all dreamed of
the ocean, of the deep sea. Were we not dreaming now?

Sometimes the thunder and tremor deep below us
rolled again, but it was faint now, far away; as far away as
our memory of the thunder and the tremor and the fire and
the towers falling, long ago. Neither the sound nor the
memory frightened us. We knew them.

The sapphire light brightened overhead to green, almost green-gold. We looked up. The tops of the highest
towers were hard to see, glowing in the radiance of light.
The streets and doorways were darker, more clearly defined.

In one of those long, jewel-dark streets something was
moving: something not composed of planes and angles, but
of curves and arcs. We all turned to look at it, slowly, wondering as we did so at the slow ease of our own motion, our
freedom. Sinuous, with a beautiful flowing, gathering, rolling movement, now rapid and now tentative, the thing drifted across the street from a blank garden wall to the recess
of a door. There, in the dark blue shadow, it was hard to
see for a while. We watched. A pale blue curve appeared at
the top of the doorway. A second followed, and a third. The
moving thing clung or hovered there, above the door, like a
swaying knot of silvery cords or a boneless hand, one
arched finger pointing carelessly to something above the
lintel of the door, something like itself, but motionless — a
carving. A carving in jade light. A carving in stone.

Delicately and easily the long curving tentacle followed
the curves of the carved figure, the eight petal limbs, the
round eyes. Did it recognise its image?

The living one swung suddenly, gathered its curves in a
loose knot, and darted away down the street, swift and sinuous. Behind it a faint cloud of darker blue hung for a min-

ute and dispersed, revealing again the carved figure above the door: the sea flower, the cuttlefish, quick, great-eyed, graceful, evasive, the cherished sign, carved on a thousand walls, worked into the design of cornices, pavements, handles, lids of jewel boxes, canopies, tapestries, tabletops, gateways.

Down another street, at about the level of the first-floor windows, came a flickering drift of hundreds of motes of silver. With a single motion all turned towards the cross street, and glittered off into the dark blue shadows.

There were shadows, now.

We looked up, up from the flight of silver fish, up from the streets where the jade-green currents flowed and the blue shadows fell. We moved and looked up, yearning, to the high towers of our city. They stood, the fallen towers. They glowed in the ever-brightening radiance, not blue or blue-green, up there, but gold. Far above them lay a vast, circular, trembling brightness: the sun's light on the surface of the sea.

We are here. When we break through the bright circle into life, the water will break and stream white down the white sides of the towers, and run down the steep streets back into the sea. The water will glitter in dark hair, on the eyelids of dark eyes, and dry to a thin white film of salt.

We are here.

Whose voice? Who called to us?

He was with me for twelve days. On January 28th the crats came from the Bureau of Health Education and Welfare and said that since he was receiving unemployment compensation while suffering from an untreated illness, the Government must look after him and restore him to health, because health is the inalienable right of the citizens of a democracy. He refused to sign the consent forms, so the chief Health Officer signed them. He refused to get up, so two of the policemen pulled him up off the bed. He started to try to fight them. The chief Health Officer pulled his gun and said that if he continued to struggle he would shoot him for resisting welfare, and arrest me for conspiracy to defraud the Government. The man who was holding my arms behind my back said they could always arrest me for unreported pregnancy with intent to form a nuclear family. At that Simon stopped trying to get free. It was really all he was trying to do, not to fight them, just to get his arms free. He looked at me, and they took him out.

He is in the Federal Hospital in Salem. I have not been able to find out whether he is in the regular hospital or the mental wards.

It was on the radio again yesterday, about the rising land masses in the South Atlantic and the Western Pacific. At Max's the other night I saw a TV special explaining about geophysical stresses, and subsidence, and faults. The U.S. Geodetic Service is doing a lot of advertising around town; the commonest one is a big billboard that says "It's Not Our Fault!" with a picture of a beaver pointing to a schematic map that shows how even if Oregon has a major earthquake and subsidence as California did last month, it will not affect Portland, or only the western suburbs perhaps. The news also said that they plan to halt the tidal waves in Florida by dropping nuclear bombs where Miami was. Then they will re-attach Florida to the mainland with landfill. They are already advertising real estate for housing developments on the landfill. The President is staying at the Mile High White House in Aspen, Colorado. I don't think it will do him much good. Houseboats down on the Willamette are selling for $500,000. There are no trains or busses running south from Portland, because all the highways were badly damaged by the tremors and landslides last week, so I will have to see if I can get to Salem on foot. I still have the rucksack I bought for the Mount Hood Wilderness Week. I got some dry lima beans and raisins with my Federal Fair Share Super Value Green Stamp minimal ration book for February — it took the whole book —

and Phil Drum made me a tiny camp stove powered with the solar cell. I didn't want to take the Primus, it's too bulky, and I did want to be able to carry the viola. Max gave me a half pint of brandy. When the brandy is gone I expect I will stuff this notebook into the bottle and put the cap on tight and leave it on a hillside somewhere between here and Salem. I like to think of it being lifted up little by little by the water, and rocking, and going out to the dark sea.

Where are you?
We are here. Where have you gone?

Schrödinger's Cat

As THINGS APPEAR to be coming to some sort of climax, I have withdrawn to this place. It is cooler here, and nothing moves fast.

On the way here I met a married couple who were coming apart. She had pretty well gone to pieces, but he seemed, at first glance, quite hearty. While he was telling me that he had no hormones of any kind, she pulled herself together and, by supporting her head in the crook of her right knee and hopping on the toes of the right foot, approached us shouting, "Well what's *wrong* with a person trying to express themselves?" The left leg, the arms, and the trunk, which had remained lying in the heap, twitched and jerked in sympathy. "Great legs," the husband pointed out, looking at the slim ankle. "My wife has great legs."

A cat has arrived, interrupting my narrative. It is a striped yellow tom with white chest and paws. He has long whiskers and yellow eyes. I never noticed before that cats had whiskers above their eyes; is that normal? There is no way to tell. As he has gone to sleep on my knee, I shall proceed.

Where?

Nowhere, evidently. Yet the impulse to narrate remains.

Many things are not worth doing, but almost anything is worth telling. In any case, I have a severe congenital case of *Ethica laboris puritanica,* or Adam's Disease. It is incurable except by total decapitation. I even like to dream when asleep, and to try and recall my dreams: it assures me that I haven't wasted seven or eight hours just lying there. Now here I am, lying, here. Hard at it.

Well, the couple I was telling you about finally broke up. The pieces of him trotted around bouncing and cheeping, like little chicks, but she was finally reduced to nothing but a mass of nerves: rather like fine chicken wire, in fact, but hopelessly tangled.

So I came on, placing one foot carefully in front of the other, and grieving. This grief is with me still. I fear it is part of me, like foot or loin or eye, or may even be myself: for I seem to have no other self, nothing further, nothing that lies outside the borders of grief.

Yet I don't know what I grieve for: my wife? my husband? my children, or myself? I can't remember. Most dreams are forgotten, try as one will to remember. Yet later music strikes the note, and the harmonic rings along the mandolin strings of the mind, and we find tears in our eyes. Some note keeps playing that makes me want to cry; but what for? I am not certain.

The yellow cat, who may have belonged to the couple that broke up, is dreaming. His paws twitch now and then, and once he makes a small, suppressed remark with his mouth shut. I wonder what a cat dreams of, and to whom he was speaking just then. Cats seldom waste words. They are quiet beasts. They keep their counsel, they reflect. They reflect all day, and at night their eyes reflect. Overbred Siamese cats may be as noisy as little dogs, and then people say, "They're talking," but the noise is farther from speech than is the deep silence of the hound or the tabby. All this cat can say is meow, but maybe in his silences he will suggest to me what it is that I have lost, what I am grieving for. I have a feeling that he knows. That's why he came here. Cats look out for Number One.

It was getting awfully hot. I mean, you could touch less and less. The stove burners, for instance. Now I know that stove burners always used to get hot; that was their final cause, they existed in order to get hot. But they began to get hot without having been turned on. Electric units or gas rings, there they'd be when you came into the kitchen for breakfast, all four of them glaring away, the air above them shaking like clear jelly with the heat waves. It did no good to turn them off, because they weren't on in the first place. Besides, the knobs and dials were also hot, uncomfortable to the touch.

Some people tried hard to cool them off. The favorite technique was to turn them on. It worked sometimes, but you could not count on it. Others investigated the phenomenon, tried to get at the root of it, the cause. They were probably the most frightened ones, but man is most human at his most frightened. In the face of the hot stove burners they acted with exemplary coolness. They studied, they observed. They were like the fellow in Michelangelo's *Last Judgment,* who has clapped his hands over his face in horror as the devils drag him down to Hell — but only over one eye. The other eye is busy looking. It's all he can do, but he does it. He observes. Indeed, one wonders if Hell would exist, if he did not look at it. However, neither he, nor the people I am talking about, had enough time left to do much about it. And then finally of course there were the people who did not try to do or think anything about it at all.

When the water came out of the cold-water taps hot one morning, however, even people who had blamed it all on the Democrats began to feel a more profound unease. Before long, forks and pencils and wrenches were too hot to handle without gloves; and cars were really terrible. It was like opening the door of an oven going full blast, to open the door of your car. And by then, other people almost scorched your fingers off. A kiss was like a branding iron. Your child's hair flowed along your hand like fire.

Here, as I said, it is cooler; and, as a matter of fact, this animal is cool. A real cool cat. No wonder it's pleasant to pet his fur. Also he moves slowly, at least for the most part, which is all the slowness one can reasonably expect of a cat. He hasn't that frenetic quality most creatures acquired — all they did was ZAP and gone. They lacked presence. I suppose birds always tended to be that way, but even the hummingbird used to halt for a second in the very center of his metabolic frenzy, and hang, still as a hub, present, above the fuchsias — then gone again, but you knew something was there besides the blurring brightness. But it got so that even robins and pigeons, the heavy impudent birds, were a blur; and as for swallows, they cracked the sound barrier. You knew of swallows only by the small, curved sonic booms that looped about the eaves of old houses in the evening.

Worms shot like subway trains through the dirt of gardens, among the writhing roots of roses.

You could scarcely lay a hand on children, by then: too fast to catch, too hot to hold. They grew up before your eyes.

But then, maybe that's always been true.

I was interrupted by the cat, who woke and said meow once, then jumped down from my lap and leaned against my legs diligently. This is a cat who knows how to get fed. He also knows how to jump. There was a lazy fluidity to his leap, as if gravity affected him less than it does other creatures. As a matter of fact there were some localised cases, just before I left, of the failure of gravity; but this quality in the cat's leap was something quite else. I am not yet in such a state of confusion that I can be alarmed by grace. Indeed, I found it reassuring. While I was opening a can of sardines, a person arrived.

Hearing the knock, I thought it might be the mailman. I miss mail very much, so I hurried to the door and said, "Is it the mail?"

A voice replied, "Yah!" I opened the door. He came in, almost pushing me aside in his haste. He dumped down an enor-

mous knapsack he had been carrying, straightened up, massaged
his shoulders, and said, "Wow!"

"How did you get here?"

He stared at me and repeated, "How?"

At this my thoughts concerning human and animal speech
recurred to me, and I decided that this was probably not a man,
but a small dog. (Large dogs seldom go yah, wow, how, unless it
is appropriate to do so.)

"Come on, fella," I coaxed him. "Come, come on, that's a
boy, good doggie!" I opened a can of pork and beans for him at
once, for he looked half starved. He ate voraciously, gulping and
lapping. When it was gone he said "Wow!" several times. I was
just about to scratch him behind the ears when he stiffened, his
hackles bristling, and growled deep in his throat. He had noticed
the cat.

The cat had noticed him some time before, without interest,
and was now sitting on a copy of *The Well-Tempered Clavier*
washing sardine oil off its whiskers.

"Wow!" the dog, whom I had thought of calling Rover,
barked. "Wow! Do you know what that is? *That's Schrödinger's
cat!*"

"No it's not, not any more; it's my cat," I said, unreason-
ably offended.

"Oh, well, Schrödinger's dead, of course, but it's his cat.
I've seen hundreds of pictures of it. Erwin Schrödinger, the
great physicist, you know. Oh, wow! To think of finding it here!"

The cat looked coldly at him for a moment, and began to
wash its left shoulder with negligent energy. An almost religious
expression had come into Rover's face. "It was meant," he said
in a low, impressive tone. "Yah. It was *meant*. It can't be a mere
coincidence. It's too improbable. Me, with the box; you, with the
cat; to meet — here — now." He looked up at me, his eyes
shining with happy fervor. "Isn't it wonderful?" he said. "I'll get
the box set up right away." And he started to tear open his huge
knapsack.

While the cat washed its front paws, Rover unpacked.

While the cat washed its tail and belly, regions hard to reach gracefully, Rover put together what he had unpacked, a complex task. When he and the cat finished their operations simultaneously and looked at me, I was impressed. They had come out even, to the very second. Indeed it seemed that something more than chance was involved. I hoped it was not myself.

"What's that?" I asked, pointing to a protuberance on the outside of the box. I did not ask what the box was as it was quite clearly a box.

"The gun," Rover said with excited pride.

"The gun?"

"To shoot the cat."

"To shoot the cat?"

"Or to *not shoot* the cat. Depending on the photon."

"The photon?"

"Yah! It's Schrödinger's great Gedankenexperiment. You see, there's a little emitter here. At Zero Time, five seconds after the lid of the box is closed, it will emit one photon. The photon will strike a half-silvered mirror. The quantum mechanical probability of the photon passing through the mirror is exactly one half, isn't it? So! If the photon passes through, the trigger will be activated and the gun will fire. If the photon is deflected, the trigger will not be activated and the gun will not fire. Now, you put the cat in. The cat is in the box. You close the lid. You go away! You stay away! What happens?" Rover's eyes were bright.

"The cat gets hungry?"

"The cat gets shot — or not shot," he said, seizing my arm, though not, fortunately, in his teeth. "But the gun is silent, perfectly silent. The box is soundproof. There is no way to know whether or not the cat has been shot, until you lift the lid of the box. There is *no* way! Do you see how central this is to the whole of quantum theory? Before Zero Time the whole system, on the quantum level or on our level, is nice and simple. But after Zero Time the whole system can be represented only by a linear combination of two waves. We cannot predict the behavior of the photon, and thus, once it has behaved, we cannot predict the state of the system it has determined. We cannot predict it! God plays dice with the world! So it is beautifully demonstrated that if you desire certainty, any certainty, you must create it yourself!"

"How?"

"By lifting the lid of the box, of course," Rover said, looking at me with sudden disappointment, perhaps a touch of suspicion, like a Baptist who finds he has been talking church matters not to another Baptist as he thought, but a Methodist, or even, God forbid, an Episcopalian. "To find out whether the cat is dead or not."

"Do you mean," I said carefully, "that until you lift the lid of the box, the cat has neither been shot nor not been shot?"

"Yah!" Rover said, radiant with relief, welcoming me back to the fold. "Or maybe, you know, both."

"But why does opening the box and looking reduce the system back to one probability, either live cat or dead cat? Why don't we get included in the system when we lift the lid of the box?"

There was a pause. "How?" Rover barked, distrustfully.

"Well, we would involve ourselves in the system, you see, the superposition of two waves. There's no reason why it should only exist *inside* an open box, is there? So when we came to look, there we would be, you and I, both looking at a live cat, and both looking at a dead cat. You see?"

A dark cloud lowered on Rover's eyes and brow. He barked twice in a subdued, harsh voice, and walked away. With his back turned to me he said in a firm, sad tone, "You must not complicate the issue. It is complicated enough."

"Are you sure?"

He nodded. Turning, he spoke pleadingly. "Listen. It's all we have — the box. Truly it is. The box. And the cat. And they're here. The box, the cat, at last. Put the cat in the box.

Will you? Will you let me put the cat in the box?"

"No," I said, shocked.

"Please. Please. Just for a minute. Just for half a minute! Please let me put the cat in the box!"

"Why?"

"I can't stand this terrible uncertainty," he said, and burst into tears.

I stood some while indecisive. Though I felt sorry for the poor son of a bitch, I was about to tell him, gently, No; when a curious thing happened. The cat walked over to the box, sniffed around it, lifted his tail and sprayed a corner to mark his territory, and then lightly, with that marvellous fluid ease, leapt into it. His yellow tail just flicked the edge of the lid as he jumped, and it closed, falling into place with a soft, decisive click.

"The cat is in the box," I said.

"The cat is in the box," Rover repeated in a whisper, falling to his knees. "Oh, wow. Oh, wow. Oh, wow."

There was silence then: deep silence. We both gazed, I afoot, Rover kneeling, at the box. No sound. Nothing happened. Nothing would happen. Nothing would ever happen, until we lifted the lid of the box.

"Like Pandora," I said in a weak whisper. I could not quite recall Pandora's legend. She had let all the plagues and evils out of the box, of course, but there had been something else, too. After all the devils were let loose, something quite different, quite unexpected, had been left. What had it been? Hope? A dead cat? I could not remember.

Impatience welled up in me. I turned on Rover, glaring. He returned the look with expressive brown eyes. You can't tell me dogs haven't got souls.

"Just exactly what are you trying to prove?" I demanded.

"That the cat will be dead, or not dead," he murmured submissively. "Certainty. All I want is certainty. To know for *sure* that God *does* play dice with the world."

I looked at him for a while with fascinated incredulity.

"Whether he does, or doesn't," I said, "do you think he's going to leave you a note about it in the box?" I went to the box, and with a rather dramatic gesture, flung the lid back. Rover staggered up from his knees, gasping, to look. The cat was, of course, not there.

Rover neither barked, nor fainted, nor cursed, nor wept. He really took it very well.

"Where is the cat?" he asked at last.

"Where is the box?"

"Here."

"Where's here?"

"Here is now."

"We used to think so," I said, "but really we should use larger boxes."

He gazed about him in mute bewilderment, and did not flinch even when the roof of the house was lifted off just like the lid of a box, letting in the unconscionable, inordinate light of the stars. He had just time to breathe, "Oh, wow!"

I have identified the note that keeps sounding. I checked it on the mandolin before the glue melted. It is the note A, the one that drove the composer Schumann mad. It is a beautiful, clear tone, much clearer now that the stars are visible. I shall miss the cat. I wonder if he found what it was we lost?

North

Two Delays on the Northern Line

1. Going to Paraguananza

THE RIVER was in flood, embankments under water clear down the line from Brailava to Krasnoy. A two-hour train trip had stretched into an afternoon of shunting, waiting, crawling from one village siding to another all through the hills of the upper Molsen province in heavy, inexhaustible rain. Rain was bringing down an early twilight on the tracks, the thistles, the tin roofs, the far-off barn and single poplar tree of an outlying farm of a nameless village somewhere west of the capital, when this scene, which had sat in self-contained enigmatic patience outside the window for fifty minutes, was eclipsed by a screeching rush of blackness. "There's the freight! Now we'll get on," said the salesman, who knew everything, and the family from Mesoval rejoiced. When the tracks, thistles, roofs, barn, and tree had reappeared, the train did begin to move, and quietly, unchanged, indifferent, these things disappeared backwards forever into the rainy dusk. The family from Mesoval and the salesman congratulated one another, "Now we're off, it can't be over half an hour, Krasnoy at last." Eduard Orte reopened his book.

When he looked up after reading a page or two it had got quite dark outside. Lights of a lone car on a road far away swung round and were lost. In the dark, deep in glimmering rain, he saw the line of the green window blind and under it his face.

He looked with assurance at that face. At twenty he had disliked it. At forty he owned it. Deep lines, long nose, long chin, that was Eduard Orte; he looked at him as an equal, without admiration or contempt. But he saw in the shape of the brows what people had seen when they used to say, "How you take after her," "Eduard has his mother's eyes," stupidly, as if they were not his eyes, as if he had no claim to see the world for himself. But in the second twenty years he had made his claim good.

Despite the divagations and false starts of this day's journey he knew where he was going and what would happen. His brother Nikolas would meet him at North Station, drive him eastward through the rainy city to the house where they had been born. Their mother would be sitting up in bed under the pink lamp. If this had been a mild attack she would look rather childlike and her voice would be thin; if it had been severe enough to frighten her into resistance, she would be alert and cheerful. They would ask each other questions and answer them. Then dinner downstairs, and a chat with Nikolas and his quiet wife, and to bed, hearing the rain on the windows of the bedroom where he had slept the first twenty years. Almost certainly his sister Retsia would not be there; she would have remembered she had left three small children in Solariy, and rushed back to them in a panic, just as she had rushed away from them. Nikolas would never have wired him, would simply have telephoned after the attack to give him the doctor's report, but Retsia thrived on commotion, flew to bedsides, fired off telegrams, COME AT ONCE, with more sense for the dramatic than of the ludicrous. Their mother, entirely content with Nikolas's twice-weekly visits, had not the faintest desire to "see" either Eduard or Retsia, to have her routines disrupted and her hoarded vitality called upon for an expenditure of specious interest in their doings, which had not interested her for years. But Retsia needed the expectable, the conventional, so badly that she regularly employed the inconvenient to achieve it. When wired COME AT ONCE to the sick mother's bedside, one comes. To certain moves in chess only certain responses are possible. Eduard Orte, a stronger and more conscious adherent of convention than his sister, submitted his will to the rules without complaint. But it was like chess without a board, this tracking back and forth for nothing: the same pointless trip three times in two years, or was it three years since the first attack? — so pointless, such a waste of time that he scarcely cared if the train went on all night as it had done all afternoon, shifting from siding to siding in the hills, off the main line and getting no closer; it made no difference.

When he got off the train and found in the wet hubbub of the platform and the glare and echoes of North Station nobody to meet him, he felt let down, betrayed. The emotion was quite inappropriate. Nikolas would hardly have stayed to meet a train five hours late. Eduard considered calling the house to say he had arrived, and then wondered why the thought had entered his head. It had risen from his stupid disappointment at not being met. He went out to get a taxi. At the bus stop near the taxi stand, a 41 was waiting; without hesitation he walked to it and got onto it. It had been how long, ten years, fifteen, no, longer than that, since he had ridden a bus crosstown through the loud streets of Krasnoy, dark and flashing in the March night, street lamps stretching reflections down into the rivers of black asphalt, as when he was a student riding home after late class at the University. The 41 stopped at the old stop at the foot of the Hill and a couple of students got on, pale, grave girls. The Molsen under Old Bridge ran very high in its stone embankments; everyone craned to see, and somebody behind him said, "It's up over the warehouses down below Rail Bridge." The bus groaned, swayed, stopped, lurched its way through the long straight

streets of the Trasfiuve. Orte was the last but one to get off. The
bus with its solitary passenger gasped its door shut and went on,
leaving a quietness in its wake, the suburban quietness. Rain fell
steadily. At the corner near a street lamp a young tree stood
startled by light, its new leaves piercing green. There were no
further delays or changes of route. Orte walked the last half
block home.

He knocked softly, pushed the unlocked door open, and entered. For some reason the hall was brightly lighted. A loud
voice was talking in the sitting room, a stranger's voice. Was
there a party going on? As he took off his topcoat to hang it on
the hall coatrack, a boy came careening past, stopped at a distance, and stared with bright, bold eyes.

"Who are you?" Orte asked, as the boy asked the same
question, and as he answered, "Eduard Orte," the boy gave the
same answer.

For a moment his head spun with the dizziness that he
dreaded, the abyss opening, the falling.

"I'm your uncle," he said, tapping the rain off his hat and
hanging it up. "Is your mother here?"

"In the piano room. With the funerals man." The boy kept
gazing, studying him, self-possessed, as if in his own house. Why
did he not stand out of the way? I cannot go past him, Orte
thought.

Retsia came into the hallway, saw him, cried, "Oh, Eduard!"
and burst instantly into tears. "Oh, poor Eduard!"

She drew him with her, relinquishing him only to Nikolas,
who shook his hand softly and seriously, saying in his even voice,
"You'd left. We couldn't reach you. Very easy, much suddener
than expected, but very easy at the end. . . ."

"I see, yes," Orte said. The abyss hung under him, he held
his brother's hand. "The train," he said.

"At two o'clock almost exactly," Nikolas said.

Retsia said, "We've been calling the station all afternoon.
The whole railway above Aris is under water. You must be worn

out, poor Eduard! And not knowing, all day long, the whole afternoon!" Tears ran down her face as plentiful and simple as
rain running down the windows of the train.

Orte had intended to ask several questions of Nikolas before he went up to see his mother: Had it in fact been a severe
attack? Is she on the same medication? Has there been much
angina? Now he still wanted to ask these questions, which after
all had not been answered. Nikolas continued to tell him about
the death, but he had not asked about that. It was not fair. He
still felt a little light-headed, but that was from travelling all
day. The abyss had closed and he had let go Nikolas's hand.
Retsia hovered close, smiling, tearful. Nikolas, he noticed,
looked strained and tired, his eyes rather swollen behind his
thick spectacles. What did he look like himself? Did he show
any such signs of grief? Did he feel grief? He looked into himself with apprehension, finding nothing except the continuing
slight unpleasant dizziness. One could not call that grief. Should
he not wish to cry?

"Is she upstairs?"

Nikolas explained the new government regulations. "They
have been most efficient and considerate," he said. The body
had been taken to the East District Crematory; a man had come
by with the papers, to arrange for the display and service; they
had just been completing the arrangements when Eduard arrived. They all moved about, went to the music room, the man
was introduced. It was his voice Orte had first heard coming
into the house, the loud voice and bright lights, like a party.
Nikolas showed the man out. "I met," Eduard Orte said to his
sister, then hesitated — "young Eduard." Then wished he had
not spoken, because the nephew named for him could not be
that boy, who was much too old, and who had said his name was
Orte, had he not? when it must be Paren; Retsia's married name
was Paren. But who was the boy, then?

"Yes, I did want the children here," Retsia was saying.
"Tomas will drive up tomorrow morning. I do hope it stops rain-

ing, the roads must be terrible." He noticed her strong ivory teeth. She must be, it was impossible, thirty-eight. He would not have known her had they passed on the street. Her eyes were greyish blue. She was looking at him. "You're tired," she said in the way that had used to irritate him, telling people what they felt; but the words were welcome to him. He was not aware of being particularly tired, but if he looked tired, or was tired without knowing it, perhaps also he had feelings he was unaware of, appropriate feelings. "Come and have some supper, now that man's gone. You must be starving! The children are eating in the kitchen. Oh, Eduard, everything is so strange!" she said, leading him briskly on.

The kitchen was warm and full of people. The cook-housekeeper Vera, who had come after his time but had been there for years now, greeted him mumbling. She was upset, and he understood that; how was an old woman with bad legs to get a new job? But no doubt Nikolas and Nina would take her in. Retsia's children were all at the kitchen table: the boy he had met in the hall, and the older sister, and the little boy, whom they had called Riri last time Orte had seen them, but were calling Raul now; and there was another one, that sister or cousin of Retsia's husband who lived with them, a short, sullen girl of twenty or more. Nikolas's wife Nina came from behind the table to greet him with an embrace. As she spoke, he remembered what he had not thought of since Nikolas's letter about it a couple of weeks ago, that Nikolas and Nina had adopted a baby — had Nikolas written that it was a boy? It had all seemed so artificial to him that he had read the letter carelessly, finding the matter distasteful and embarrassing, and now he could not recall what Nikolas had written. It would not do to ask Nina about it. Old Vera insisted on making tea for him to show that she was necessary, and he had to sit down with them all in the bright noisy kitchen and eat a little, wait for the tea and drink it. The noise abated. Nobody spoke to him much; Nina glanced at him with her sad, dark eyes. He began to re-

alise with relief that his habitual gravity of manner might be
taken for emotion controlled, might serve him as a façade behind which he could keep to himself his lack of sorrow, like a
locked and empty room.

He was not allowed to sleep in his old room upstairs after
all. Nothing he had expected happened. The house was full up.
It seemed that since the adoption Nikolas and Nina had given
up their flat in Old Quarter and moved back here till they came
in line for a larger flat. They were in Eduard's old room, and
their baby was in Nikolas's old room; Retsia and her three were
in the nursery; the cousin slept on the living-room couch; there
was nothing left for him but the leather couch in the glassed-in
porch off the music room, downstairs. Only the mother's room
was empty. He did not see it. He did not go upstairs. Retsia
brought down blankets, then a quilt, finally a warm dressing
gown of Nikolas's. "It's terrible out here, terrible, poor Eduard.
If you sleep in this it might help you stay warm. Oh, how
strange everything is!" Her hair was braided for sleep, she wore
a pink wool wrapper. She looked broad, competent, maternal,
beautiful; her face was illuminated as if she were listening to
music. That is grief, he thought.

"It's all right," he said.

"But you always get cold feet at night. It's terrible to stick
you out here. I don't know what we'll do when Tomas comes.
Oh, Eduard, I do so wish that you'd got married, I hate for
people to be alone! I know you don't mind, but I do. The curtains won't close, will they? Oh, Christ, I've torn the side hem.
Well, there's nothing to shut out here but the rain." The ready
tears stood in her eyes; her warmth and strength enveloped him
a moment as she hugged him. "Good night!" she said and left,
shutting the curtained glass door behind her, and he heard her
voice and the cousin's in the next room.

She went upstairs. The house grew silent. He rearranged
the blankets and quilt and lay down on the couch. He read the
book he had read on the train, a long-term project for goals and

fund allocations in the department that would, in May, come under the administration of his bureau. Rain brushed the windows above the couch. His hands grew cold. Silently and suddenly the light in the next room went out, leaving the curtained glass door black, and the light from his small reading lamp very dim. The cousin was in that room. The house was full of people he did not know. This porch, cold, in night and rain, was strange to him. They never used the porch except in summer, on hot days. This was not the trip he had started out on. To come home, that was one true direction, but now it had lost its sense, he had ended up in a strange place. Was this confusion what they called grief? She is dead, he thought, she is dead, as he lay fairly comfortably propped against the arm of the couch, the book open against his raised knees under the quilt, gazing at the page numbers 144, 145, and waited for the reaction. But he had left home so long ago, after all. 144, 145. His eyes returned to the paragraph he had been reading. He read on to the end of the section. His watch said two-thirty. He turned off the bronze-shaded reading lamp and huddled down under the blankets and quilts; he heard the rain brush quietly against the windows. "I am going to Paraguay," he told the salesman, annoyed at being asked. "To Paraguananza, the capital of the nation." But they met with long delays along the line from floods of water, and when he got there, across terrible abysses, to Paraguananza, it was no different from here.

2. Metempsychosis

WHEN THE LAWYER'S LETTER CAME, Eduard Russe thought nothing at first about the house that had been willed to him, but tried only to dredge up from the shifty bogs of memory some shard or fragment, a cranium, a fingerbone, of that great-uncle, his mother's father's brother, who had seen fit, or been forced by a paucity of survivors, to leave him the house in Brailava. He had always lived in Krasnoy; when he was nine or ten he had gone with his mother to visit their Northern relatives, but of that journey he could recall only the most trivial things — a hen with her brood of chicks in a back yard by a basket, a man standing and singing aloud on a street corner directly under (so his child's eye averred) a huge, dark-blue mountain. Of the grandfather who had then owned the house, of the great-uncle who had next inherited it, nothing remained but a discomfort of dark rooms and loud old voices. Old men, deaf, not the same species as himself, no kin. Crossed swords with basket grips and curved blades hanging on a chimney: sabres. He had never seen a sabre. He was not allowed to play with them. The old men did nothing with them, did not keep them polished. If they had let him take them down he would have polished them. He was ashamed, now, of this ingratitude of mind which left him only his own childish envies and not one glimpse of the man who had given him a house — even if he did not want the house and could wish the old man had, equally, forgotten him. What was he to do with a house in Brailava? What was he supposed to reply to the lawyer's letter? Employed in the Bureau of Housing, on modest salary, he had never had any use for lawyers and had kept well clear of the breed. His wife would have known how to answer the letter; she had good sense about such things, and good manners too. Following what he imagined Elena might have written, he produced a short, civil acknowledgment of the lawyer's communication, posted it, and then, in fact, altogether forgot about the great-uncle, the legacy, the property in Brailava. He was busy, having undertaken an extra task of the kind he was good at, a reorganisation and simplification of record-keeping. People would say he was trying to lose himself in his work, but though he had always liked his work and still did, he knew there was no way to lose himself in it. Rather he found himself in it constantly, met himself in the work he had done, in the people he worked with. On every street corner on the way to the Bureau he met himself coming back from work to the apartment on Sidres Street where Elena, who taught in the College of

Applied Arts, would be home already, unless it was Wednesday night when she had a class from four to six —

His days were punctuated by these dashes, not periods but breaks, empty spaces in which he stopped himself from finishing the thought, or from trying to finish the thought which no longer had an end, since in this case Elena had no class from four to six on Wednesday, because she was dead of an aneurysm of the heart and had been dead for three months, and in any case all thoughts led to this same non-end or stopping place and were there, as in the cremator's fire, destroyed.

He knew he could manage his misery in a wiser way, without these breaks and terrible repetitions, if he could sleep well. But he could never sleep, now, more than two or three hours at a time, and then would wake and lie awake as long as he had slept. He tried drinking, and he tried the sleeping pills a friend at work recommended. Both gave him five hours' sleep, two hours' nightmare, and a day of sick despair. He went back to reading during his night wakings. He read anything, but preferred history, the histories of other countries. Sometimes, at three in the morning, he cried, as he read the history of Renaissance Spain, ignoring his tears. He had no dreams. She had taken his dreams, and they had gone with her too far, by now, to find their way back to him. They had got lost and petered out, dried up, somewhere in that thick, rock-ridden darkness through which Elena had very slowly gone, tunnelling her way forward, heavily, without breathing. He felt that she was beyond that now, in some other region, but not one he was able to imagine.

A second letter arrived from the law firm in Brailava. The envelope was double-weight manila, heavy, portentous. Resigned, he opened it. The lawyer's letter was short and only moderately obscure, appearing to suggest, with due caution, that as things stood (and undoubtedly given his professional affiliation he was far better informed on this subject than the writer), he might find, if he decided to consider selling the house, that it was possible to get a good price for it; dissociating himself promptly, the lawyer, whom Eduard now envisaged as almost inevitably sixty and clean-shaven with a long upper lip, went on to remark that there were several reputable real-property agents in Krasnoy with Northern branches, if he did not wish to be troubled with the business himself. However, personal belongings left in the house might demand, at least briefly, his presence and decision as to whether the furniture, papers, books, etc., were of value, monetary or sentimental. With the letter were some documents, evidently deeds, descriptions, and so on, concerning the property, and, in an old, soft, rather mangy leather pouch, a steel ring on which were six keys.

It was curious that he should have sent them without waiting to hear from Eduard again, to identify him more securely, to meet him. It was the keys that had made the envelope misshapen and heavy. Eduard spread them out fanwise on his left palm with his right forefinger and studied them with uneasy curiosity. Two, identical, looked like old-fashioned, respectable front-door keys. The other four were wildly various: one that might fit a big padlock, one with a barrel like a clock key, one plain iron all-purpose that suggested a pantry or cellar door, and one of brass with delicately intricate wards, probably the key to some old piece of furniture, a wardrobe or escritoire. He imagined, with continuing unease, the brass keyhole in the curved mahogany, shelves behind glass, meaningless papers in half-empty drawers.

He requested two days off work at the end of the month. He would go up to Brailava on the Wednesday evening train, come back on the Sunday. Efficiency. See the lawyer, see the house, arrange to have it cleared out and put up for sale. While looking after all this he would be able to see something of the city where his mother had been born and lived as a child. With the money from the sale of the house he would go to Spain. Unearned money should be spent at once, otherwise it festered. What would it cost to go to Egypt? He had always wanted to see the pyramids. Red-coated, waving sabres, cinematic English

soldiers charged thinly across a waste of gold behind the back of
the indifferent Sphinx and petered out, like water poured onto
sand. The Sahara, a furnace, an empty place. The train jerked
forward tentatively and stopped again. No one else was in the
compartment at the moment; the young couple who had taken
the facing seat were standing in the corridor. They had been
joking with friends on the platform. Now they shouted and
waved and banged the windows childishly as the train, quiet and
purposeful, began to glide forward. Eduard's eyes filled up with
tears and his breath stuck in an audible sob. Appalled by the
ambush, by the overwhelming advantage grief had over him, he
clenched his hands, shut his eyes, feigned sleep, although his
face was hot and his breath would not come evenly. He fore-
swore Egypt, damn Egypt, damn Toledo and Madrid. The tears
dried in his eyes. He watched the northern suburbs slide past
beyond the viaducts in the soft, amniotic haze of the September
afternoon.

The young couple came back into the compartment, no
longer talking or smiling; their animation had been all for their
friends in North Station. Eduard continued to gaze out the window as the train ran steadily north on the level embankments by
the Molsen. The river was wide, serene, a pale silken blue color
between low banks. Willows stood in the late sunlight by the
river. The haze was thickening; it looked like rain ahead, in the
north, a heavy blueness of clouds. He had got off work early to
catch the five o'clock express. They would be in Brailava by half
past six, following the river all the way. He got a little drowsy,
looking at the silken water.

At a quarter to six there was a tremendous noise and a
subsequent absolute silence. As Eduard picked himself up from
the floor of the compartment where for some reason he had arrived, the young man kicked him in the shoulder. "Watch that!"
Eduard said furiously, and retrieved his briefcase, which had
also slid across the floor. There was now a strange, thin commotion of voices in the corridor. "Oh, oh, oh, oh," the young wom-

an was saying in a silly voice. The commotion grew to a hubbub like that of an audience at intermission, both inside the car and outside along the tracks, shouts, exclamations, descriptions, comparisons, complaints, as it became clear that the engine had hit a hay truck stalled at a crossing, and that though nobody was hurt except for the truck driver, who had been killed, the engine had derailed and there was going to be a delay while they brought a relief engine down from Brailava. Another break, a dash not a period; non-arrival. Eduard walked up and down the tracks a while in the late long sunlight. It was almost seven when a relief engine arrived, from the south not the north, and pulled the train back to a siding at the local station called Isestno, which was not even mentioned on the Krasnoy–Brailava schedule of the Northern Line; and there it waited, while night fell and the rain came on, until the tracks were mended and the relief engine from Brailava came and hauled it on in, arriving at Sumeny Station at half past ten.

There had been nothing whatever to eat on the train and no vendors at mournful Isestno siding, but Eduard did not feel hungry as he walked under the bright cavernous dome of Sumeny, carrying the briefcase which was all he had brought. Now that he was off the train at last, he felt shaken. He had planned to arrive at half past six, find a hotel near the station, have dinner, but now he did not want to stay up and eat out among strangers, he wanted to go home. Other men hurried past him through the high doors into the rainy night.

"Taxi?"

"All right," he said.

"Where to, sir?"

"Fourteen Kamenny Street."

"That'll be up Underhill," the taxi driver said, confirming Eduard's memory of the name of the district and of the dark-blue crags hunched over a singing man, a man under a hill, and took off, doors and smeared windows rattling. It was dark in the cab and the smell was comfortable. Eduard roused himself, confused, almost from sleep, and sank back into it, almost.

"Fourteen, was it?"

"Right."

"This one, looks like. There's Twelve."

He could see no street number. There was a house; there was rain, trees, darkness. He paid the driver, who said good night to him in the dry, civil, Northern voice.

Three stone steps, flanked by shrubs and some kind of iron fence or grille: "14" over the rather ornate wooden doorframe. A strange city, a strange street, whose house? The first of the twin keys fit the lock. He opened the door, looked in, took a couple of steps in, but left the door ajar behind him, to be certain of escape.

Pitch dark; dry; cool. Sound of rain above on high roofs. No other sound.

The light switch came under his hand to the right of the door. He felt that he should say, "I'm here." To whom? He turned on the light.

The hall was much smaller than it had seemed in darkness. He had, he now realised, felt himself to be in an almost limitless space, but it was only the quiet shabby front hall of an old house on a rainy night. The strip of carpet on the handsome black and grey tiles was worn and not very clean. Somebody's hat, his great-uncle's hat, an old felt, lay forlorn on a small sideboard. The light fixture was of yellowish cloudy glass.

The door was still ajar behind him. He returned and closed it, and automatically put the key ring into his trousers pocket.

Stairs went up to the left. The hall went on past them: a door to the right and an end door, both shut. The sitting room would be that one to the right, the end one would lead back to the kitchen. There was a dining room, maybe on the way to the kitchen; it was in a dark dining room that he had heard the loud old voices. He should look into the rooms, but he was tired. He had been sleeping very badly for several nights, and the train trip with its shock and unfelt death and long delay had left him shaky. The hall was all right, the old hat was all right, but he could not take much more. The yellowish light illuminated the stairs as well as the hall. He went up the stairs, his right hand on the narrow heavily varnished railing. At the top he turned and went down the hall to the end door, opened it, and turned on the light. He did not know why he chose that door, or whether he had been upstairs in the house as a child. This was the front bedroom, probably the largest. It might be the room his great-uncle had slept in, perhaps died in, unless he had died in hospital, or it might have been the grandfather's room, or have stood unused for thirty years. It was clean and sparse, bed, table, chair, two windows, fireplace. The bed was made, tight and neat, an old blue coverlet pulled tight. The overhead light in its glass shade was dim, and there was no lamp.

Eduard put down his briefcase by the bed.

The washroom was at the other end of the hall. He thought at first the water had been cut off, for the pipe groaned when he turned the faucet, but then it spat rust, belched red, and ran clear. He was thirsty. He drank from the faucet. The water was rusty and cold and tasted of the north.

There was an old bookcase with glassed shelves in the hall, and he stopped before it for a minute, but the light was faint and the titles of the books meant nothing. He could not read. He went into the front bedroom and turned back the blue coverlet. The bed was made up with heavy linen sheets and a dark blanket. He took off his clothes, hung his coat and trousers in the empty closet, turned off the light, got into the cold bed in the dark room made tremulous by a distant street lamp shining through rain or the shadows of leaves; he stretched out and laid his head back on the hard pillow, and slept.

He woke in sunlit morning, lying on his side, looking at the swords, cavalry sabres, hung crossed on the chimneypiece.

They were tools, he thought, expressing purpose as simply as a needle or a hammer, their purpose, their reason or meaning, being death; they were made to kill men with; the slightly curved and still unpolished blades were death, were in fact his own death, which he saw with clarity and relaxation; for as his eyes were occupied with looking at that his mind was wandering to the other rooms, which he had not seen last night, the rooms whose doors, for which he had the keys, would lead to his life, his request for a transfer to the Bureau here in Brailava, the wild cherry flowering in the mountains in March, his second marriage, all that, but for the moment enough, this room, the swords, the sunlight; he had arrived.

SQ

I THINK what Dr. Speakie has done is wonderful. He is a wonderful man. I believe that. I believe that people need beliefs. If I didn't have my belief I really don't know what would happen.

And if Dr. Speakie hadn't truly believed in his work he couldn't possibly have done what he did. Where would he have found the courage? What he did proves his genuine sincerity.

There was a time when a lot of people tried to cast doubts on him. They said he was seeking power. That was never true. From the very beginning all he wanted was to help people and make a better world. The people who called him a power-seeker and a dictator were just the same ones who used to say that Hitler was insane and Nixon was insane and all the world leaders were insane and the arms race was insane and our misuse of natural resources was insane and the whole world civilisation was insane and suicidal. They were always saying that. And they said it about Dr. Speakie. But he stopped all that insanity, didn't he? So he was right all along, and he was right to believe in his beliefs.

I came to work for him when he was named the Chief of

the Psychometric Bureau. I used to work at the U.N., and when the World Government took over the New York U.N. Building they transferred me up to the thirty-fifth floor to be the head secretary in Dr. Speakie's office. I knew already that it was a position of great responsibility, and I was quite excited the whole week before my new job began. I was so curious to meet Dr. Speakie, because of course he was already famous. I was there right at the dot of nine on Monday morning, and when he came in it was so wonderful. He looked so kind. You could tell that the weight of his responsibilities was always on his mind, but he looked so healthy and positive, and there was a bounce in his step — I used to think it was as if he had rubber balls in the toes of his shoes. He smiled and shook my hand and said in such a friendly, confident voice, "And you must be Mrs. Smith! I've heard wonderful things about you. We're going to have a wonderful team here, Mrs. Smith!"

Later on he called me by my first name, of course.

That first year we were mostly busy with Information. The World Government Presidium and all the Member States had to be fully informed about the nature and purpose of the SQ Test, before the actual implementation of its application could be eventualised. That was good for me too, because in preparing all that information I learned all about it myself. Often, taking dictation, I learned about it from Dr. Speakie's very lips. By May I was enough of an "expert" that I was able to prepare the Basic SQ Information Pamphlet for publication just from Dr. Speakie's notes. It was such fascinating work. As soon as I began to understand the SQ Test Plan I began to believe in it. That was true of everybody in the office and in the Bureau. Dr. Speakie's sincerity and scientific enthusiasm were infectious. Right from the beginning we had to take the Test every quarter, of course, and some of the secretaries used to be nervous before they took it, but I never was. It was so obvious that the Test was *right*. If you scored under 50 it was nice to know that you were sane, but even if you scored over 50 that was fine too, because then you could be *helped*. And anyway it is always best to know the truth about yourself.

As soon as the Information service was functioning smoothly Dr. Speakie transferred the main thrust of his attention to the implementation of Evaluator training, and planning for the structurisation of the Cure Centers, only he changed the name to SQ Achievement Centers. It seemed a very big job even then. We certainly had no idea how big the job would finally turn out to be!

As he said at the beginning, we were a very good team. We all worked hard, but there were always rewards.

I remember one wonderful day. I had accompanied Dr. Speakie to the Meeting of the Board of the Psychometric Bureau. The emissary from the State of Brazil announced that his State had adopted the Bureau Recommendations for Universal Testing — we had known that that was going to be announced. But then the delegate from Libya and the delegate from China announced that their States had adopted the Test too! Oh, Dr. Speakie's face was just like the sun for a minute, just *shining*. I wish I could remember exactly what he said, especially to the Chinese delegate, because of course China was a very big State and its decision was very influential. Unfortunately I do not have his exact words because I was changing the tape in the recorder. He said something like, "Gentlemen, this is a historic day for humanity." Then he began to talk at once about the effective implementation of the Application Centers, where people would take the Test, and the Achievement Centers, where they would go if they scored over 50, and how to establish the Test Administrations and Evaluations infrastructure on such a large scale, and so on. He was always modest and practical. He would rather talk about doing the job than talk about what an important job it was. He used to say, "Once you know what you're doing, the only thing you need to think about is how to do it." I believe that that is deeply true.

From then on, we could hand over the Information program

to a subdepartment and concentrate on How to Do It. Those were exciting times! So many States joined the Plan, one after another. When I think of all we had to do I wonder that we didn't all go crazy! Some of the office staff did fail their quarterly Test, in fact. But most of us working in the Executive Office with Dr. Speakie remained quite stable, even when we were on the job all day and half the night. I think his presence was an inspiration. He was always calm and positive, even when we had to arrange things like training 113,000 Chinese Evaluators in three months. "You can always find out 'how' if you just know the 'why'!" he would say. And we always did.

When you think back over it it really is quite amazing what a big job it was — so much bigger than anybody, even Dr. Speakie, had realised it would be. It just changed everything. You only realise that when you think back to what things used to be like. Can you imagine, when we began planning Universal Testing for the State of China, we only allowed for 1,100 Achievement Centers, with 6,800 Staff? It really seems like a joke! But it is not. I was going through some of the old files yesterday, making sure everything is in order, and I found the first China Implementation Plan, with those figures written down in black and white.

I believe the reason why even Dr. Speakie was slow to realise the magnitude of the operation was that even though he was a great scientist he was also an optimist. He just kept hoping against hope that the average scores would begin to go down, and this prevented him from seeing that universal application of the SQ Test was eventually going to involve everybody either as Inmates or as Staff.

When most of the Russias and all the African States had adopted the Recommendations and were busy implementing them, the debates in the General Assembly of the World Government got very excited. That was the period when so many bad things were said about the Test and about Dr. Speakie. I used to get quite angry, reading the *World Times* reports of debates. When I went as his secretary with Dr. Speakie to General Assembly meetings I had to sit and listen in person to people insulting him personally, casting aspersions on his motives and questioning his scientific integrity and even his sincerity. Many of those people were very disagreeable and obviously unbalanced. But he never lost his temper. He would just stand up and prove to them, again, that the SQ Test did actually literally scientifically show whether the testee was sane or insane, and the results could be proved, and all psychometrists accepted them. So the Test Ban people couldn't do anything but shout about freedom and accuse Dr. Speakie and the Psychometric Bureau of trying to "turn the world into a huge insane asylum." He would always answer quietly and firmly, asking them how they thought a person could be "free" if they lacked mental health. What they called freedom might well be a delusional system with no contact with reality. In order to find out, all they had to do was to become testees. "Mental health *is* freedom," he said. " 'Eternal vigilance is the price of liberty,' they say, and now we have an eternally vigilant watchdog: the SQ Test. *Only the testees can be truly free!*"

There really was no answer they could make to that. Sooner or later the delegates even from Member States where the Test Ban movement was strong would volunteer to take the SQ Test to prove that their mental health was adequate to their responsibilities. Then the ones that passed the test and remained in office would began working for Universal Application in their home State. The riots and demonstrations, and things like the burning of the Houses of Parliament in London in the State of England (where the Nor-Eurp SQ Center was housed), and the Vatican Rebellion, and the Chilean H-Bomb, were the work of insane fanatics appealing to the most unstable elements of the populace. Such fanatics, as Dr. Speakie and Dr. Waltraute pointed out in their Memorandum to the Presidium, deliberately aroused and used the proven instability of the crowd, "mob psychosis." The only response to mass delusion of that kind was

immediate implementation of the Testing Program in the disturbed States, and immediate amplification of the Asylum Program.

That was Dr. Speakie's own decision, by the way, to re-
name the SQ Achievement Centers "Asylums." He took the
word right out of his enemies' mouths. He said: "An asylum
means a place of *shelter*, a place of *cure*. Let there be no stigma
attached to the word 'insane,' to the word 'asylum,' to the words
'insane asylum'! No! For the asylum is the haven of mental
health — the place of cure, where the anxious gain peace,
where the weak gain strength, where the prisoners of inadequate
reality assessment win their way to freedom! Proudly let us use
the word 'asylum.' Proudly let us go to the asylum, to work to
regain our own God-given mental health, or to work with others
less fortunate to help them win back their own inalienable right
to mental health. And let one word be written large over the
door of every asylum in the world — 'WELCOME!'"

Those words are from his great speech at the General Assembly on the day World Universal Application was decreed by
the Presidium. Once or twice a year I listen to my tape of that
speech. Although I am too busy ever to get really depressed,
now and then I feel the need of a tiny "pick-me-up," and so I
play that tape. It never fails to send me back to my duties in-
spired and refreshed.

Considering all the work there was to do, as the Test scores
continued to come in always a little higher than the Psychometric Bureau analysts estimated, the World Government Presidium did a wonderful job for the two years that it administered
Universal Testing. There was a long period, six months, when
the scores seemed to have stabilised, with just about half of the
testees scoring over 50 and half under 50. At that time it was
thought that if forty percent of the mentally healthy were assigned to Asylum Staff work, the other sixty percent could keep
up routine basic world functions such as farming, power supply,
transportation, etc. This proportion had to be reversed when

they found that over sixty percent of the mentally healthy were volunteering for Staff work, in order to be with their loved ones in the Asylums. There was some trouble then with the routine basic world functions functioning. However, even then contingency plans were being made for the inclusion of farmlands, factories, power plants, etc., in the Asylum Territories, and the assignment of routine basic world functions work as Rehabilitation Therapy, so that the Asylums could become totally self-supporting if it became advisable. This was President Kim's special care, and he worked for it all through his term of office. Events proved the wisdom of his planning. He seemed such a nice wise little man. I still remember the day when Dr. Speakie came into the office and I knew at once that something was wrong. Not that he ever got really depressed or reacted with inopportune emotion, but it was as if the rubber balls in his shoes had gone just a little bit flat. There was the slightest tremor of true sorrow in his voice when he said, "Mary Ann, we've had a bit of bad news I'm afraid." Then he smiled to reassure me, because he knew what a strain we were all working under, and certainly didn't want to give anybody a shock that might push their score up higher on the next quarterly Test! "It's President Kim," he said, and I knew at once — I knew he didn't mean the President was ill or dead.

"Over 50?" I asked, and he just said quietly and sadly, "55."

Poor little President Kim, working so efficiently all that three months while mental ill health was growing in him! It was very sad and also a useful warning. High-level consultations were begun at once, as soon as President Kim was committed; and the decision was made to administer the Test monthly, instead of quarterly, to anyone in an executive position.

Even before this decision, the Universal scores had begun rising again. Dr. Speakie was not distressed. He had already predicted that this rise was highly probable during the transition period to World Sanity. As the number of the mentally healthy living outside the Asylums grew fewer, the strain on them kept growing greater, and they became more liable to break down under it — just as poor President Kim had done. Later, he predicted, when the Rehabs began coming out of the Asylums in ever increasing numbers, this stress would decrease. Also the crowding in the Asylums would decrease, so that the Staff would have more time to work on individually orientated therapy, and this would lead to a still more dramatic increase in the number of Rehabs released. Finally, when the therapy process was completely perfected, there would be no Asylums left in the world at all. Everybody would be either mentally healthy or a Rehab, or "neonormal," as Dr. Speakie liked to call it.

It was the trouble in the State of Australia that precipitated the Government crisis. Some Psychometric Bureau officials accused the Australian Evaluators of actually falsifying Test returns, but that is impossible since all the computers are linked to the World Government Central Computer Bank in Keokuk. Dr. Speakie suspected that the Australian Evaluators had been falsifying *the Test itself*, and insisted that they themselves all be tested immediately. Of course he was right. It had been a conspiracy, and the suspiciously low Australian Test scores had resulted from the use of a false Test. Many of the conspirators tested higher than 80 when forced to take the genuine Test! The State Government in Canberra had been unforgivably lax. If they had just admitted it everything would have been all right. But they got hysterical, and moved the State Government to a sheep station in Queensland, and tried to withdraw from the World Government. (Dr. Speakie said this was a typical mass psychosis: reality evasion, followed by fugue and autistic withdrawal.) Unfortunately the Presidium seemed to be paralysed. Australia seceded on the day before the President and Presidium were due to take their monthly Test, and probably they were afraid of overstraining their SQ with agonising decisions. So the Psychometric Bureau volunteered to handle the episode. Dr. Speakie himself flew on the plane with the H-bombs, and helped to drop the information leaflets. He never lacked personal courage.

When the Australian incident was over, it turned out that most of the Presidium, including President Singh, had scored over 50. So the Psychometric Bureau took over their functions temporarily. Even on a long-term basis this made good sense, since all the problems now facing the world Government had to do with administering and evaluating the Test, training the Staff, and providing full self-sufficiency structuration to all Asylums.

What this meant in personal terms was that Dr. Speakie, as Chief of the Psychometric Bureau, was now Interim President of the United States of the World. As his personal secretary I was, I will admit it, just terribly proud of him. But he never let it go to his head.

He was so modest. Sometimes he used to say to people, when he introduced me, "This is Mary Ann, my secretary," he'd say with a little twinkle, "and if it wasn't for her I'd have been scoring over 50 long ago!"

There were times, as the World SQ scores rose and rose, that I would become a little discouraged. Once the week's Test figures came in on the readout, and the *average* score was 71. I said, "Doctor, there are moments I believe the whole world is going insane!"

But he said, "Look at it this way, Mary Ann. Look at those people in the Asylums — 3.1 billion inmates now, and 1.8 billion staff — but look at them. What are they doing? They're pursuing their therapy, doing rehabilitation work on the farms and in the factories, and striving all the time, too, to *help* each other towards mental health. The preponderant inverse sanity quotient is certainly very high at the moment; they're mostly insane, yes. But you have to admire them. They are fighting for mental health. They will — they *will* win through!" And then he dropped his voice and said as if to himself, gazing out the window and bouncing just a little on the balls of his feet, "If I didn't believe that, I couldn't go on."

And I knew he was thinking of his wife.

Mrs. Speakie had scored 88 on the very first American Universal Test. She had been in the Greater Los Angeles Territory Asylum for years now.

Anybody who still thinks Dr. Speakie wasn't sincere should think about that for a minute! He gave up everything for his belief.

And even when the Asylums were all running quite well, and the epidemics in South Africa and the famines in Texas and the Ukraine were under control, still the workload on Dr. Speakie never got any lighter, because every month the personnel of the Psychometric Bureau got smaller, since some of them always flunked their monthly Test and were committed to Bethesda. I never could keep any of my secretarial staff any more for longer than a month or two. It was harder and harder to find replacements, too, because most sane young people volunteered for Staff work in the Asylums, since life was much easier and more sociable inside the Asylums than outside. Everything so convenient, and lots of friends and acquaintances! I used to positively envy those girls! But I knew where my job was.

At least it was much less hectic here in the U.N. Building, or the Psychometry Tower as it had been renamed long ago. Often there wouldn't be anybody around the whole building all day long but Dr. Speakie and myself, and maybe Bill the janitor (Bill scored 32 regular as clockwork every quarter). All the restaurants were closed, in fact most of Manhattan was closed, but we had fun picnicking in the old General Assembly Hall. And there was always the odd call from Buenos Aires or Reykjavik, asking Dr. Speakie's advice as Interim President about some problem, to break the silence.

But last November 8, I will never forget the date, when Dr. Speakie was dictating the Referendum for World Economic Growth for the next five-year period, he suddenly interrupted himself. "By the way, Mary Ann," he said, "how was your last score?"

We had taken the Test two days before, on the sixth. We always took the Test every first Monday. Dr. Speakie never would have dreamed of excepting himself from Universal Testing regulations.

"I scored 12," I said, before I thought how strange it was of him to ask. Or, not just to ask, because we often mentioned our scores to each other; but to ask *then*, in the middle of executing important world government business.

"Wonderful," he said, shaking his head. "You're wonderful, Mary Ann! Down two from last month's Test, aren't you?"

"I'm always between 10 and 14," I said. "Nothing new about that, Doctor."

"Some day," he said, and his face took on the expression it had when he gave his great speech about the Asylums, "some day, this world of ours will be governed by men fit to govern it. Men whose SQ score is Zero. Zero, Mary Ann!"

"Well, my goodness, Doctor," I said jokingly — his intensity almost alarmed me a little — "even *you* never scored lower than 3, and you haven't done that for a year or more now!"

He stared at me almost as if he didn't see me. It was quite uncanny. "Some day," he said in just the same way, "nobody in the world will have a Quotient higher than 50. Some day, nobody in the world will have a Quotient higher than 30! Higher than 10! The Therapy will be perfected. I was only the diagnostician. But the Therapy will be perfected! The cure will be found! Some day!" And he went on staring at me, and then he said, "Do you know what my score was on Monday?"

"7," I guessed promptly. The last time he had told me his score it had been 7.

"92," he said.

I laughed, because he seemed to be laughing. He had always had a puckish sense of humor. But I thought we really should get back to the World Economic Growth Plan, so I said laughingly, "That really is a very bad joke, Doctor!"

"92," he said, "and you don't believe me, Mary Ann, but that's because of the cantaloupe."

I said, "What cantaloupe, Doctor?" and that was when he jumped across his desk and began to try to bite through my jugular vein.

I used a judo hold and shouted to Bill the janitor, and when he came I called a robo-ambulance to take Dr. Speakie to Bethesda Asylum.

That was six months ago. I visit Dr. Speakie every Saturday. It is very sad. He is in the McLean Area, which is the Violent Ward, and every time he sees me he screams and foams. But I do not take it personally. One should never take mental ill health personally. When the Therapy is perfected he will be completely rehabilitated. Meanwhile, I just hold on here. Bill keeps the floors clean, and I run the World Government. It really isn't as difficult as you might think.

Small Change

"SMALL CHANGE," my aunt said as I put the obol on her tongue. "I'll need more than that where I'm going."

It is true that the change was very small. She looked exactly as she had looked a few hours before, except that she was not breathing.

"Goodbye, Aunt," I said.

"I'm not going yet!" she snapped. I always tried her patience. "There are rooms in this house I've never even opened the door of!"

I did not know what she was talking about. Our house has two rooms.

"This obol tastes funny," she said after a long silence. "Where did you get it?"

I did not want to tell her that it was a good-luck piece, a copper sequin, not money though it was round like a coin, which I had carried for a year or more in my pocket, ever since I picked it up by the gate of the bricklayer's yard. I had rubbed it clean, of course, but my aunt had a keen tongue, and it was trodden mud, dog turds, brick dust, and the inside of my pocket that she was tasting, along with the dry-blood taste of copper. I pretended that I had not understood her question.

"A wonder you had it at all," my aunt said. "If you have a penny in your pocket after a month without me, I'll be surprised. Poor thing!" She would have sighed if she had been breathing. I had not known that she would continue to worry about me after she died. I began to cry.

"That's good," my aunt said with satisfaction. "Just don't keep it up too long. I'm not going far, now. I just want very much to find out what room that door leads to."

She looked younger when she got up, younger than she was when I was born. She went across the room lightly and opened a door I had not known was there.

I heard her say in a pleased, surprised voice, "Lila!" Lila was the name of her sister, my mother.

"For goodness' sake, Lila," my aunt said, "you haven't been waiting in here for eleven years?"

I could not hear what my mother said.

"I'm very sorry about leaving the girl," my aunt said. "I did what I could, I tried my best. She's a good girl. But what will become of her now!"

My aunt never cried, and now she had no tears; but her anxiety over me made me cry again in alarm and self-pity.

My mother came out of that new room in the form of a lacewing fly and saw me crying. Tears taste salt to the living but sweet to the dead, and they have a taste for sweets, at first. I did not know all that, then. I was just glad to have my mother with me even as a tiny fly. It was a gladness the size of a fly.

That was all there was left of my mother in the house, and she had got what she wanted; so my aunt went on.

The room she was in was large and rather shadowy, lighted only by a skylight, like a storeroom. Along one wall stood distaffs full of spun flax, in a row, and in the place where the light fell from the skylight stood a loom. My aunt had been a notable spinster and weaver all her life, and was sorely tempted now by those rolls of fine, even thread, as well spun as any she had ever spun herself; the loom was warped, and there lay the shuttle ready. But linen weaving is a careful art. If she began a shroud now she would be at it for a long time, and much as she wanted a proper shroud, she never had been one to start a job and then drop it unfinished. So it was that she kept worrying about what would become of me. But she had already made up her mind to leave the housework undone (since housework is never done anyhow), and now she admitted that she must let other people see to her winding sheet. She hoped she could trust me to choose a clean sheet, at least, and a well-patched one. But she could not resist picking up the end thread of one of the distaffs and feeding out a length between her thumb and finger to test it for evenness and strength; and she kept the thread running between thumb and finger as she walked on.

It was well that she did so, as the new room opened onto a corridor along which were many doorways, each one leading to other halls and rooms, a maze in which she would certainly have lost her way but for the thread of flax.

The rooms were clean, a little dusty, and unfurnished. In one of them my aunt found a toy lying on the floor, a wooden horse. It was crudely carved, the forelegs all of a piece and the hind legs the same, a kind of a two-legged horse with round, flat eyes, which she thought she remembered, though she was not sure.

In another long, narrow room many unused kitchen tools and pans lay on a counter, and three horn buttons in a row.

At the end of a long corridor into which she was drawn by a gleam or a reflection at the far end, there stood an engine of some kind, which was certainly nothing my aunt had ever seen before.

In one small room with no skylight an intense, pungent smell hung in the air, filling up the room like a living creature caught in it. My aunt left that room hurriedly, upset.

Though her curiosity had been roused by finding all these rooms she had not known in her house, her explorations, and the

silence, brought on her a sense of oppression and unease. She
stood for a moment outside the door of the room where the
strong smell was, making up her mind. That never took her long.
She began to follow the thread back, winding it about the fingers of her left hand as she took it up. This process needed more
attention than the paying out, and lifting her eyes from a tangle
in the thread she was puzzled to find herself in a room which
she did not recall passing through, but could hardly have crossed
without noticing, for it was very large. The walls were of a beautiful fine-grained stone of a pale grey hue, in which certain figures like astrologers' charts of the constellations, fine lines con-
necting stars or clusters of stars, were inlaid in gold wire. The
ceiling was light and high, the floor of worn, dark marble. It was
like a church, my aunt thought, but not a religious church (that
is what she thought). The patterns on the walls were like the
illustrations in books of learning, and the room itself was like
the hall of the great library in the city; there were no books, but
the place was majestic and reposeful, having about it a collected
stillness very pleasant to the spirit of my aunt. She was tired of
walking, and decided to rest there.

She sat down, since there was no furniture, on the floor in
the corner nearest the door to which the thread had led her. My
aunt was a woman who liked a wall at her back. The invasions
had left her uneasy in open spaces, always looking over her
shoulder. Though who could hurt her now? as she said to herself, sitting down. But, as she said to herself, you never can be
sure.

The lines of gold wire on the walls led her eye along them
as she sat resting. Some of the figures they made seemed familiar. She began to think that these figures or patterns were a map
of the maze which she was in, the wires representing passages
and the stars, rooms; or perhaps the stars represented the doors
into rooms, the walls of which were not outlined. She could pretty certainly retrace the first corridor back to the room of the
distaffs; but on the far side of that, where the old part of our

house ought to be, the patterns continued, looking a good deal
more like the familiar constellations of the sky in early winter.
She was not certain she understood the map at all, but she continued to study it, to let her mind follow the lines from star to
star, until she began to see her way. She got up then, and went
back, pursuing the flaxen thread and taking it up in her left
hand, till she came back.

There I was in the same room still crying. My mother was
gone. Lacewing flies wait years to be born, but they live only a
day. The undertaker's men were just leaving, and I had to follow
them, so my aunt came along to her funeral, though she did not
want to leave the house. She tried to bring her ball of thread
with her, but it broke as she crossed the threshold. I could hear
her swear under her breath, the way she always did when she
broke a thread or spilled the sugar — "Damn!" in a whisper.

Neither of us enjoyed the funeral at all. My aunt grew pan-
icky as they began to throw the dirt back into the grave. She
cried aloud, "I can't breathe! I can't breathe!" — which frightened me so much that I thought it was myself speaking, myself
suffocating, and I fell down. People had to help me get up, and
help me get home. I was so ashamed and confused among them
that I lost my aunt.

One of the neighbors, who had never been particularly
pleasant to us, took pity on me, and behaved with much kindness. She talked so wisely to me that I got up the courage to ask
her, "Where is my aunt? Will she come back?" But she did not
know, and only said things meant to comfort me. I am not as
clever as most people, but I knew there was no comfort for me.

The neighbor made sure I could look after myself, and that
evening she sent one of her children over with dinner in a dish
for me. I ate it, and it was very good. I had not eaten anything
while my aunt was away in the other part of the house.

At night, after dark, I lay down all alone in the bedroom.
At first I felt well and cheerful, because of the food I had eaten,
and I pretended my aunt was there sleeping in the same room,

the way it had always been. Then I got frightened, and the fright grew in the darkness.

My aunt came up out of the floor in the middle of the room. The red tiles humped up and cracked apart. Her hair and her head pushed through the tiles, and then her body. She looked very dark, like dirt, and she was much smaller than she had been.

"Let me be!" she said.

I was too terrified to speak.

"Let me go!" my aunt said. But it was not truly my aunt; it was only an old part of her that had come back underground from the graveyard, because I had been wanting her. I did not like that part of her, or want it there. I cried, "Go away! Go back!" and hid my head in my arms.

My aunt made a little creaking sound like a wicker basket. I kept my eyes hidden so long that I nearly fell asleep. When I looked, no one was there, or only a kind of darker place in the air, and the tiles were not cracked apart. I went to sleep.

Next morning when I woke up the sunlight was in the window and things were all right, but I could not walk across that part of the floor where my aunt had come up through the tiles.

I was afraid to cry after that night, since crying might bring her back to taste the sweetness or to scold me. But it was lonely in the house now that she was buried and gone. I had no idea what to do without her. The neighbor came in and talked about finding me work, and gave me food again; but the next day a man came, who said he had been sent by a creditor. He took away the chest of clothes and bedding. Later that day, in the evening, he came back, because he had seen that I was alone there. I kept the door locked this time. He spoke smoothly at first, trying to make me let him in, and then he began saying in a low voice that he would hurt me, but I kept the door locked and never answered. The next day somebody else came, but I had pushed the bedstead up against the door. It may have been the neighbor's child that came, but I was afraid to look. I felt safe staying in the back room. Other people came and knocked, but I never answered, and they went away again.

I stayed in the back room until at last I saw the door that my aunt had gone through, that day. I went and opened it. I was sure she would be there. But the room was empty. The loom was gone, and the distaffs were gone, and no one was there.

I went on to the corridor beyond, but no farther. I could never find my way by myself through all those halls and rooms, or understand the patterns of the stars. I was so afraid and wretched that I went back, and crawled into my own mouth, and hid there.

My aunt came to fetch me. She was very cross. I always tried her patience. All she said was, "Come on!" And she pulled me along by the hand. Once she said, "Shame on you!" When we got to the riverbank she looked me over very sternly. She washed my face with the dark water of that river, and pressed my hair down with the palms of her hands. She said, "I should have known."

"I'm sorry, Aunt," I said.

"Oh, yes," she said. "Come along, now. Look sharp!"

For the boat had come across the river and was tying up at the wharf. We walked down to the wharf among the reeds in the twilight. It was after sunset, and there was no moon or stars, and no wind blowing. The river was so wide I could not see the other shore.

My aunt dickered with the ferryman. I let her do that, since people always cheated me. She had taken the obol off her tongue, and was talking fast. "My niece, can't you see how it is? Of course they didn't give her the fare! She's not responsible! I came along with her to look after her. Here's the fare. Yes, it's for us both. No, you don't," and she drew back her hand, having merely shown him a glimpse of the bit of copper. "Not till we're both safe across!"

The ferryman glowered, but began to loosen the painter.

"Come along, then!" my aunt said. She stepped into the boat, and held out her hand to me. So I followed her.

East

The First Report of the Shipwrecked Foreigner to the Kadanh of Derb

WHAT YOU ASK of me, my lord, is manifestly impossible. How can one person describe a world? One may indeed use a small pencil to describe a large circle, but if the circle is so large that one cannot make out the curve of it even from the top of a tower, why then the pencil will wear out before it has fairly begun its task. How many tones can one voice take? How can I describe even a single rock, and which rock should I describe? If I began by telling you that the Earth is the third planet of a system of nine, orbiting a middle-sized yellow sun at a mean distance of 93 million miles, with a 365-day period of revolution and a 24-hour period of rotation, and that it has a companion moon, what would I have told you but that a year is a year, a month is a month, and a day is a day, which you know already?

But since I know that you know that what you have been pleased to ask of me is impossible, and yet that you have asked it neither lightly nor cruelly, all I can do is answer; knowing that you know that my answer, in all its words, may mean nothing in the end beyond: Forgive me.

A moment ago as I glimpsed from the tail of my eye the enormous task that awaits me, like a mountain range to be climbed, it occurred to me that there may be an ulterior motive to your request. In asking me to describe my world to you, you may not be seeking information about my world at all. You may not plan to listen to my words, but only to the silences between the sentences, from which you will learn a good deal about your own world. If this is the case, I have no objection; indeed I prefer the arrangement. My job then is not to describe my world in general terms such as apply to all worlds, the language of astronomy, physics, chemistry, biology, etc., but rather to dwell upon the individual and transient, the fortuitous and peculiar; not to describe the class of flowering plants, but to mention the acrid odor of a Cecile Bruner rose full-blown on a balcony overlooking a great bay encircled by the lights of cities on a mild, foggy evening of September; not to give an outline of the evolution of intelligence or the course of human history, but to tell you, perhaps at considerable length, about my great-aunt Elizabeth. No general historical narrative, not even a close examination of the westward migration of the white peoples as it culminated and ended in the treks of the pioneers across the Great Plains, the Rockies, the Sierra, to the Pacific Shore, would give you an honest conviction of the necessity of the existence of my great-aunt Elizabeth. Even if I carried the narrative into such details as the fortunes of the individual families of the settlers of Wyoming, the existence of my great-aunt would continue to appear fortuitous. Only if I were to describe her, her life, her death, might you gain some understanding of the absolute necessity of her existence, and, through that, perhaps some comprehension of that millennial movement to the west which ended on the beaches of an immense fog-breeding sea; and, through that, perhaps a new understanding of some ancient migration of your own people, or the lack of any migratory movements in the history of your people; or of the nature of failure, or the character of your own great-aunt, or your own soul.

My lord, I see that instead of apologising and procrastinating I should simply thank you for the utterly unexpected and welcome opportunity to talk about my great-aunt, and begin at once to do so. It is not an opportunity often given to the Second Officer of a ship of the Terran Interstellar Fleet.

But I do not think I will begin with my great-aunt. She is a difficult subject, and it has occurred to me, as I gain the courage to take a few quick glances directly at the appalling mountains which I am to climb (and from whose summits what fog-bound ocean will I see?), that it does not matter where I begin, and that I need not even stick precisely to the facts. Whatever I tell you, if you are listening to the silences between the sentences, you will hear the truth. As in music, when one has caught the rhythm, the pattern of the sounds and silences, then one hears the tune. There is, after all, only one tune I can sing. So I shall begin with a fairy tale.

Once upon a time there was a city. All other cities of all times and places were alike in many ways. This city was unlike them all, in many ways; and yet it manifested more fully than any of the others the Idea of a city. It was populated by birds, cats, people, and winged lions, in roughly equal proportions. The lions were all literate. Seldom did one see a lion without a book in its paw. The cats were illiterate, but highly civilised. Observing a large family group at ease in the shrubbery of a shady garden fenced from all intrusion, or a ritual confrontation of toms on the moonlit stones of a city square, or the leisurely progress from roof to roof of a silken and silvery maiden, one might well conclude not only that the city had been built for, but that the art of living in it had been brought to perfection by, the cats. But as soon as one looked at a lion one would have to question this; for, with all their resemblances to the cats in form and feature, the complete tranquillity of the lions, their universal expression of benevolent pride and conscious mastery, surely indicated a state of mind transcending mere happiness, approaching joy. You might see the corpse of a cat floating under a bridge along with soft-drink bottles and rotten oranges, but looking up from that sorry sight you would see by the steps of the bridge a lion frowning beatifically through his mane, his stone wings folded; for what better place could he ever fly to?

It is easy to assume that the birds were the least happy inhabitants of the city. Many of them lived in cages. These prisoners certainly did not appear to be unhappy, singing ornate cadenzas in the style of Vivaldi from dawn to evening across the narrow ways, pecking at their birdseed and staring rapt at their little yellow reflections in the Christmas-tree ornaments hung in their airy cages. But all the same, they lived in cages. The pigeons lived free, but only as sturdy beggars. Daily they answered the summons of the bells for their handout, and in between handouts they pestered the tourists for more handouts. Perhaps it was their resentment at being thus reduced to the status of dependents, disenfranchised, their obscure anger at having been given few trees to perch in and few dangers to flee from, that made their excrement so corrosive. Whatever their motive, the pigeons were destroying some of the most exquisite elements of the city's fabric, by shitting persistently and ruinously on the perishable stone of cornices, pinnacles, carvings. Not even the lions could escape the pigeons. In this work of destruction the pigeons were, however, surpassed by the people, whose factories on the nearby mainland emitted vapors far exceeding the corrosive powers of the most class-conscious pigeon, and whose motorboats were furiously engaged in trying to sink the city before it crumbled.

For the quality in which Venice differed most clearly from all other cities and yet in which it exemplified and described them all, every one, most exactly, was its fragility.

A city, a splendid, old, crowded, active city full of thousands of busy lives, that might be destroyed by a pigeon — or a motorboat — or a wisp of gas? Ridiculous!

But then what is it that destroys cities? Why have the mighty fallen? Look, and you find a toy horse; a brass key; a couple of men chatting over wine; a change in the weather; the arrival of a few Spaniards. Nothing at all. A pigeon, a motorboat, a click on a Geiger counter.

The first lesson of Venice, then, is mortality.

Misread by Germans and other barbarians from the north (the city has always been besieged by Germans, and was in fact founded out in the deepest part of its lagoon in an effort to remove itself from the compulsive visitations of Langobard tourists — an effort which failed, in the long run), this perfectly straightforward message has been interpreted, with all the magnificent obtuseness of Teutonic thought, to mean that because Venice is more than usually mortal therefore Venice is a city of death, of dying, of disease, decadent, a city without healthy business, surviving like its pigeons as a parasite on visitors, a fever-dream city of morbidity, a place where aging pederasts go to die. This is, of course, rubbish. What is most mortal is most alive. There is no place in the world where the green beautiful murky tides of life run so high, where one is so vividly aware of the presence of living birds, cats, lions, and people walking, talking, singing, quarrelling, rolling metal shop blinds up and down, cooking dinner, eating breakfast, getting married, holding funerals, transporting Coca-Cola and zucchini from place to place in Coca-Cola and zucchini boats, making speeches, playing radios and musical instruments, selling electrified yo-yos that glow like fireflies as they roll up and down their strings in the dusk before the doors of the great cathededral, playing truant from school, kicking soccer balls, fighting, fishing, kissing, throwing tear gas at demonstrators, demonstrating, shortening their life expectancy by blowing incredibly fragile baubles of colored glass, etc., etc. — in other words, living. If I were an aging German pederast with a death wish, I should feel a terrible fool in Venice. Right out of my depth.

I have heard two Venetian housewives on the steps of a green canal discuss the qualities of various makes of electric food blenders for twenty minutes straight, in detail and with enormous vigor. The conversation was not notable for hectic and death-haunted ecstasy. Indeed, one reason why life is so strong there is that you can hear it. In other cities it is drowned out by the sound of motors. What you hear in the other cities is the noise engines make. What you hear in Venice, mostly, is the noise people make. The birds, too; the cats when they are in love; the lions make no noise worth mentioning, though the book they hold says softly, *Pax tibi, Marce, evangelista meus.* And thus the silence of Venice is the noisiest silence imaginable.

When I have been out in the vacuum between the stars, and have listened to it and been terrified, I have found a way to pull free from that absorbing terror (which Pascal mentioned, although he had never flown in a space ship) and rejoin myself: I pretend that I am waking up rather early in the morning in a hotel room in Venice. At first it is still, deeply still, the stillness of the level, misty, bluish-green lagoon, the stillness of the small canal between stone house walls around the corner. I know that the bridge near the hotel entrance is reflected, its arch making a perfect circle, in that stillness. Beyond that bridge is another bridge, and another beyond that, each borne up entire by its reflection: air, water, stone, glass, one. A pigeon up on the tiles outside the dormer window goes *oocooloo roo.* That is the first sound; that, and the faint whicker of wind in the pigeon's wings, alighting. Footsteps come down the street past the hotel entrance, across the arched bridge, die away: the second sound, or pattern of sounds and silences. Somebody breaks some glass down in the courtyard of the hotel. They always break glass in Venetian hotel courtyards in the morning; it may be a ritual observance of the dawn, or a way of getting rid of the baubles unsold to tourists in the gewgaw shops yesterday, I do not know. Maybe it is how they wash dishes in Venice. A startling sound, but not unmusical, followed by loud swearing and a laugh. By now I am almost safe from the terrors of the hygienic void. Down in the courtyard a radio is playing while they sweep up the glass. Somebody on one of the bridges shouts something I cannot quite understand in the Venetian dialect to someone on another bridge; and then the great bells of the Campanile and the small bells of three neighborhood churches all undertake more or less simultaneously to invite parishioners to early Mass. It is all music, and I am home safe, listening to the profound, extraordinary silence of the city of life.

I was not born there and have never lived there. When I say "home safe" I am using a metaphor from the game of baseball.

I have visited Venice four times, each time for four days only. Each time it was a little lower in the water.

If you were to ask me pointblank (as you have asked me to describe the Earth) whether I want to go back to Earth and why, I might well answer, "Yes: to see Venice in the winter." I have seen it only in late spring and summer. In winter, they tell me, it is terribly cold, and the museums are closed even more often than in summer, so that you cannot go warm yourself at the red and golden fires of Titian and Veronese. The white fog seeps among the stones. In the storms of winter St. Mark's Square, that loveliest living room ever built, whose ceiling is the opalescent sky, has often been flooded. The cathedral itself has been invaded by the sea, waves and mosaics interchanging their netted and glittering reflections, the five gold domes floating like balloons above the breakers, the four bronze horses of Neptune snorting and trembling as they scent their native element. No doubt the lions continued to gaze downward with detached and frowning approbation, scarcely troubling to stir their folded wings. The gondolas, I suppose, floated tied to the very tops of their striped mooring poles, or else were put away, knocking on the ceilings of flooded boathouses; or did they drift across the great square beneath the horses and the gold balloons, the procession of the Angel and the Three Kings, the bell tower which fell down in 1903 but got right up again, the agitated pigeons searching for their daily handout on the shallow, cold, grey waves? Beneath the waves at evening did the electric yo-yos flicker up and down their strings, attracting the ghosts of long-drowned Langobards?

Winter and summer, the gondolas were black. They were

painted black a long time ago in mourning for something —
the loss of a battle, the fall of the Republic, the death of a baby
— I cannot remember why gondolas went into mourning. They
were the most elegant boats people have ever made, more elegant even than the boat that brought me here. The warning cry
of the gondolier, as he guided his craft towards the sunlight at
the end of a narrow side canal under balconies and arched
bridges, through a trembling of shadows, was soft and yet carried clearly along the ways of stone and water: "Hoy-y-y," he
called, and the cats and lions on the sun-warmed angles of the
bridges listened and said nothing, as you, my lord, do now.

The Diary of the Rose

30 August

DR. NADES RECOMMENDS that I keep a diary of my work.
She says that if you keep it carefully, when you reread it you
can remind yourself of observations you made, notice errors and
learn from them, and observe progress in or deviations from positive thinking, and so keep correcting the course of your work by
a feedback process.

I promise to write in this notebook every night, and reread
it at the end of each week.

I wish I had done it while I was an assistant, but it is even
more important now that I have patients of my own.

As of yesterday I have six patients, a full load for a scopist,
but four of them are the autistic children I have been working
with all year for Dr. Nades's study for the Nat'l Psych. Bureau
(my notes on them are in the cli psy files). The other two are
new admissions:

Ana Jest, 46, bakery packager, md., no children, diag. depression, referral from city police (suicide attempt).

Flores Sorde, 36, engineer, unmd., no diag., referral from

TRTU (Psychopathic behavior — Violent).

Dr. Nades says it is important that I write things down each night just as they occurred to me at work: it is the spontaneity that is most informative in self-examination (just as in autopsychoscopy). She says it is better to write it, not dictate onto tape, and keep it quite private, so that I won't be self-conscious. It is hard. I never wrote anything that was private before. I keep feeling as if I was really writing it for Dr. Nades! Perhaps if the diary is useful I can show her some of it, later, and get her advice.

My guess is that Ana Jest is in menopausal depression and hormone therapy will be sufficient. There! Now let's see how bad a prognostician I am.

Will work with both patients under scope tomorrow. It is exciting to have my own patients, I am impatient to begin. Though of course teamwork was very educational.

31 August

Half-hour scope session with Ana J. at 8:00. Analyzed scope material, 11:00–17:00. N.B.: Adjust right-brain pickup next session! Weak visual Concrete. Very little aural, weak sensory, erratic body image. Will get lab analyses tomorrow of hormone balance.

It is amazing how banal most people's minds are. Of course the poor woman is in severe depression. Input in the Con dimension was foggy and incoherent, and the Uncon dimension was deeply open, but obscure. But the things that came out of the obscurity were so trivial! A pair of old shoes, and the word "geography"! And the shoes were dim, a mere schema of a pair-of-shoes, maybe a man's maybe a woman's, maybe dark blue maybe brown. Although definitely a visual type, she does not see anything clearly. Not many people do. It is depressing. When I was a student in first year I used to think how wonderful other people's minds would be, how wonderful it was going to be to share in all the different worlds, the different colors of their passions and ideas. How naïve I was!

I realised this first in Dr. Ramia's class when we studied a tape from a very famous successful person, and I noticed that the subject had never looked at a tree, never touched one, did not know any difference between an oak and a poplar, or even between a daisy and a rose. They were all just "trees" or "flowers" to him, apprehended schematically. It was the same with people's faces, though he had tricks for telling them apart: mostly he saw the name, like a label, not the face. That was an Abstract mind, of course, but it can be even worse with the Concretes, whose perceptions come in a kind of undifferentiated sludge — bean soup with a pair of shoes in it.

But aren't I "going native"? I've been studying a depressive's thoughts all day and have got depressed. Look, I wrote up there, "It is depressing." I see the value of this diary already. I know I am over-impressionable.

Of course, that is why I am a good psychoscopist. But it is dangerous.

No session with F. Sorde today, since sedation had not worn off. TRTU referrals are often so drugged that they cannot be scoped for days.

REM scoping session with Ana J. at 4:00 tomorrow. Better go to bed!

1 September

Dr. Nades says the kind of thing I wrote yesterday is pretty much what she had in mind, and invited me to show her this diary again whenever I am in doubt. Spontaneous thoughts — not the technical data, which are recorded in the files anyhow. Cross nothing out. Candor all-important.

Ana's dream was interesting but pathetic. The wolf who turned into a pancake! Such a disgusting, dim, hairy pancake, too. Her visuality is clearer in dream, but the feeling tone remains low (but remember: *you* contribute the affect — don't read it in). Started her on hormone therapy today.

F. Sorde awake, but too confused to take to scope room for session. Frightened. Refused to eat. Complained of pain in side. I thought he was unclear what kind of hospital this is, and told him there was nothing wrong with him physically. He said, "How the hell do you know?" which was fair enough, since he was in straitjacket, due to the V notation on his chart. I examined and found bruising and contusion, and ordered X-ray, which showed two ribs cracked. Explained to patient that he had been in a condition where forcible restraint had been necessary to prevent self-injury. He said, "Every time one of them asked a question the other one kicked me." He repeated this several times, with anger and confusion. Paranoid delusional system? If it does not weaken as the drugs wear off, I will proceed on that assumption. He responds fairly well to me, asked my name when I went to see him with the X-ray plate, and agreed to eat. I was forced to apologise to him, not a good beginning with a paranoid. The rib damage should have been marked on his chart by the referring agency or by the medic who admitted him. This kind of carelessness is distressing.

But there's good news too. Rina (Autism Study subject 4) saw a first-person sentence today. Saw it: in heavy, black, primer print, all at once in the high Con foreground: *I want to sleep in the big room.* (She sleeps alone because of the feces problem.) The sentence stayed clear for over 5 seconds. She was reading it in her mind just as I was reading it on the holoscreen. There was weak subverbalisation, but not subvocalisation, nothing on the audio. She has not yet spoken, even to herself, in the first person. I told Tio about it at once and he asked her after the session, "Rina, where do you want to sleep?" — "Rina sleep in the big room." No pronoun, no conative. But one of these days she will say *I want* — aloud. And on that build a personality, maybe, at last: on that foundation. I want, therefore I am.

There is so much fear. Why is there so much fear?

4 September

Went to town for my two-day holiday. Stayed with B. in

her new flat on the north bank. Three rooms to herself!!! But I
don't really like those old buildings, there are rats and roaches,
and it feels so old and strange, as if somehow the famine years
were still there, waiting. Was glad to get back to my little room
here, all to myself but with others close by on the same floor,
friends and colleagues. Anyway I missed writing in this book. I
form habits very fast. Compulsive tendency.

Ana much improved: dressed, hair combed, was knitting.
But session was dull. Asked her to think about pancakes, and
there it came filling up the whole Uncon dimension, the hairy,
dreary, flat wolf-pancake, while in the Con she was obediently
trying to visualise a nice cheese blintz. Not too badly: colors and
outlines already stronger. I am still willing to count on simple
hormone treatment. Of course they will suggest ECT, and a co-
analysis of the scope material would be perfectly possible, we'd
start with the wolf-pancake, etc. But is there any real point to
it? She has been a bakery packager for 24 years and her physical health is poor. She cannot change her life situation. At least
with good hormone balance she may be able to endure it.

F. Sorde: rested but still suspicious. Extreme fear reaction
when I said it was time for his first session. To allay this I sat
down and talked about the nature and operation of the psychoscope. He listened intently and finally said, "Are you going to
use only the psychoscope?"

I said Yes.

He said, "Not electroshock?"

I said No.

He said, "Will you promise me that?"

I explained that I am a psychoscopist and never operate the
electroconvulsive therapy equipment, that is an entirely different
department. I said my work with him at present would be diagnostic, not therapeutic. He listened carefully. He is an educated
person and understands distinctions such as "diagnostic" and
"therapeutic." It is interesting that he asked me to *promise*.
That does not fit a paranoid pattern, you don't ask for promises
from those you can't trust. He came with me docilely, but when

we entered the scope room he stopped and turned white at sight of the apparatus. I made Dr. Aven's little joke about the dentist's chair, which she always used with nervous patients. F.S. said, "So long as it's not an electric chair!"

I believe that with intelligent subjects it is much better not to make mysteries and so impose a false authority and a feeling of helplessness on the subject (see T. R. Olma, *Psychoscopy Technique*). So I showed him the chair and electrode crown and explained its operation. He has a layman's hearsay knowledge of the psychoscope, and his questions also reflected his engineering education. He sat down in the chair when I asked him. While I fitted the crown and clasps he was sweating profusely from fear, and this evidently embarrassed him, the smell. If he knew how Rina smells after she's been doing shit paintings. He shut his eyes and gripped the chair arms so that his hands went white to the wrist. The screens were almost white too. After a while I said in a joking tone, "It doesn't really hurt, does it?"

"I don't know."

"Well, does it?"

"You mean it's on?"

"It's been on for ninety seconds."

He opened his eyes then and looked around, as well as he could for the head clamps. He asked, "Where's the screen?"

I explained that a subject never watches the screen live, because the objectification can be severely disturbing, and he said, "Like feedback from a microphone?" That is exactly the simile Dr. Aven used to use. F.S. is certainly an intelligent person. N.B.: Intelligent paranoids are dangerous!

He asked, "What do you see?" and I said, "Do be quiet, I don't want to see what you're saying, I want to see what you're thinking," and he said, "But that's none of your business, you know," quite gently, like a joke. Meanwhile the fear-white had gone into dark, intense, volitional convolutions, and then, a few seconds after he stopped speaking, a rose appeared on the whole Con dimension: a full-blown pink rose, beautifully sensed and visualised, clear and steady, whole.

He said presently, "What am I thinking about, Dr. Sobel?" and I said, "Bears in the Zoo." I wonder now why I said that. Self-defense? Against what? He gave a laugh and the Uncon went crystal-dark, relief, and the rose darkened and wavered. I said, "I was joking. Can you bring the rose back?" That brought back the fear-white. I said, "Listen, it's really very bad for us to talk like this during a first session, you have to learn a great deal before you can co-analyse, and I have a great deal to learn about you, so no more jokes, please? Just relax physically, and think about anything you please."

There was flurry and subverbalisation on the Con dimension, and the Uncon faded into grey, suppression. The rose came back weakly a few times. He was trying to concentrate on it, but couldn't. I saw several quick visuals: myself, my uniform, TRTU uniforms, a grey car, a kitchen, the violent ward (strong aural images — screaming), a desk, the papers on the desk. He stuck to those. They were the plans for a machine. He began going through them. It was a deliberate effort at suppression, and quite effective. Finally I said, "What kind of machine is that?" and he began to answer aloud but stopped and let me get the answer subvocally in the earphone: "Plans for a rotary engine assembly for traction," or something like that, of course the exact words are on the tape. I repeated it aloud and said, "They aren't classified plans, are they?" He said, "No," aloud, and added, "I don't know any secrets." His reaction to a question is intense and complex, each sentence is like a shower of pebbles thrown into a pool, the interlocking rings spread out quick and wide over the Con and into the Uncon, responses rising on all levels. Within a few seconds all that was hidden by a big signboard that appeared in the high Con foreground, deliberately visualised like the rose and the plans, with auditory reinforcement as he read it over and over: KEEP OUT! KEEP OUT! KEEP OUT!

It began to blur and flicker, and somatic signals took over, and soon he said aloud, "I'm tired," and I closed the session (12.5 min.).

After I took off the crown and clamps I brought him a cup of tea from the staff stand in the hall. When I offered it to him he looked startled and then tears came into his eyes. His hands were so cramped from gripping the armrests that he had trouble taking hold of the cup. I told him he must not be so tense and afraid, we are trying to help him not to hurt him.

He looked up at me. Eyes are like the scope screen and yet you can't read them. I wished the crown was still on him, but it seems you never catch the moments you most want on the scope. He said, "Doctor, why am I in this hospital?"

I said, "For diagnosis and therapy."

He said, "Diagnosis and therapy of *what?*"

I said he perhaps could not now recall the episode, but he had behaved strangely. He asked how and when, and I said that it would all come clear to him as therapy took effect. Even if I had known what his psychotic episode was, I would have said the same. It was correct procedure. But I felt in a false position. If the TRTU report was not classified, I would be speaking from knowledge and the facts. Then I could make a better response to what he said next:

"I was waked up at two in the morning, jailed, interrogated, beaten up, and drugged. I suppose I did behave a little oddly during that. Wouldn't you?"

"Sometimes a person under stress misinterprets other people's actions," I said. "Drink up your tea and I'll take you back to the ward. You're running a temperature."

"The ward," he said, with a kind of shrinking movement, and then he said almost desperately, "Can you really not know why I'm here?"

That was strange, as if he has included me in his delusional system, *on "his side."* Check this possibility in Rheingeld. I should think it would involve some transference and there has not been time for that.

Spent pm analysing Jest and Sorde holos. I have never seen any psychoscopic realisation, not even a drug-induced hallucination, so fine and vivid as that rose. The shadows of one petal on another, the velvety damp texture of the petals, the pink color full of sunlight, the yellow central crown — I am sure the scent was there if the apparatus had olfactory pickup — it wasn't like a mentifact but a real thing rooted in the earth, alive and growing, the strong thorny stem beneath it.

Very tired, must go to bed.

Just reread this entry. Am I keeping this diary right? All I have written is what happened and what was said. Is that spontaneous? But it was *important* to me.

5 September

Discussed the problem of conscious resistance with Dr. Nades at lunch today. Explained that I have worked with unconscious blocks (the children, and depressives such as Ana J.) and have some skill at reading through, but have not before met a conscious block such as F.S.'s KEEP OUT sign, or the device he used today, which was effective for a full 20-minute session: a concentration on his breathing, bodily rhythms, pain in ribs, and visual input from the scope room. She suggested that I use a blindfold for the latter trick, and keep my attention on the Uncon dimension, as he cannot prevent material from appearing there. It is surprising, though, how large the interplay area of his Con and Uncon fields is, and how much one resonates into the other. I believe his concentration on his breathing rhythm allowed him to achieve something like "trance" condition. Though of course most so-called "trance" is mere occultist fakirism, a primitive trait without interest for behavioral science.

Ana thought through "a day in my life" for me today. All so grey and dull, poor soul! She never thought even of food with pleasure, though she lives on minimum ration. The single thing that came bright for a moment was a child's face, clear dark eyes, a pink knitted cap, round cheeks. She told me in post-session discussion that she always walks by a school playground on the way to work because "she likes to see the little ones running and yelling." Her husband appears on the screen as a big bulky suit of work clothes and a peevish, threatening mumble. I wonder if she knows that she hasn't seen his face or heard a word he says for years? But no use telling her that. It may be just as well she doesn't.

The knitting she is doing, I noticed today, is a pink cap.

Reading De Cams's *Disaffection: A Study,* on Dr. Nades's recommendation.

6 *September*

In the middle of session (breathing again) I said loudly: "Flores!"

Both psy dimensions whited out but the soma realisation hardly changed. After 4 seconds he responded aloud, drowsily. It is not "trance," but autohypnosis.

I said, "Your breathing's monitored by the apparatus. I don't need to know that you're still breathing. It's boring."

He said, "I like to do my own monitoring, Doctor."

I came around and took the blindfold off him and looked at him. He has a pleasant face, the kind of man you often see running machinery, sensitive but patient, like a donkey. That is stupid. I will not cross it out. I am supposed to be spontaneous in this diary. Donkeys do have beautiful faces. They are supposed to be stupid and balky but they look wise and calm, as if they had endured a lot but held no grudges, as if they knew some reason why one should not hold grudges. And the white ring around their eyes makes them look defenseless.

"But the more you breathe," I said, "the less you think. I need your cooperation. I'm trying to find out what it is you're afraid of."

"But I know what I'm afraid of," he said.

"Why won't you tell me?"

"You never asked me."

"That's most unreasonable," I said, which is funny, now I think about it, being indignant with a mental patient because he's unreasonable. "Well, then, now I'm asking you."

He said, "I'm afraid of electroshock. Of having my mind destroyed. Being kept here. Or only being let out when I can't remember anything." He gasped while he was speaking.

I said, "All right, why won't you think about that while I'm watching the screens?"

"Why should I?"

"Why not? You've said it to me, why can't you think about it? I want to see the color of your thoughts!"

"It's none of your business, the color of my thoughts," he said angrily, but I was around to the screen while he spoke, and saw the unguarded activity. Of course it was being taped while we spoke, too, and I have studied it all afternoon. It is fascinating. There are two subverbal levels running aside from the spoken words. All sensory-emotive reactions and distortions are vigorous and complex. He "sees" me, for instance, in at least three different ways, probably more, analysis is impossibly difficult! And the Con-Uncon correspondences are so complicated, and the memory traces and current impressions interweave so rapidly, and yet the whole is unified in its complexity. It is like that machine he was studying, very intricate but all one thing in a mathematical harmony. Like the petals of the rose.

When he realised I was observing he shouted out, "Voyeur! Damned voyeur! Let me alone! Get out!" and he broke down and cried. There was a clear fantasy on the screen for several seconds of himself breaking the arm and head clamps and kicking the apparatus to pieces and rushing out of the building, and there, outside, there was a wide hilltop, covered with short dry grass, under the evening sky, and he stood there all alone. While he sat clamped in the chair sobbing.

I broke session and took off the crown, and asked him if he wanted some tea, but he refused to answer. So I freed his arms, and brought him a cup. There was sugar today, a whole box full.

I told him that and told him I'd put in two lumps.

After he had drunk some tea he said, with an elaborate ironical tone, because he was ashamed of crying, "You know I like sugar? I suppose your psychoscope told you I liked sugar?"

"Don't be silly," I said, "everybody likes sugar if they can get it."

He said, "No, little doctor, they don't." He asked in the same tone how old I was and if I was married. He was spiteful. He said, "Don't want to marry? Wedded to your work? Helping the mentally unsound back to a constructive life of service to the Nation?"

"I like my work," I said, "because it's difficult, and interesting. Like yours. You like your work, don't you?"

"I did," he said. "Goodbye to all that."

"Why?"

He tapped his head and said, "*Zzzzzzt!* — All gone. Right?"

"Why are you so convinced you're going to be prescribed electroshock? I haven't even diagnosed you yet."

"Diagnosed me?" he said. "Look, stop the playacting, please. My diagnosis was made. By the learned doctors of the TRTU. Severe case of disaffection. Prognosis: Evil! Therapy: Lock him up with a roomful of screaming thrashing wrecks, and then go through his mind the same way you went through his papers, and then burn it . . . burn it out. Right, Doctor? Why do you have to go through all this posing, diagnosis, cups of tea? Can't you just get on with it? Do you have to paw through everything I am before you burn it?"

"Flores," I said very patiently, "*you're* saying 'Destroy me' — don't you hear yourself? The psychoscope destroys nothing. And I'm not using it to get evidence, either. This isn't a court, you're not on trial. And I'm not a judge. I'm a doctor."

He interrupted — "If you're a doctor, can't you see that I'm not sick?"

"How can I see anything so long as you block me out with

your stupid KEEP OUT signs?" I shouted. I did shout. My patience *was* a pose and it just fell to pieces. But I saw that I had
reached him, so I went right on. "You look sick, you act sick —
two cracked ribs, a temperature, no appetite, crying fits — is
that good health? If you're not sick, then prove it to me! Let me
see how you are inside, inside all that!"

He looked down into his cup and gave a kind of laugh and
shrugged. "I can't win," he said. "Why do I talk to you? You
look so honest, damn you!"

I walked away. It is shocking how a patient can hurt one.
The trouble is, I am used to the children, whose rejection is
absolute, like animals that freeze, or cower, or bite, in their terror. But with this man, intelligent and older than I am, first
there is communication and trust and then the blow. It hurts
more.

It is painful writing all this down. It hurts again. But it is
useful. I do understand some things he said much better now. I
think I will not show it to Dr. Nades until I have completed
diagnosis. If there is any truth to what he said about being arrested on suspicion of disaffection (and he is certainly careless in
the way he talks) Dr. Nades might feel that she should take over
the case, due to my inexperience. I should regret that. I need the
experience.

7 September

Stupid! That's why she gave you De Cams's book. Of
course she knows. As Head of the Section she has access to the
TRTU dossier on F.S. She gave me this case deliberately.

It is certainly educational.

Today's session: F.S. still angry and sulky. Intentionally
fantasized a sex scene. It was memory, but when she was heav-
ing around underneath him he suddenly stuck a caricature of
my face on her. It was effective. I doubt a woman could have
done it, women's recall of having sex is usually darker and
grander and they and the other do not become meat-puppets like

that, with switchable heads. After a while he got bored with the performance (for all its vividness there was little somatic participation, not even an erection) and his mind began to wander. For the first time. One of the drawings on the desk came back. He must be a designer, because he changed it, with a pencil. At the same time there was a tune going on the audio, in mental puretone; and in the Uncon lapping over into the interplay area, a large, dark room seen from a child's height, the windowsills very high, evening outside the windows, tree branches darkening, and inside the room a woman's voice, soft, maybe reading aloud, sometimes joining with the tune. Meanwhile the whore on the bed kept coming and going in volitional bursts, falling apart a little more each time, till there was nothing left but one nipple. This much I analysed out this afternoon, the first sequence of over 10 sec. that I have analysed clear and entire.

When I broke session he said, "What did you learn?" in the satirical voice.

I whistled a bit of the tune.

He looked scared.

"It's a lovely tune," I said, "I never heard it before. If it's yours, I won't whistle it anywhere else."

"It's from some quartet," he said, with his "donkey" face back, defenseless and patient. "I like classical music. Didn't you — "

"I saw the girl," I said. "And my face on her. Do you know what I'd like to see?"

He shook his head. Sulky, hangdog.

"Your childhood."

That surprised him. After a while he said, "All right. You can have my childhood. Why not? You're going to get all the rest anyhow. Listen. You tape it all, don't you? Could I see a playback? I want to see what you see."

"Sure," I said. "But it won't mean as much to you as you think it will. It took me eight years to learn to observe. You start with your own tapes. I watched mine for months before I recognised anything much."

I took him to my seat, put on the earphone, and ran him 30 sec. of the last sequence.

He was quite thoughtful and respectful after it. He asked, "What was all that running-up-and-down-scales motion in the, the background I guess you'd call it?"

"Visual scan — your eyes were closed — and subliminal proprioceptive input. The Unconscious dimension and the Body dimension overlap to a great extent all the time. We bring the three dimensions in separately, because they seldom coincide entirely anyway, except in babies. The bright triangular motion at the left of the holo was probably the pain in your ribs."

"I don't see it that way!"

"You don't see it; you weren't consciously feeling it, even, then. But we can't translate a pain in the rib onto a holoscreen, so we give it a visual symbol. The same with all sensations, affects, emotions."

"You watch all that at once?"

"I told you it took eight years. And you do realise that that's only a fragment? Nobody could put a whole psyche onto a four-foot screen. Nobody knows if there are any limits to the psyche. Except the limits of the universe."

He said after a while, "Maybe you aren't a fool, doctor. Maybe you're just very absorbed in your work. That can be dangerous, you know, to be so absorbed in your work."

"I love my work, and I hope that it is of positive service," I said. I was alert for symptoms of disaffection.

He smiled a little and said, "Prig," in a sad voice.

Ana is coming along. Still some trouble eating. Entered her in George's mutual-therapy group. What she needs, at least one thing she needs, is companionship. After all why should she eat? Who needs her to be alive? What we call psychosis is sometimes simply realism. But human beings can't live on realism alone.

F.S.'s patterns do not fit any of the classical paranoid psychoscopic patterns in Rheingeld.

The De Cams book is hard for me to understand. The terminology of politics is so different from that of psychology. Everything seems backwards. I must be genuinely attentive at P.T. sessions Sunday nights from now on. I have been lazy-minded. Or, no, but as F.S. said, too absorbed in my work — and so inattentive to its context, he meant. Not thinking about what one is working *for*.

10 September

Have been so tired the last two nights I skipped writing this journal. All the data are on tape and in my analysis notes, of course. Have been working really hard on the F.S. analysis. It is very exciting. It is a truly unusual mind. Not brilliant, his intelligence tests are good average, he is not original or an artist, there are no schizophrenic insights, I can't say what it is, I feel honored to have shared in the childhood he remembered for me. I can't say what it is. There was pain and fear of course, his father's death from cancer, months and months of misery while F.S. was twelve, that was terrible, but it does not come out pain in the end, he has not forgotten or repressed it but it is all changed, by his love for his parents and his sister and for music and for the shape and weight and fit of things and his memory of the lights and weathers of days long past and his mind always working quietly, reaching out, reaching out to be whole.

There is no question yet of formal co-analysis, it is far too early, but he cooperates so intelligently that today I asked him if he was aware consciously of the Dark Brother figure that accompanied several Con memories in the Uncon dimension. When I described it as having a matted shock of hair he looked startled and said, "Dokkay, you mean?"

That word had been on the subverbal audio, though I hadn't connected it with the figure.

He explained that when he was five or six Dokkay had been his name for a "bear" he often dreamed or daydreamed about. He said, "I rode him. He was big, I was small. He smashed down walls, and destroyed things, bad things, you know, bullies, spies, people who scared my mother, prisons, dark alleys I was afraid to cross, policemen with guns, the pawnbroker. Just knocked them over. And then he walked over all the rubble on up to the hilltop. With me riding on his back. It was quiet up there. It was always evening, just before the stars come out. It's strange to remember it. Thirty years ago! Later on he turned into a kind of friend, a boy or man, with hair like a bear. He still smashed things, and I went with him. It was good fun."

I write this down from memory as it was not taped; session was interrupted by power outage. It is exasperating that the hospital comes so low on the list of Government priorities.

Attended the Pos. Thinking session tonight and took notes. Dr. K. spoke on the dangers and falsehoods of liberalism.

11 September

F.S. tried to show me Dokkay this morning but failed. He laughed and said aloud, "I can't see him any more. I think at some point I turned into him."

"Show me when that happened," I said, and he said, "All right," and began at once to recall an episode from his early adolescence. It had nothing to do with Dokkay. He saw an arrest. He was told that the man had been passing out illegal printed matter. Later on he saw one of these pamphlets, the title was in his visual bank, "Is There Equal Justice?" He read it, but did not recall the text or managed to censor it from me. The arrest was terribly vivid. Details like the young man's blue shirt and the coughing noise he made and the sound of the hitting, the TRTU agents' uniforms, and the car driving away, a big grey car with blood on the door. It came back over and over, the car driving away down the street, driving away down the street. It was a traumatic incident for F.S. and may explain the exaggerated fear of the violence of national justice justified by national security which may have led him to behave irrationally when investigated and so appeared as a tendency to disaffection, falsely I believe.

I will show why I believe this. When the episode was done I

said, "Flores, think about democracy for me, will you?"

He said, "Little doctor, you don't catch old dogs quite that easily."

"I am not catching you. Can you think about democracy or can't you?"

"I think about it a good deal," he said. And he shifted to right-brain activity, music. It was a chorus of the last part of the Ninth Symphony by Beethoven, I recognised it from the Arts term in high school. We sang it to some patriotic words. I yelled, "Don't censor!" and he said, "Don't shout, I can hear you." Of course the room was perfectly silent, but the pickup on the audio was tremendous, like thousands of people singing together. He went on aloud, "I'm not censoring. I'm thinking about democracy. That is democracy. Hope, brotherhood, no walls. All the walls unbuilt. You, we, I make the universe! Can't you hear it?" And it was the hilltop again, the short grass and the sense of being up high, and the wind, and the whole sky. The music was the sky.

When it was done and I released him from the crown I said, "Thank you."

I do not see why the doctor cannot thank the patient for a revelation of beauty and meaning. Of course the doctor's authority is important but it need not be domineering. I realise that in politics the authorities must lead and be followed but in psychological medicine it is a little different, a doctor cannot "cure" the patient, the patient "cures" himself with our help, this is not contradictory to Positive Thinking.

14 September

I am upset after the long conversation with F.S. today and will try to clarify my thinking.

Because the rib injury prevents him from attending work therapy, he is restless. The Violent ward disturbed him deeply so I used my authority to have the V removed from his chart and have him moved into Men's Ward B, three days ago. His bed is next to old Arca's, and when I came to get him for session they were talking, sitting on Arca's bed. F.S. said, "Dr. Sobel, do you know my neighbor, Professor Arca of the Faculty of Arts and Letters of the University?" Of course I know the old man, he has been here for years, far longer than I, but F.S. spoke so courteously and gravely that I said, "Yes, how do you do, Professor Arca?" and shook the old man's hand. He greeted me politely as a stranger — he often does not know people from one day to the next.

As we went to the scope room F.S. said, "Do you know how many electroshock treatments he had?" and when I said no he said, "Sixty. He tells me that every day. With pride." Then he said, "Did you know that he was an internationally famous scholar? He wrote a book, *The Idea of Liberty,* about twentieth-century ideas of freedom in politics and the arts and sciences. I read it when I was in engineering school. It existed then. On bookshelves. It doesn't exist any more. Anywhere. Ask Dr. Arca. He never heard of it."

"There is almost always some memory loss after electroconvulsive therapy," I said, "but the material lost can be relearned, and is often spontaneously regained."

"After sixty sessions?" he said.

F.S. is a tall man, rather stooped, even in the hospital pajamas he is an impressive figure. But I am also tall, and it is not because I am shorter than he that he calls me "little doctor." He did it first when he was angry at me and so now he says it when he is bitter but does not want what he says to hurt me, the me he knows. He said, "Little doctor, quit faking. You know the man's mind was deliberately destroyed."

Now I will try to write down exactly what I said, because it is important.

"I do not approve of the use of electroconvulsive therapy as a general instrument. I would not recommend its use on my patients except perhaps in certain specific cases of senile melancholia. I went into psychoscopy because it is an integrative rather than a destructive instrument."

That is all true, and yet I never said or consciously thought it before.

"What will you recommend for me?" he said.

I explained that once my diagnosis is complete my recommendation will be subject to the approval of the Head and Assistant Head of the Section. I said that so far nothing in his history or personality structure warranted the use of ECT but that after all we had not got very far yet.

"Let's take a long time about it," he said, shuffling along beside me with his shoulders hunched.

"Why? Do you like it?"

"No. Though I like you. But I'd like to delay the inevitable end."

"Why do you insist that it's inevitable, Flores? Can't you see that your thinking on that one point is quite irrational?"

"Rosa," he said, he has never used my first name before, "Rosa, you can't be reasonable about pure evil. There are faces reason cannot see. Of course I'm irrational, faced with the imminent destruction of my memory — my self. But I'm not inaccurate. You know they're not going to let me out of here un . . ." He hesitated a long time and finally said, "unchanged."

"One psychotic episode — "

"I had no psychotic episode. You must know that by now."

"Then why were you sent here?"

"I have some colleagues who prefer to consider themselves rivals, competitors. I gather they informed the TRTU that I was a subversive liberal."

"What was their evidence?"

"Evidence?" We were in the scope room by now. He put his hands over his face for a moment and laughed in a bewildered way. "Evidence? Well, once at a meeting of my section I talked a long time with a visiting foreigner, a fellow in my field, a designer. And I have friends, you know, unproductive people, bohemians. And this summer I showed our section head why a design he'd got approved by the Government wouldn't work. That was stupid. Maybe I'm here for, for imbecility. And I read. I've read Professor Arca's book."

"But none of that matters, you think positively, you love your country, you're not disaffected!"

He said, "I don't know. I love the idea of democracy, the hope, yes, I love that. I couldn't live without that. But the country? You mean the thing on the map, lines, everything inside the lines is good and nothing outside them matters? How can an adult love such a childish idea?"

"But you wouldn't betray the nation to an outside enemy."

He said, "Well, if it was a choice between the nation and humanity, or the nation and a friend, I might. If you call that betrayal. I call it morality."

He *is* a liberal. It is exactly what Dr. Katin was talking about on Sunday.

It is classic psychopathy: the absence of normal affect. He said that quite unemotionally — "I might."

No. That is not true. He said it with difficulty, with pain. It was I who was so shocked that I felt nothing — blank, cold.

How am I to treat this kind of psychosis, a *political* psychosis? I have read over De Cams's book twice and I believe I do understand it now, but still there is this gap between the political and the psychological, so that the book shows me how to think but does not show me how to *act* positively. I see how F.S. should think and feel, and the difference between that and his present state of mind, but I do not know how to educate him so that he can think positively. De Cams says that disaffection is a negative condition which must be filled with positive ideas and emotions, but this does not fit F.S. The gap is not in him. In fact that gap in De Cams between the political and the psychological is exactly where *his* ideas apply. But if they are wrong ideas how can this be?

I want advice badly, but I cannot get it from Dr. Nades. When she gave me the De Cams she said, "You'll find what you need in this." If I tell her that I haven't, it is like a confession of helplessness and she will take the case away from me. Indeed I think it is a kind of test case, testing me. But I need this experience, I am learning, and besides, the patient trusts me and talks freely to me. He does so because he knows that I keep what he tells me in perfect confidence. Therefore I cannot show this journal or discuss these problems with anyone until the cure is under way and confidence is no longer essential.

But I cannot see when that could happen. It seems as if confidence will always be essential between us.

I have got to teach him to adjust his behavior to reality, or he will be sent for ECT when the Section reviews cases in November. He has been right about that all along.

9 October

I stopped writing in this notebook when the material from F.S. began to seem "dangerous" to him (or to myself). I just reread it all over tonight. I see now that I can never show it to Dr. N. So I am going to go ahead and write what I please in it. Which is what she said to do, but I think she always expected me to show it to her, she thought I would want to, which I did, at first, or that if she asked to see it I'd give it to her. She asked about it yesterday. I said that I had abandoned it, because it just repeated things I had already put into the analysis files. She was plainly disapproving but said nothing. Our dominance-submission relationship has changed these past few weeks. I do not feel so much in need of guidance, and after the Ana Jest discharge, the autism paper, and my successful analysis of the T. R. Vinha tapes she cannot insist upon my dependence. But she may resent my independence. I took the covers off the notebook and am keeping the loose pages in the split in the back cover of my copy of Rheingeld, it would take a very close search to find them there. While I was doing that I felt rather sick at the stomach and got a headache.

Allergy: A person can be exposed to pollen or bitten by

fleas a thousand times without reaction. Then he gets a viral
infection or a psychic trauma or a bee sting, and next time he
meets up with ragweed or a flea he begins to sneeze, cough, itch,
weep, etc. It is the same with certain other irritants. One has to
be sensitized.

"Why is there so much fear?" I wrote. Well now I know.
Why is there no privacy? It is unfair and sordid. I cannot read
the "classified" files kept in her office, though I work with the
patients and she does not. But I am not to have any "classified"
material of my own. Only persons in authority can have secrets.
Their secrets are all good, even when they are lies.

Listen. Listen Rosa Sobel. Doctor of Medicine, Deg. Psy-
chotherapy, Deg. Psychoscopy. Have you gone native?

Whose thoughts are you thinking?

You have been working 2 to 5 hours a day for 6 weeks
inside one person's mind. A generous, integrated, sane mind.
You never worked with anything like that before. You have only
worked with the crippled and the terrified. You never met an
equal before.

Who is the therapist, you or he?

But if there is nothing wrong with him what am I supposed
to cure? How can I help him? How can I save him?

By teaching him to lie?

(Undated)

I spent the last two nights till midnight reviewing the diagnostic scopes of Professor Arca, recorded when he was admitted,
eleven years ago, before electroconvulsive treatment.

This morning Dr. N inquired why I had been "so far back
in the files." (That means that Selena reports to her on what
files are used. I know every square centimeter of the scope room
but all the same I check it over daily now.) I replied that I was
interested in studying the development of ideological disaffection in intellectuals. We agreed that intellectualism tends to fos-
ter negative thinking and may lead to psychosis, and those suf-

fering from it should ideally be treated, as Prof. Arca was
treated, and released if still competent. It was a very interesting
and harmonious discussion.

I lied. I lied. I lied. I lied deliberately, knowingly, well. She
lied. She is a liar. She is an intellectual too! She is a lie. And a
coward, afraid.

I wanted to watch the Arca tapes to get perspective. To
prove to myself that Flores is by no means unique or original.
This is true. The differences are fascinating. Dr. Arca's Con
dimension was splendid, architectural, but the Uncon material
was less well integrated and less interesting. Dr. Arca knew very
much more, and the power and beauty of the motions of his
thought was far superior to Flores's. Flores is often extremely
muddled. That is an element of his vitality. Dr. Arca is an, was
an Abstract thinker, as I am, and so I enjoyed his tapes less. I
missed the solidity, spatiotemporal realism, and intense sensory
clarity of Flores's mind.

In the scope room this morning I told him what I had been
doing. His reaction was (as usual) not what I expected. He is
fond of the old man and I thought he would be pleased. He said,
"You mean they saved the tapes, and destroyed the mind?" I
told him that all tapes are kept for use in teaching, and asked
him if that didn't cheer him, to know that a record of Arca's
thoughts in his prime existed: wasn't it like his book, after all,
the lasting part of a mind which sooner or later would have to
grow senile and die anyhow? He said, "No! Not so long as the
book is banned and the tape is classified! Neither freedom nor
privacy even in death? That is the worst of all!"

After session he asked if I would be able or willing to destroy his diagnostic tapes, if he is sent to ECT. I said such things
could get misfiled and lost easily enough, but that it seemed a
cruel waste. I had learned from him and others might, later, too.
He said, "Don't you see that I will not serve the people with
security passes? I will not be used, that's the whole point. You
have never used me. We have worked together. Served our term
together."

Prison has been much in his mind lately. Fantasies, day-dreams of jails, labor camps. He dreams of prison as a man in prison dreams of freedom.

Indeed as I see the way narrowing in I would get him sent to prison if I could, but since he is *here* there is no chance. If I reported that he is in fact politically dangerous, they will simply put him back in the Violent ward and give him ECT. There is no judge here to give him a life sentence. Only doctors to give death sentences.

What I can do is stretch out the diagnosis as long as possi-ble, and put in a request for full co-analysis, with a strong prog-nosis of complete cure. But I have drafted the report three times already and it is very hard to phrase it so that it's clear that I know the disease is ideological (so that they don't just override my diagnosis at once) but still making it sound mild and curable enough that they'd let me handle it with the psy-choscope. And then, why spend up to a year, using expensive equipment, when a cheap and simple instant cure is at hand? No matter what I say, they have that argument. There are two weeks left until Sectional Review. I have got to write the report so that it will be really impossible for them to override it. But what if Flores is right, all this is just playacting, lying about lying, and they have had orders right from the start from TRTU, "wipe this one out" —

(Undated)

Sectional Review today.

If I stay on here I have some power, I can do some good No no no but I don't I don't even in this one thing even in this what can I do now how can I stop

(Undated)

Last night I dreamed I rode on a bear's back up a deep gorge between steep mountainsides, slopes going steep up into a dark sky, it was winter, there was ice on the rocks

(Undated)

Tomorrow morning will tell Nades I am resigning and requesting transfer to Children's Hospital. But she must approve the transfer. If not I am out in the cold. I am in the cold already. Door locked to write this. As soon as it is written will go down to furnace room and burn it all. There is no place any more.

We met in the hall. He was with an orderly.

I took his hand. It was big and bony and very cold. He said, "Is this it, now, Rosa — the electroshock?" in a low voice. I did not want him to lose hope before he walked up the stairs and down the corridor. It is a long way down the corridor. I said, "No. Just some more tests — EEG probably."

"Then I'll see you tomorrow?" he asked, and I said yes.

And he did. I went in this evening. He was awake. I said, "I am Dr. Sobel, Flores. I am Rosa."

He said, "I'm pleased to meet you," mumbling. There is a slight facial paralysis on the left. That will wear off.

I am Rosa. I am the rose. The rose, I am the rose. The rose with no flower, the rose all thorns, the mind he made, the hand he touched, the winter rose.

The White Donkey

THERE WERE snakes in the old stone place, but the grass grew so green and rank there that she brought the goats back every day. "The goats are looking fat," Nana said. "Where are you grazing them, Sita?" And when Sita said, "At the old stone place, in the forest," Nana said, "It's a long way to take them," and Uncle Hira said, "Look out for snakes in that place," but they were thinking of the goats, not of her; so she did not ask them, after all, about the white donkey.

She had seen the donkey first when she was putting flowers on the red stone under the pipal tree at the edge of the forest. She liked that stone. It was the Goddess, very old, round, sitting comfortably among the roots of the tree. Everybody who passed by there left the Goddess some flowers or poured a bit of water on her, and every spring her red paint was renewed. Sita was giving the Goddess a rhododendron flower when she looked round, thinking one of the goats was straying off into the forest; but it wasn't a goat. It was a white animal that had caught her eye, whiter than a Brahminee bull. Sita followed it to see what it was. When she saw the neat round rump and the tail like a rope with a tassel, she knew it was a donkey; but such a beautiful donkey! And whose? There were three donkeys in the village, and Chandra Bose owned two, all of them grey, bony, mournful, laborious beasts. This was a tall, sleek, delicate donkey, a wonderful donkey. It could not belong to Chandra Bose, or to anybody in the village, or to anybody in the other village. It wore no halter or harness. It must be wild; it must live in the forest alone.

Sure enough, when she brought the goats along by whistling to clever Kala, and followed where the white donkey had gone into the forest, first there was a path, and then they came to the place where the old stones were, blocks of stone as big as houses all half buried and overgrown with grass and kerala vines; and there the white donkey was standing looking back at her from the darkness under the trees.

She thought then that the donkey was a god, because it had a third eye in the middle of its forehead like Shiva. But when it turned she saw that that was not an eye, but a horn — not curved like a cow's or a goat's horns, a straight spike like a deer's — just the one horn, between the eyes, like Shiva's eye. So it might be a kind of god donkey; and in case it was, she picked a yellow flower off the kerala vine and offered it, stretching out her open palm.

The white donkey stood a while considering her and the goats and the flower; then it came slowly back among the big stones towards her. It had split hooves like the goats, and walked even more neatly than they did. It accepted the flower. Its nose was pinkish-white, and very soft where it snuffled on Sita's palm. She quickly picked another flower, and the donkey accepted it too. But when she wanted to stroke its face around the short, white, twisted horn and the white, nervous ears, it moved away, looking sidelong at her from its long dark eyes.

Sita was a little afraid of it, and thought it might be a little afraid of her; so she sat down on one of the half-buried rocks and pretended to be watching the goats, who were all busy grazing on the best grass they had had for months. Presently the donkey came close again, and standing beside Sita, rested its curly-bearded chin on her lap. The breath from its nostrils moved the thin glass bangles on her wrist. Slowly and very gently she stroked the base of the white, nervous ears, the fine, harsh hair at the base of the horn, the silken muzzle; and the white donkey stood beside her, breathing long, warm breaths.

Every day since then she brought the goats there, walking carefully because of snakes; and the goats were getting fat; and her friend the donkey came out of the forest every day, and accepted her offering, and kept her company.

"One bullock and one hundred rupees cash," said Uncle Hira, "you're crazy if you think we can marry her for less!"

"Moti Lal is a lazy man," Nana said. "Dirty and lazy."

"So he wants a wife to work and clean for him! And he'll take her for only one bullock and one hundred rupees cash!"

"Maybe he'll settle down when he's married," Nana said.

So Sita was betrothed to Moti Lal from the other village, who had watched her driving the goats home at evening. She had seen him watching her across the road, but had never looked at him. She did not want to look at him.

"This is the last day," she said to the white donkey, while the goats cropped the grass among the big, carved, fallen stones, and the forest stood all about them in the singing stillness. "Tomorrow I'll come with Uma's little brother to show him the way here. He'll be the village goatherd now. The day after tomorrow is my wedding day."

The white donkey stood still, its curly, silky beard resting against her hand.

"Nana is giving me her gold bangle," Sita said to the donkey. "I get to wear a red sari, and have henna on my feet and hands."

The donkey stood still, listening.

"There'll be sweet rice to eat at the wedding," Sita said; then she began to cry.

"Goodbye, white donkey," she said. The white donkey looked at her sidelong, and slowly, not looking back, moved away from her and walked into the darkness under the trees.

The Phoenix

THE RADIO on the chest of drawers hissed and crackled like burning acid. Through the crackle a voice boasted of victories. "Butchers!" she snarled at the voice. "Butchers, liars, fools!" But there was an expression in the librarian's eyes which brought her rage up short like a dog on a chain, clawing at the air, choked off.

"You can't be a Partisan!"

The librarian said nothing. He might well have said nothing even if he had been able to say anything.

She turned the radio down — you could never turn it off, lest you should miss the last act, the denouement — and came up close to the librarian on the bed. Familiar to her now were the round, sallow face, the dark eyes with bloodshot whites, the dark, wiry hair on his head, and the hair on his forearms and the backs of his hands and fingers, and the hair under his arms and on his chest and groin and legs, and the whole of his stocky, sweaty, suffering body, which she had been trying to look after for thirty hours while the city blew itself apart street by street and nerve by nerve and the radio twitched from lies to static to lies.

"Come on, don't tell me that!" she said to his silence. "You weren't with them. You were against them."

Without a word, with the utmost economy, he evinced a denial.

"But I saw you! I saw exactly what you did. You locked the library. Why do you think I came there looking for you? You don't think I'd have crossed the street to help one of them!" A one-note laugh of scorn, and she awarded the well-delivered line the moment of silence that was its due. The radio hissed thinly, drifting back to static. She sat down on the foot of the bed, directly in the librarian's line of sight, front and center.

"I've known you by sight for I don't know how long — a couple of years, it must be. My other room, there, looks out on the square. Right across to the library. I've seen you opening it up in the morning a hundred times. This time I saw you closing it, at two in the afternoon. Running those wrought-iron gates across the doors in a rush. So what's he up to? Then I heard the cars and those damned motorcycles. I drew the curtain right away. But then I stood behind the curtain and watched. That was strange, you know? I'd have sworn I'd be hiding under the bed in here as soon as I knew they were that close. But I stood there and watched. It was like watching a play!" she said with the expansiveness of inaccuracy. In fact, peering out between the curtain and the window frame with a running thrill of not disagreeable terror, she had inevitably felt that she was sizing up the house. Was it that revival of emotion that had moved her, so soon afterwards, to act?

"They pulled the flag down first. I suppose even terrorists have to do things in the proper order. Probably in fact no one is more conventional. They have to do everything that's expected of them. . . . Well, I'd seen you go round to that side door, the basement entrance, after you'd locked the gates. I think I'd noticed your coat, without noticing that I noticed, you know; that yellowish-brown color. So, after they'd been all over the front steps, and broken in at the side door — like ants on meat, I kept thinking — and finally all come out again and got onto their damned motorcycles and roared off to go wreck something else, and I was wondering if it was smoke or just dust that was hanging around that side door — then I thought of your coat, because of the color of the smoke, that yellowish brown. I thought, I never saw that coat again. They didn't bring the librarian out with them. Well, so I thought probably they'd shot you, inside there with the books. But I kept thinking how you'd locked the doors and locked the gates and then gone back inside. I didn't know why you'd done that. You could have locked up and left, got away, after all. I kept thinking about that. And there wasn't a soul down in the square. All us rats hiding in our rat-holes. So finally I thought, Well, I can't live with this, and went over to look for you. I walked right across the square. Empty as four A.M. It was peaceful. I wasn't afraid. I was only frightened of finding you dead. A wound, blood. Blood turns me faint, I detest it. So I go in, and my mouth's dry and my ears are singing, and then I see you coming with an armload of books!" She laughed, but this time her voice cracked. She turned left profile to him, glancing at him once sidelong.

"Why did you go back in? And when they were in there, what did you do? You hid, I suppose. And when they left you came out and tried to put out the fire."

He shook his head slightly.

"You did," she said. "You did put it out. There was water on the floor, and a mop bucket."

He did not deny this.

"I shouldn't have thought books would catch fire easily. Or did they pull out some newspapers, or the catalogue, or the overdue file? They certainly got something burning. All that smoke, it was awful. I was choking as soon as I came in, I don't know how you breathed at all up there on the main floor. Anyway, you put out the fire, and you had to get out because of the smoke, or you weren't sure the fire was really out; so you quick picked up some valuable books and headed for the door — "

Again he shook his head. Was he smiling?

"You did! You were crawling towards the stairs, crawling on your knees, trying to carry those books, when I came up. I don't know if you would have got out or not, but you were trying to."

He nodded, and tried to whisper something.

"Never mind. Don't talk. Just tell me, no, don't tell me, how you can be a Partisan, after that. After giving your life, all but, for a few books!"

He forced the whisper, like a steel brush on brass, that was all the smoke had left of his voice: "Not valuable," he said.

She had leaned forward to catch his words. She straightened up, smoothed her skirt, and presently spoke with some disdain.

"I don't know that we are really very well qualified to judge whether our life is or is not valuable."

But he shook his head again and whispered, voiceless, meaningless, obstinate: "The books."

"You're saying that the *books* aren't valuable?"

He nodded, his face relaxing, relieved at having explained himself at last, at having got it all straight.

She stared at him, incredulous, angrier than she had been at the radio, and then the anger flipped over like a coin from a thumb, and she laughed. "You're crazy!" she said, putting her hand on his.

His hand was thickset like the rest of him, firm but uncallused, a desk worker's hand. It was hot to her touch.

"You ought to be in hospital," she said with remorse. "I know you shouldn't talk, I can't help talking, but don't answer. I know you should have gone to the hospital. But how could you get there, no taxis, and God knows what the hospitals are like now. Or who they're willing to take. If it ever quiets down and the telephone works again I'll try to call a doctor. If there are any doctors left. If there's anything left when this is over."

It was the silence that made her say that. It was a silent

day. On the silent days you almost wanted to hear the motorcycles, the machine guns.

His eyes were closed. Yesterday evening, and from time to time all night, he had had spasms of struggling for breath, like asthma or a heart attack, terrifying. He breathed short and hard even now, but however worn out and uncomfortable, he was resting; he must be better. What could a doctor do for smoke inhalation, anyhow? Probably not much. Doctors were not much good for things like lack of breath, or old age, or civil disorders. The librarian was suffering from what his country was dying of, his sickness was his citizenship of this city. Weeks now, the loudspeakers, the machine guns, the explosions, the helicopters, the fires, the silences; the body politic was incurable, its agony went on and on. You went miles for a cabbage, a kilo of meal. Then next day the sweet shop at the corner was open, children buying orange drink. And the next day it was gone, the corner building blown up, burnt out. The carcase politic. Faces of people like façades of buildings downtown, the great hotels, blank and furtive, all blinds down. And last Saturday night they had thrown a bomb into the Phoenix. Thirty dead, the radio had said, and later sixty dead, but it was not the deaths that outraged her. People took their chances. They had gone to see a play in the middle of a civil war, they had taken their chance and lost. There was both gallantry and justice there. But the old Phoenix, the house itself: the stage where she had played how many pert housemaids, younger sisters, confidantes, dowagers, Olga Prozorova, and for the great three weeks Nora; the red curtain, the red plush seats, the dirty chandelier and gilt plaster mouldings, all that fake grandeur, that box of toys, that defenseless and indefensible strutting place for the human soul — to hurt that was contemptible. Better if they threw their damned bombs into churches. There surely the startled soul would be plucked straight up to downy heaven before it noticed that its body had been blown to stewmeat. With God on your side, in God's house, how could anything go wrong? But there was no protection in some dead playwright and a lot of stagehands and fool actors. Everything could go wrong, and always did. Lights out, and screaming and pushing, trampling, an unspeakable sewer stink, and so much for Molière, or Pirandello, or whoever they'd been playing Saturday night at the Phoenix. God had never been on that side. He'd take the glory, all right, but not the blame. What God was, in fact, was a doctor, a famous surgeon: don't ask questions, I don't answer them, pay your fees, I'll save you if I care to but if I don't it's your own fault.

She got up to rearrange the bedside table, reproving herself for vulgarity of thought. She had to be angry at somebody; there was nobody there but God and the librarian, and she did not want to be angry at the librarian. Like the city, he was too sick. And anger would disturb the purity of her strong erotic attraction to him, which had been giving her great pleasure. She had not so enjoyed looking at a man for years; she had thought that joy lost, withered away. Her age took advantage from his illness. In the normal course of things he would not have seen her as a woman but as an old woman, and his blindness would have blinded her: she would not have looked at him. But, having undressed him and looked after his body, she was spared hypocrisy, and could admire that stocky and innocent body with the innocent joy of desire. Of his mind and spirit she knew almost nothing, only that he had courage, which was a good thing. She did not need to know more. Indeed she did not want to. She was sorry he had spoken at all, had said those two stupid, boastful words, "Not valuable," whether meaning his own life, or the books he had tried to save at the risk of his life. In either case what he had meant was that to a Partisan nothing was valuable but the cause. The existence of a branch librarian, the existence of a few books — trash. Nothing mattered but the future.

But if he was a Partisan, why had he tried to save the books?

Would a Loyalist have stayed alone in that terrible brownish-yellow room of smoke trying to put out the fire, to keep the books from burning?

Of course, she answered herself. According to his opinions,

his theories, his beliefs, yes, certainly, of course! Books, statues, buildings, lamp posts bearing lighted lamps not strangled corpses, Molière at eight-thirty, conversation at dinner, schoolgirls in blue with satchels, order, decency, the past that ensures a future, for this the Loyalist stood. Staunchly he stood. But would he also crawl across a floor coughing out his lungs, trying to hang on to a few of the books? — not even valuable books, that's what the librarian had been trying to say, she understood him now, not even valuable ones; there probably were no valuable books in this branch library. Just books, any books, not because he had opinions, not because he had beliefs, there with his life forfeit, but because he was a librarian. A person who looked after books. The one responsible.

"Is that what you meant?" she asked him, softly, because he had fallen asleep. "Is that why I brought you here?"

The radio hissed, but she did not need applause. His sleep was her audience.

Zenith

Intracom

CAPTAIN: Good morning, good morning, good morning everybody. How many of us are there, aboard this space ship? Well, let's see. This is, of course, the Captain speaking. There is the First Mate, about whom there is something, well, different. But not the ears. I've seen First Mates with funny ears, but that isn't this one's problem. Well, then there is the Chief Engineer, whose vocabulary is limited to symptoms of valvular malfunction. And the Insane Second Mate, who is locked up in the Crew Recreation Lounge, busy pulling the stuffing out of chairs and sofas, and throwing pool balls at the indirect lighting fixtures. Then there is the Communications Officer, forever wearing headphones and hunched above the hissing radio. The hiss, I understand, is the noise stars make. It is quite a loud noise, out here. Is that all of us? I can't think of anybody else. It is a small crew, but a select one, being composed entirely of officers. How many does it come to? Six, doesn't it?

FIRST MATE: Five.

CAPTAIN: Only five? Are you sure of that, Mr. Balls?

FIRST MATE: Affirmative.

CAPTAIN: Very well, five, then. I know you're good with mathematics. But I keep having this feeling there's somebody else.

FIRST MATE: Conceivably, sir, you are thinking of yourself in your capacity as Cook.

CAPTAIN: Don't call me "sir," Mr. Balls. All right, then. Here we are, the personnel of the space ship *Mary Jane Hewett,* Class F, b-1951, Type 36-25-38, Size 13, outward bound from Earth (Terra, 3 Solis) on an exploratory voyage in the direction of the South Orion Arm, with a cargo of breadfruit trees. We have travelled a tremendous distance already, light-years and light-years, though there are times it hardly seems we're moving at all.

Excuse me. I have to go make lunch.

It isn't easy to feed the Insane Second Mate, since she plugged the soup chute full of sofa stuffing. We have cut a little hole in the door of the Crew Recreation Lounge, like a mail slot. We wait until the Insane Second Mate is asleep, because when she's awake, if she hears us at the door, she sticks her hands through and makes obscene gestures with the middle finger of her left hand, or throws pool balls at us. While she is asleep, or sulking, we hastily force her dinner through the slot. After a certain time has passed, if one places one's ear to the lower half of the door, the Insane Second Mate may be heard munching the food. Uneaten portions are returned through the slot. Lately very little has been returned. Evidently she is eating all the food, or doing something else with it. From time to time I have wondered if there could be someone else in there with her. She seems to eat inordinately, for a female Insane Second Mate of average size.

Chief Engineer, before I go to the galley may I have your daily report for the Ship's Log.

CHIEF ENGINEER: Aye, weel, compressed hydrogen tank A-30 is

leaking. Leakage not contained at present time. Stoppage in forward conduit FC-599 continues, causing buildup of pressure in central coolant storage area CCS-2. Hairline crack in casing of Anti-Matter Isolater is being investigated with intention of presenting report on viability of implementation of repair procedures.

CAPTAIN: What procedure is indicated if repair implementation proves non-feasible?

CHIEF ENGINEER: Automatic Self-Destruct.

CAPTAIN: Good God.

CHIEF ENGINEER: Log entry continued: Vane One has suffered extensive meteor damage and is not currently functioning at full gather-power. Vane Two has been shortened by 81,000 miles to offset the slow spin imparted by imbalance in vane function. Results should be discernible within five to thirteen days (Ship Time). Automatic self-destruct units of ship are no longer functioning, due to suspected short circuit causing automatic self-destruct units to automatically self-destruct.

CAPTAIN: You mean the automatic self-destruct units are all self-destructed?

CHIEF ENGINEER: Aye, that's about the size of it, Captain.

CAPTAIN: You mean we can't destruct the ship, if the crack in the Anti-Matter Isolater widens? But if we can't self-destruct, and the Anti-Matter Isolater blows, we'll take the fifty nearest stars and all their planets with us — we'll blow up this whole region of space — if the anti-matter meets an F-2 star, the destruction might become a chain reaction and the entire Galaxy could be destructed!

CHIEF ENGINEER: Weel, we're working hard on that crack, Captain.

CAPTAIN: We? What do you mean, we? There's only one of you down there in the Engine Room. Isn't there?

CHIEF ENGINEER: Aye. But I wish there was a few more.

CAPTAIN: I know you do, at times like this, "Bolts." But we have the utmost faith in you. You're a fantastically good Chief Engineer, for a woman.

CHIEF ENGINEER: Thank you, Captain. I'll be going back to my wee crack now.

CAPTAIN: Very well, and I'm on my way to the galley.

It's odd. Just now as I glanced over my shoulder I could have sworn I saw somebody going down Corridor G. Now Corridor G leads to a totally disused section of the ship, the Athletic Supporter Storage Room. Who's got any business there? Mr. Balls? Mr. Balls, are you there?

FIRST MATE: I am in the Computer Center, sir.

CAPTAIN: Will you please not call me "sir," Mr. Balls. It estranges me. "Sparks," where are you? "Sparks"? Report to Bridge by intracom at once. "Sparks"?

COMMUNICATIONS OFFICER: Shhh. I'm listening to the radio. Roger. Over and out.

CAPTAIN: All right. And "Bolts" is down with the Anti-Matter Isolater; and I'm here on the Bridge trying to get to the galley. That's four. Five, five, who's five? Oh, yes. Insane Second Mate, report current whereabouts to Bridge by intracom at once.

INSANE SECOND MATE: I am clinging by the skin of my teeth and the nails of my toes to a cliff that towers above a raging sea of salt, lashed by great winds into waves and breakers whiter and heavier than ever water was. If I let go I will fall and be broken against the rocks and buried under tons of roaring salt, drowned in the dry sea. If I do not let go I have to keep holding on here, and holding on, and holding on, what for? I am so bored I could scream. I am screaming loudly but no one can hear it over the howl of the wind and the thunder of collapsing salt. I hope the rest of you are enjucting yourselves.

CAPTAIN: What?

INSANE SECOND MATE: Before the ship self-destructs, I hope

you are emplucting your time in enjuctable diversions. I
think I shall let go now.

CAPTAIN: Wait! Listen, "Bats," is there anybody else there in
the Crew Recreation Lounge with you?

INSANE SECOND MATE: Here I go. Eeeee-yahhhhhh! — Jesus
Christ! it's sugar.

CAPTAIN: Well, that seems to account for all six of us. There
couldn't have been anybody in Corridor G. I just thought
there was.

FIRST MATE: Captain, there are only five persons aboard.

CAPTAIN: What makes you so sure of that, Mr. Balls?

FIRST MATE: Mathematics. Simple addition of real numbers.
Yourself, 1, myself, 1, "Bolts," 1, "Sparks," 1, "Bats," 1. 1
plus 1 plus 1 plus 1 plus 1 equals 5.

CAPTAIN: That may be. You can prove anything with statistics.
But what if there's one 1 you haven't counted?

FIRST MATE: Who?

CAPTAIN: That's what I'm asking *you,* Mr. Balls.

FIRST MATE: Captain, may I respectfully suggest that it is time
for lunch, or dinner, or whatever time it is time for.

CAPTAIN: And what about irrational numbers, Mr. Balls? Eh?

FIRST MATE: Captain, may I respectfully suggest that you leave
mathematics to me and the onboard computers.

CAPTAIN: All right, all right. What do you want for lunch?

FIRST MATE: Whatever you please, Captain.

CAPTAIN: I am sick and tired of having to think about it, planning meals all the time. I'm going to open a can of Camp-
bell's Tomato Rice Soup and if you don't like it it's too bad.
Every time I'm on the verge of really understanding something, every time an insight is just within outgrope, every
time I really realise that I am the Captain of a great ship, I
have to turn around and decide whether it's to be macaroni
and cheese or rice pilaf. Why can't somebody else do the
cooking for a while?

FIRST MATE: Nobody else knows how.

CAPTAIN: Any one of you can heat a can of soup as well as I can.

FIRST MATE: Remember when the Second Mate tried?

CAPTAIN: Well, almost any of you. A robot could do it. Why don't we have galley robots? Why weren't we designed properly? The real trouble is that this is a lazy, uncoordinated, incoherent crew. And the center of the trouble, the real source of the disintegration, the stumbling block to all my efforts to run a tight ship, is one person, one single member of the crew, and I think you all know who I'm talking about.

FIRST MATE: Affirmative.

CHIEF ENGINEER: Oh, aye.

INSANE SECOND MATE: Not me. But poor Tom's a-cold.   .

CAPTAIN: "Sparks," are you listening? "Sparks," come in please. Come in please.

COMMUNICATIONS OFFICER: Shhh. I'm listening to the radio. Roger. Over and —

CAPTAIN: No! Now you take off those damned headphones and listen to me for a minute, "Sparks."

COMMUNICATIONS OFFICER: Captain, I wish I could take off the headphones. Sometimes I even wish I could turn off the radio. But I can't. It does fade sometimes, you know. There'll be days at a time, weeks, months, when I can't pick up a thing, not even star hiss. But I have to keep listening, in case it comes back, in case a message comes through. That's the way it is now. I haven't picked up a message for five days (Ship Time). But what if one is just about to come through? What if it came through and I was in the galley heating soup? What if it's coming through right now and I'm missing it because I'm talking on the intracom? It isn't that I have anything against the rest of you, or that I want to be a stumbling block, but that's the nature of a Communications Officer. Over and —

CAPTAIN: No. Now stay on the intracom and listen to *this* message. Other ships have Communications Officers, you

know, and they don't act like you at all. They don't just sit
there with their damned head between the earphones and
their mouth hanging open all the time. They *communicate*.
They talk with other ships of the Fleet. They receive news
and directives, and exchange all sorts of information and
friendly chitchat to beguile the interminable boredom of
space. Why don't you ever do that? Don't you realise the
rest of us would like to talk with the rest of the Fleet now
and then?

COMMUNICATIONS OFFICER: But I don't listen on the Fleet
wavelength.

CAPTAIN: Why not?

COMMUNICATIONS OFFICER: Because I'm trying to pick up the
message.

CAPTAIN: What message?

COMMUNICATIONS OFFICER: The one we haven't heard before.

CAPTAIN: What for?

COMMUNICATIONS OFFICER: Well, it might indicate where we're
going — we and all the other ships of the Fleet.

CAPTAIN: What does it matter where we're going, so long as
we're going? Listen, "Sparks," I don't like to berate you
like this. We'd like to have the upmost faith in you. You're
a fantastically good Communications Officer, for a woman.
But —

COMMUNICATIONS OFFICER: Excuse me, Captain, I'm getting
star hiss. Over and out.

CAPTAIN: Oh, hell. Mr. Balls, will you please proceed to Bridge.
I'll be in the galley, heating soup.

FIRST MATE: Captain, wait. There's something funny in the air.
Something in the ship's atmospheric circulation system.

CAPTAIN: Probably just some of "Bolts's" hydrogen leaking.

FIRST MATE: It doesn't smell like hydrogen. It's a *strange* smell.
Or is it a vibration? Or is it a noise?

CAPTAIN: Mr. Balls, are you all right? You don't sound like
yourself.

FIRST MATE: Affirmative. Captain, I wish to report suspected presence of an alien aboard this ship.

CAPTAIN: An alien?

FIRST MATE: Affirmative. Alert. Alert. Red Alert. All hands to combat posts. Alien presence suspected on ship. Chief Engineer, report on conditions in Engine Room.

CHIEF ENGINEER: Weel, noo, everything's dandy in the Engine Room, sir.

CAPTAIN: What about the Anti-Matter Isolater?

CHIEF ENGINEER: We mended the wee crack wi' a wee Band-Aid, Captain, and it's as good as new.

CAPTAIN: What about the ship's self-destruct capacity?

CHIEF ENGINEER: Weel, noo, we're working on that. But otherwise I may say that things in the Engine Room have never been better.

FIRST MATE: Red Alert! Red Alert! Chief Engineer, proceed instantly to repair automatic self-destruct units in Central Propulsion Zone, and as soon as repairs are completed place automatic self-destruct units on Imminent status.

CAPTAIN: Mr. Balls, what are you shouting about?

FIRST MATE: There's an alien in this ship with us, Captain!

CAPTAIN: How do you know?

FIRST MATE: A slimy, unspeakable alien!

CAPTAIN: Have you seen it, Mr. Balls? Is it in the Athletic Supporter Storage Room?

FIRST MATE: No, I haven't seen it. I don't want to see it. I can *feel* it. It's in here, Captain. It's in the ship — something that doesn't belong here. It's not one of us. It came from Outer Space. From outside. To take us over. It's waiting, waiting somewhere in the very bowels of the ship, waiting, and growing —

CAPTAIN: Good gracious. Get a hold of yourself, Mr. Balls.

INSANE SECOND MATE: I told you poor Tom was a-cold. Now poor Tom's a-flipped.

FIRST MATE: It's in there, in the Crew Recreation Lounge, with you, isn't it, "Bats"? You've known about it for days, weeks. You've been hiding it from us. You traitor! I'm coming in. I'm coming in there, "Bats," and I'm going to kill that thing, that unspeakable, amorphous Thing that you've been hiding from us and feeding with our food —

CAPTAIN: Mr. Balls! Where are you? What are you doing?

FIRST MATE: I'm breaking down the door of the Crew Recreation Lounge, Captain. Don't worry. I'll handle this. You just keep things running there on the Bridge, and the ship on course, and all.

CAPTAIN: I'm not on the Bridge. I'm in the galley.

FIRST MATE: For God's sake, Captain, get back to the Bridge! The Thing will try to take control of the ship, if it escapes me! — All right, "Bats," where is it? Where is it hiding? Show the Thing to me, or I'll — Aagh! Aaaggghhh! Ow!

CHIEF ENGINEER: Captain? Captain Cook? Would there be a wee bit o' trouble up there?

COMMUNICATIONS OFFICER: Please be quieter, everybody. I'm receiving.

CAPTAIN: Mr. Balls, report current conditions in Crew Recreation Lounge. Mr. Balls, report please.

INSANE SECOND MATE: This is the Insane Second Mate speaking. The First Mate is temporarily incapacitated.

CAPTAIN: Report, please, Second Mate.

INSANE SECOND MATE: Well, he came busting in shouting about how he was going to do something to the alien, and I got in his way, and he tried to karate chop me. But as you know, Captain, I'm extraordinarily strong, even for an Insane Second Mate. I hit him on the head with a copy of the *I Ching,* and he folded.

CAPTAIN: Report current condition of First Mate, please.

INSANE SECOND MATE: He is lying on the floor breathing.

CAPTAIN: Very good. "Bats," I suppose you'd better get up to the Bridge and keep an eye on flight control. Last time I looked Arcturus seemed to have drifted a bit. If I don't get lunch ready, tempers are going to be getting short.

INSANE SECOND MATE: Aye aye, Captain.

CAPTAIN: By the way, *is* there an alien aboard?

INSANE SECOND MATE: Oh, yes, Captain.

CAPTAIN: I thought so all along. I knew Mr. Balls couldn't count. You'd better take it up to the Bridge with you and keep an eye on it.

INSANE SECOND MATE: Captain, I can't do that. I have to leave it here in the Crew Recreation Lounge.

CAPTAIN: Why?

INSANE SECOND MATE: Well, see, it sort of fits in here. We can feed it through the slot in the door. Frankly, I'm just as glad to get out. Things were getting a little crowded in here. As Mr. Balls noticed, it's been growing. You wouldn't believe it. It was just a speck of a thing to start with.

CAPTAIN: And how is Mr. Balls?

INSANE SECOND MATE: He's sitting up now, but he looks a bit catatonic. It's the shock. I'll walk him back to his quarters.

FIRST MATE: Oh my God I can't stand it horrible vile like a giant worm slimy battening on us fattening on us invading us a vampire a parasite using us growing *growing* GROWING get me out get me out Red Alert Self-Destruct SELF-DESTRUCT!

INSANE SECOND MATE: There, there, Balls. Now. Come on. Here's your own nice cozy quarters, see? And you can lock the door, and shut It out, and do mathematics all by yourself.

FIRST MATE: My God, you're worse than It is! Get out of here! Out! Captain Cook! Captain Cook1 This officer is insane!

CAPTAIN: What officer?

INSANE SECOND MATE: Me.

CAPTAIN: Oh, now, we just call you that, because you won't use secondary process thinking.

FIRST MATE: Captain Cook! Order Engine Room personnel to activate automatic self-destruct units! Abort mission! Abort mission!

CAPTAIN: How's that again?

FIRST MATE: Abort! Abort! We are being emplucted by an alien creature for unknown purposes! It is taking over the officers' minds! This ship is a peril to the Universe!

INSANE SECOND MATE: Goodness, he talks almost the way I do.

CAPTAIN: It's quite interesting, actually, looked at dispassionately. I wonder if Mr. Balls resents the presence of the alien because he too has always been, in a sense, an alien presence on this ship. Psychologists call the phenomenon "projection," I believe.

FIRST MATE: Can't you realise how horrible it is, horrible, horrible!

COMMUNICATIONS OFFICER: Please order the First Mate to shut up, Captain. All this shouting is very annucting. I'm getting some interesting material on the radio.

CAPTAIN: Where from? I certainly could use some advice.

COMMUNICATIONS OFFICER: I'm not sure. Seems very close. Loud signal.

CAPTAIN: What does it say?

COMMUNICATIONS OFFICER: It doesn't speak English.

INSANE SECOND MATE: This is "Bats" reporting from the Bridge. All well here.

CAPTAIN: All right, everybody. Lunchtime. Mouth to the soup chute, mates! Ready?

INSANE SECOND MATE: Ready.

CHIEF ENGINEER: Ready.

FIRST MATE: Ready.

COMMUNICATIONS OFFICER: Ready.

CAPTAIN: Soup's on!

CHIEF ENGINEER: Ahh.

FIRST MATE: Mmmm.

INSANE SECOND MATE: Yum.

COMMUNICATIONS OFFICER: Yum.

CAPTAIN: Yum.

INSANE SECOND MATE: What about the alien?

CHIEF ENGINEER: I'll see to the puir wee beastie. Send me an-
    other chute of soup, Captain, and I'll catch it in an oilcan
    and pour it in through the slot. Aye, that's it. Now then.
    Here I am. Are you ready, beastie? Here it comes!

ALIEN: Num, num.

CHIEF ENGINEER: There's a bonnie beastie. Go to sleep now.
    Captain, how do you think the beastie got aboard?

CAPTAIN: I've been thinking about that.

INSANE SECOND MATE: It didn't "get" aboard. It's autochtho-
    nous. It's ours, all ours.

CAPTAIN: It doesn't happen that way, "Bats." Not with ad-
    vanced space ships of our type. At least, not without a Spe-
    cial Dispensation. Personally, I think the only time it could
    have got into the Crew Recreation Lounge was through the
    tubes, when we rendezvoused with that cruiser near Deneb.
    The hatches were open several times, if you recall, during
    that exchange.

CHIEF ENGINEER: Oh, aye, a lovely ship, that cruiser. Sleek and
    slim and tapered, and power enough to rattle my pipes.

COMMUNICATIONS OFFICER: Yes, damn it, it kept interfering
    with my reception. Jammed the radio with a lot of senti-
    mental nonsense for a week. Kept signalling us as "Honey
    Pot."

FIRST MATE: Do you mean to imply, Captain, that that cruiser
    deliberately stowed this monster away aboard our ship? A
    cruiser of the Fleet?

CAPTAIN: Well, no, not deliberately. Those things simply hap-
    pen, sometimes, if precautions haven't been taken. If the
    Second Mate, for instance, failed to activate the hatch
    forcefields, and to remind me to go through decontamina-
    tion procedure — which has happened before —

INSANE SECOND MATE: I hate activating those forcefields.
    They're unnatural. They drive me crazy. All those vibra-
    tions. And worrying about getting the phases timed just
    right. They're not good for the ship, in the long run.
    "Bolts" will back me up on that.

CHIEF ENGINEER: Aye, they're a strain on the engines. Besides, why do *we* have to take all the precautions?

INSANE SECOND MATE: So I forgot to turn them on.

CAPTAIN: There you are.

FIRST MATE: You're all psychotic — subhuman. You let us be infected, invaded, taken over by this alien. You deliberately invited it to happen, and now that it's happened, you're allowing it to go on happening — and it's sitting there, growing, *growing* —

CHIEF ENGINEER: There, there, puir wee First Mate. Dinna let it fash ye.

FIRST MATE: Captain Cook! Listen to me! You've always listened to me sometimes, you've always been superbly rational more or less. Think about it, *think* about it — the danger, the danger to the ship. It's taking us over, don't you see? And we have a mission! How long are you going to let it go on? The sooner we act, the safer and easier it'll be —

CAPTAIN: Well, how long has it been aboard?

INSANE SECOND MATE: About fifty days (Ship Time). That's when the cruiser left, anyhow.

CAPTAIN: That leaves, let's see, wait, fifty from 280 —

FIRST MATE: 230.

CAPTAIN: Right. Yes. So. About 230 days (Ship Time) to go. If it follows the usual pattern. This isn't the first time an alien has got aboard a Ship of the Fleet, you know, Mr. Balls. Nor will it be the last. We know, barring accidents, pretty well what to expect. Perhaps you should glance over the *Handbook of Onboard Aliens* to freshen up your information on the subject.

FIRST MATE: Captain, aren't you even scared?

CAPTAIN: Mr. Balls, I am scared shitless. But what can I do?

FIRST MATE: Get rid of it! Now! Quick! While we still can! Before it gets any bigger! Let me stuff it into the Disposal Hatch! Unlock my door — just let me out — it won't take any time at all — the rest of the Fleet won't even know —

INSANE SECOND MATE: Listen, little Balls. I am on the Bridge
now. And I think I'll continue to be on the Bridge for the
next 230 days (Ship Time). The Captain is needed in the
galley. Your door is locked and will remain locked, until
you come to terms with the situation. You may not like my
being in charge. I know you feel I'm untrustworthy, and
useful only in a subordinate position. And in normal conditions and most situations that's quite true. I *am* untrustworthy, unpredictable, and devious. I can't even count on myself. When I leap into a roaring seething ocean of salt, it
turns out to be powdered sugar. When I look out the Bridge
viewport at the stars, I don't see the stars. I see dragons,
swans, whales, scorpions, bears, huntsmen, chariots, crosses,
signs, omens, and writings in huge shining words I cannot
read. When I set my finger on the buttons on the Main
Control Panel, the buttons turn into a dog's hind paws, and
my finger explodes like a firecracker. When I walk across
the Bridge to check the computer readouts, I can't see the
floor; I see an abyss, the dark underpit where pale shapes
writhe and shoulder in the gloom, turning vast rudimentary
faces, eye spots, mouth holes, up towards me, their country-
woman, mincing across the Bridge high above them on my
thin wire, clutching at my flying trapeze. I do not belong on
the Bridge of a ship of this class, except during the night
shift when you and the Captain are asleep — and during
certain exceptional situations, such as this. The fact is,
granted all my peculiarities, at this point I'm the only one
who can bring us through.

FIRST MATE: Captain, Captain Cook, listen to me. Don't listen
to that maniac, that mutineer. Listen to me. Captain, you
know I have the utmost faith in you, almost. You're a fantastically good captain, for a woman. Don't let the Second
Mate take over the Bridge!

CAPTAIN: I can't stop her, Mr. Balls. It's the influence of the
alien, I suppose. We've all changed, don't you see?

FIRST MATE: Changed?

CAPTAIN: Yes. "Bats" has acquired tremendous strength — as you must have noticed when she hit you with the *I Ching* — and a driving sense of purpose. "Bolts" isn't complaining any more about engine malfunctions; she's happy as a lark down there, singing "Scots Wha Hae wi' Wallace Bled." "Sparks" has gone completely out of touch — right, "Sparks"? — "Sparks"? — See? As for myself, I don't know exactly what the change involves, except that the Second Mate makes better sense to me than she used to, and you don't; but I do know that since we've had the alien aboard I've felt a different person.

FIRST MATE: And I, Captain? I haven't changed.

CAPTAIN: No. That's the trouble, Mr. Balls. You haven't. You aren't really cut out to cope with this. But it's not your fault; and in the long run it may be a good thing. It maintains a certain continuity aboard the ship. We don't want to become totally alienated, after all.

FIRST MATE: Captain, you're not as civilised as I am, but you are pretty much a product of civilisation — unlike the rest of this crew. And what I don't understand is how, being a civilised person, you can stand the humiliation of it. The being *used* — like a bucket, or a Petri dish. We aren't a mere vehicle, a vessel for aliens to get fat in, a damned yeast culture! We are a ship, a Ship of the Fleet, sailing under our own power, embarked on the Great Journey to the Unknown End.

CAPTAIN: But you know, Mr. Balls, that in fact we probably won't get there.

FIRST MATE: I know. But there was a chance. Now there isn't. We won't get there, we won't get anywhere, weighted down with this alien, and with all of you paying no more attention to anything outside the ship. I'll bet, right now, that the Second Mate can't give us a star fix. What's our inclination to Arcturus, "Bats"?

INSANE SECOND MATE: Well. Let me see. Just let me press this dog's hind paw here, and adjust this earthworm. There now. Arcturus? I'm not sure; but I do see a dead queen sitting upside down in a chair off the larboard bow.

FIRST MATE: You see? You see?

CAPTAIN: Yes. And I'm not crazy about staying in the galley all the time, either. But we can be patient, Mr. Balls. The alien won't actually be aboard very long. Less than eight months to go, now. Then, you know, all we have to do is take it in tow for a while, just for a few years.

FIRST MATE: In tow? *Tow* it?

CAPTAIN: Well, of course. It's our responsibility now.

CHIEF ENGINEER: An' ye wouldna abandon the puir wee thing in the near-absolute-zero cold of interstellar space, surely, Mr. Balls?

FIRST MATE: Yes! Out the hatch! Now! Out the hatch! Out the hatch!

INSANE SECOND MATE: Shut the trap, Balls.

FIRST MATE: Captain. Now I'm talking quite quietly now, aren't I. Now do you mean to say that when we finally get rid of this monster, when it gets too big for the ship and breaks its way out, causing terrible damage to the tubes, perhaps wrecking the whole Engine Room on its way — had you thought of that, "Bolts"? — and quite possibly destructing the entire ship — that, if we survive that ordeal, you intend to turn back, take the mindless, helpless thing in tow, and limp on after the Fleet at half speed for five years, ten years, twenty years (Ship Time) — while it keeps getting bigger, and stronger, and smarter, and wilder? Captain! don't you realise that this thing is going to be the death of us?

CAPTAIN: Yes, Mr. Balls, I do. But you know, if it wasn't, something else would be. A meteor, an interstellar plague spore, the irresistible gravity well around an invisible neutron star, an extra-galactic enemy destroyer, a collision with another

Ship of the Fleet. . . . One way or another, Mr. Balls, we are going to have had it. Sometime, somewhere in the time-space continuum, there is a point-instant with our name on it. So what can we do but go on?

FIRST MATE: But we don't have to drag this thing along with us —

CAPTAIN: If we don't give it a fair start, then who's to carry our breadfruit trees on to the Unknown End when we run out of fuel?

CHIEF ENGINEER: I've thocht, Captain, that perhaps that cruiser might lend us a hand wi' the beastie, if it knew we had one.

CAPTAIN: It certainly would be a help in the towing. But the problem is getting "Sparks" to send a message to the cruiser. If only we had a normal Communications Officer!

COMMUNICATIONS OFFICER: Please be quiet, everybody. I'm receiving.

INSANE SECOND MATE: From the dead upside-down queen out there?

COMMUNICATIONS OFFICER: No; she isn't saying anything. This is from the alien, I think.

INSANE SECOND MATE: Already? Ha! I always said that a ship could communicate with its alien, if it just listened carefully. What is it saying?

COMMUNICATIONS OFFICER: It still doesn't speak English.

INSANE SECOND MATE: What's the message, then?

COMMUNICATIONS OFFICER: Hiccups.

CAPTAIN: Hiccups?

COMMUNICATIONS OFFICER: It has the hiccups. It must have been the tomato rice soup. Here, I'll put it on the intracom. Listen.

ALIEN: Hic
       Hic

CHIEF ENGINEER: Captain, there's a rattling in the forward pipes, and a high pressure area building up amidships. Should I try baking soda?

CAPTAIN: No, no, you never use soda when there's an alien aboard, haven't you read the *Handbook?* Try Maalox.

CHIEF ENGINEER: Aye aye, Captain.

ALIEN: Hic

CHIEF ENGINEER: There, there, puir wee sleekit cowerin' beastie.

FIRST MATE: Oh, my God, if only I could have shipped aboard a cruiser, where I belong! I'm going mad here! You're all mad. I'm mad.

INSANE SECOND MATE: Mr. Balls. Listen. Would it make you feel any better if there was another male on board?

FIRST MATE: Another male? Of course it would. Strength! Sanity! Logic! Cleanliness! Godliness! Virility! Yes! Yes!

INSANE SECOND MATE: Even if it was an alien?

FIRST MATE: An alien?

INSANE SECOND MATE: This might, you know, be a male alien.

CAPTAIN: Yes, there's better than a fifty percent chance of that.

FIRST MATE: My God. It might. You're right. It might.

CAPTAIN: That was a good thought, "Bats."

INSANE SECOND MATE: Well, it's not my own preference, but I thought it might stabilise Mr. Balls.

FIRST MATE: A male alien. A male. By golly. It just might be. Hey. Alien. Are you there?

ALIEN: Hic

FIRST MATE: What are you, alien? Hmm? Are you a little boy alien? Hmm?

CAPTAIN: Please, Mr. Balls, don't, as it were, go overboard. Keep your duties in mind, and the obscure dignity of your position. We need you. You'd better do some mathematics right now. As for me, I'll be starting dinner soon. Second Mate, how are things on the Bridge?

INSANE SECOND MATE: Splendid, Captain. Fiery bears and scorpions break like luminous foam and stream backward in glory from our prow. Beneath us, above us, on all sides of us is the abyss, unsounded, full of unimaginable horrors,

unpredictable disasters, undeserved beauties, and unexpected death. Like a flying yarrow stalk we shoot forward, if it
is forward, through the gulfs of probability.

CAPTAIN: Very good. "Bolts"?

CHIEF ENGINEER: Dandy, Captain. We're on Warp Five, and
the Maalox is working fine.

CAPTAIN: Very good. I shall make dinner now. Something light
but nourishing, I think. Chinese Egg Flower Soup, perhaps.

COMMUNICATIONS OFFICER: Please. Will you all be quiet a minute. I'm receiving from Cosmic Sources.

INSANE SECOND MATE: Oh, I hear them sometimes without
even a radio. What are they saying?

ALIEN: Hic

COMMUNICATIONS OFFICER: Shh. Well, here's a message just
came in from a sister ship of the Fleet. It says: *Tsk tsk.*

CAPTAIN: Never mind that. What do the Cosmic Sources say?

COMMUNICATIONS OFFICER: I can't quite make it out. There's a
lot of star hiss, and the code keeps changing. It might be
Congratulations. Or again it might not be that at all. Be
quiet, please. I'm listening.

The Eye Altering

MIRIAM STOOD at the big window of the infirmary ward and looked out at the view and thought, For twenty-five years I have been standing at this window and looking out at this view. And never once have I seen what I wanted to see.

If I forget thee, O Jerusalem —

The pain was forgotten, yes. The hatred and the fear, forgotten. In exile you don't remember the grey days and the black years. You remember the sunlight, the orchards, the white cities. Even when you try to forget it you remember that Jerusalem was golden.

The sky outside the ward window was dulled with haze. Over the low ridge called Ararat the sun was setting; setting slowly, for New Zion had a slower spin than Old Earth, and a twenty-eight-hour day; settling, rather than setting, dully down onto the dull horizon. There were no clouds to gather the colors of sunset. There were seldom any clouds. When the haze thickened there might be a misty, smothering rain; when the haze was thin, as now, it hung high and vague, formless. It never quite cleared. You never saw the color of the sky. You never saw the stars. And through the haze the sun, no, not the sun, but

NSC 641 (Class G) burned swollen and vaporous, warty as an orange — remember oranges? the sweet juice on the tongue? the orchards of Haifa? — NSC 641 stared, like a bleary eye. You could stare back at it. No glory of gold to blind you. Two imbeciles staring at each other.

Shadows stretched across the valley towards the buildings of the Settlement. In shadow the fields and woods were black; in the light they were brown, purplish, and dark red. Dirty colors, the colors you got when you scrubbed your watercolors too much and the teacher came by and said, You'd better use some fresh water, Mimi, it's getting muddy. Because the teacher had been too kind to say to a ten-year-old, That picture's a total loss, Mimi, throw it away and start fresh.

She had thought of that before — she had thought all her thoughts before, standing at this window — but this time it reminded her of Genya, because of the painting, and she turned to see how he was doing. The shock symptoms were almost gone, his face was no longer so pale and his pulse had steadied. While she held his wrist he sighed a bit and opened his eyes. Lovely eyes he had, grey in the thin face. He had never been much but eyes, poor Genya. Her oldest patient. Twenty-four years he had been her patient, right from the moment of his birth, five pounds, purplish-blue like a fetal rat, a month premature and half dead of cyanosis: the fifth child born on New Zion, the first in Ararat Settlement. A native. A feeble and unpromising native. He hadn't even had the strength, or the sense, to cry at his first breath of this alien air. Sofia's other children had been full-term and healthy, two girls, both married and mothers now, and fat Leon who could hoist a seventy-kilo sack of grain when he was fifteen. Good young colonists, strong stock. But Miriam had always loved Genya, and all the more after her own years of miscarriages and stillbirths, and the last birth, the girl who had lived two hours, whose eyes had been clear grey like Genya's. Babies never have grey eyes, the eyes of the newborn are blue, that was all sentimental rubbish. But how could you ever make sure of what color things were under this damned warty-orange sun? Nothing ever looked right. "So there you are, Gennady Borisovich," she said, "back home, eh?"

It had been their joke when he was a child; he had spent so much time in the infirmary that whenever he came in with one of his fevers or fainting spells or gasping asthma he would say, "Here I am, back home, Auntie Doctor. . . ."

"What happened?" he asked.

"You collapsed. Hoeing down in the South Field. Aaron and Tina brought you up here on the tractor. Touch of sunstroke, maybe? You've been doing all right, haven't you?"

He shrugged and nodded.

"Dizzy? Short of breath?"

"On and off."

"Why didn't you come to the clinic?"

"It's no good, Miriam."

Since he was grown he had called her Miriam. She missed "Auntie Doctor." He had grown away from her, these last few years, withdrawn from her into his painting. He had always sketched and painted, but now, all his free time and whatever energy he had left when his Settlement duties were done, he spent in the loft of the generator building where he'd made a kind of studio, grinding colors from rocks and mixing dyes from native plants, making brushes by begging pigtail ends off little girls, and painting — painting on scraps from the lumber mill, on bits of rag, on precious scraps of paper, on smooth slabs of slate from the quarry on Ararat if nothing better was at hand. Painting portraits, scenes of Settlement life, buildings, machinery, still-lifes, plants, landscapes, inner visions. Painting anything, everything. His portraits had been much in demand — people were always kind to Genya and the other sicklies — but lately he had not done any portraits; he had gone in for queer muddy jumbles of forms and lines all in a dark haze, like worlds half created. Nobody liked those paintings, but nobody ever told Genya he was wasting his time. He was a sickly; he was an artist; O.K. Healthy people had no time to be artists. There was too much work to do. But it was good to have an artist. It was human. It was like Earth. Wasn't it?

They were kind to Toby, too, whose stomach troubles were so bad that at sixteen he weighed eighty-four pounds; kind to little Shura, who was just learning to talk at six, and whose eyes wept and wept all day long, even when she was smiling; kind to all their sicklies, the ones whose bodies could not adjust to this alien world, whose stomachs could not digest the native proteins even with the help of the metabolising pills which every colonist must take twice a day every day of his life on New Zion. Hard as life was in the Twenty Settlements, much as they needed every hand to work, they were gentle with their useless ones, their afflicted. In affliction the hand of God is visible. They remembered the words civilisation, humanity. They remembered Jerusalem.

"Genya, my dear, what do you mean, it's no good?"

His quiet voice had frightened her. "It's no good," he had said, smiling. And the grey eyes not clear but veiled, hazy.

"Medicine," he said. "Pills. Cures."

"Of course you know more about medicine than I do," Miriam said. "You're a much better doctor than I am. Or are you giving up? Is that it, Genya? Giving up?" Anger had come upon her so suddenly, from so deep within, from anxiety so long and deeply hidden, that it shook her body and cracked her voice.

"I'm giving up one thing. The metas."

"Metas? Giving them up? What are you talking about?"

"I haven't taken any for two weeks."

The despairing rage swelled in her. She felt her face go hot, so that it felt twice its normal size. "Two weeks! And so, and so, and so you're here! Where did you think you'd end up, you terrible fool? Lucky you're not dead!"

"I haven't been any worse since I stopped taking them, Miriam. Better, this whole last week. Until today. It can't be that. It must have been heatstroke. I forgot to wear a hat...."

He too flushed faintly, in the eagerness of his pleading, or with shame. It was stupid to work in the fields bareheaded; for all its dull look NSC 641 could hit the unsheltered human head quite as hard as fiery Sol, and Genya was apologetic for his carelessness. "You see, I was feeling fine this morning, really good, I kept right up with the others hoeing. Then I felt a bit dizzy, but I didn't want to stop, it was so good to be able to work right with the others, I never thought about heatstroke."

Miriam found that there were tears in her eyes, and this made her so ultimately and absolutely angry that she couldn't speak at all. She got up off Genya's bed and strode down the ward between the rows of beds, four on one side, four on the other. She strode back and stood staring out the window at the mud-colored shapeless ugly world.

Genya was saying something — "Miriam, honestly, couldn't it be that the metas are worse for me than the native proteins are?" — but she did not listen; the grief and wrath and fear swelled in her and swelled in her, and broke, and she cried out, "Oh, Genya, Genya, how could you? Not you, to give up now, after fighting so long — I can't bear it! I can't bear it!" But she did not cry it out aloud. Not one word of it. Never. She cried out in her mind, and some tears came out and ran down her cheeks, but her back was turned to the patient. She looked through distorting tears at the flat valley and the dull sun and said to them, silent, "I hate you." Then after a while she could turn around and say aloud, "Lie down," — for he had sat up, distressed by her long silence — "lie down, be quiet. You'll take two metas before dinner. If you need anything, Geza's in the nurse's station." And she walked out.

As she left the infirmary she saw Tina climbing up the back path from the fields, coming to see how Genya was, no doubt. For all his wheezes and fevers Genya had never wanted for girl friends. Tina, and Shoshanna, and Bella, and Rachel, he could have had his pick. But last year when he and Rachel were living together, they had got contraceptives from the clinic regularly, and then they had separated; they hadn't married, though by his age, twenty-four, Settlement kids were married and parents. He hadn't married Rachel, and Miriam knew why. Moral genetics. Bad genes. Shouldn't pass them on to the next generation. Weed out the sicklies. No procreation for him, and therefore no marriage; he couldn't ask Rachel to live barren for the love of him. What the Settlements needed was children, plenty of healthy young natives who, with the help of the meta pills, could survive on this planet.

Rachel hadn't taken up with anybody else. But she was only eighteen. She'd get over it. Marry a boy from another Settlement, most likely, and move away, away from Genya's big grey eyes. It would be best for her. And for him.

No wonder Genya was suicidal! Miriam thought, and put the thought away from her fiercely, wearily. She was very weary. She had meant to go to her room and wash, change her clothes, change her mood, before dinner; but the room was so lonesome with Leonid away at Salem Settlement and not due back for at least another month, she couldn't stand it. She went straight across the dusty central square of the Settlement to the refectory building, and into the Living Room. To get away, clear away, from the windless haze and the grey sky and the ugly sun.

Nobody was in the Living Room but Commander Marca, fast asleep on one of the padded wooden couches, and Reine, reading. The two oldest members of the Settlement. Commander Marca was in fact the oldest person in the world. He had been forty-four when he piloted the Exile Fleet from Old Earth to New Zion; he was seventy now, and very frail. People didn't wear well here. They aged early, died at fifty, sixty. Reine, the biochemist, was forty-five now but looked twenty years older. It's a damned geriatric club, Miriam thought sourly; and it was true that the young, the Zionborn, seldom used the Living Room. They came there to read, as it held the Settlement's library of books and tapes and microfilm, but not many of them read much, or had much time to read. And maybe the April light and the pictures made them a little uneasy. They were such moral, severe, serious young people; there was no leisure in their lives, no beauty in their world; how could they approve of this luxury their elders needed, this one haven, this one place like home. . . .

The Living Room had no windows. Avram, a wizard with anything electrical, had done the indirect lighting, deliberately reproducing the color and quality of sunlight — not NSC 641 light, but sunlight — so that to enter the Living Room was to enter a room in a house on Earth on a warm sunny day of April or early May, to see all things in that clear, clean, lovely light. Avram and several others had worked on the pictures, enlarging colored photos to a meter or so square: scenes of Earth, photographs and paintings brought by the colonists — Venice, the Negev, the domes of the Kremlin, a farm in Portugal, the Dead Sea, Hampstead Heath, a beach in Oregon, a meadow in Poland, cities, forests, mountains, Van Gogh's cypresses, Bierstadt's Rocky Mountains, Monet's waterlilies, Leonardo's blue mysterious caves. Every wall of the room was covered with pictures, dozens of pictures, all the beauty of the Earth. So that the Earthborn could see and remember, so that the Zionborn could see and know.

There had been some discussion about the pictures, twenty years ago when Avram had started putting them up: Was it really wise? Should we look back? And so on. But then Commander Marca had come by on a visit, seen the Living Room of Ararat Settlement, and said, "This is where I'll stay." With every Settlement vying to have him, he had chosen Ararat. Because of the pictures of Earth, because of the light of Earth in that room, shining on the green fields, the snowy peaks, the golden forests of autumn, the flight of gulls above the sea, the white and red and rose of waterlilies on blue pools — clear colors, true, pure, the colors of the Earth.

He slept there now, a handsome old man. Outside, in the

hard, dull, orange daylight, he would look sick and old, his cheeks veined and muddy. Here you could see what he looked like.

Miriam sat down near him, facing her favorite picture, a quiet landscape by Corot, trees over a silvery stream. She was so tired that for once she was willing to just sit, in a mild stupor. Through the stupor, faintly, idly, words came floating. Couldn't it be . . . honestly, couldn't it be that the metas are worse . . . Miriam, honestly, couldn't it be . . .

"Do you think I never thought of that?" she retorted in silence. "Idiot! Do you think I don't know the metas are hard on your guts? Didn't I try fifty different combinations while you were a kid, trying to get rid of the side effects? But it's not as bad as being allergic to the whole damn planet! You know better than the doctor, do you? Don't give me that. You're trying to — " But she broke off the silent dialogue abruptly. Genya was not trying to kill himself. He was not. He would not. He had courage, that one. And brains.

"All right," she said to the quiet young man in her mind. "All right! If you'll stay in the infirmary, under observation — for two weeks, and do exactly what I say — all right, I'll try it!"

Because, said another, even quieter voice deep in her, it doesn't really matter. Whatever you do or don't do, he will die. This year; next year. Two hours; twenty-four years. The sicklies can't adjust to this world. And neither can we, neither can we. We weren't meant to live here, Genya my dear. We weren't made for this world, nor it for us. We were made of Earth, by Earth, to live on Earth, under the blue sky and the golden sun.

The dinner gong began to ring. Going into the refectory she met little Shura. The child carried a bunch of the repulsive blackish-purple native weeds, as a child at home would carry a bunch of white daisies, red poppies picked in the fields. Shura's eyes were teary as usual, but she smiled up at Auntie Doctor. Her lips looked pallid in the red-orange light of sunset through the windows. Everybody's lips looked pallid. Everybody's face looked tired, set, stoical, after the long day's work, as they went into the Settlement dining hall, all together, the three hundred exiles of Ararat on Zion, the eleventh lost tribe.

He was doing very well. She had to admit it. "You're doing well," she said, and he, with his grin, "I told you so!"

"It could be because you're not doing anything else," she said, "smart ass."

"Not doing anything? I filed health records for Geza all morning, I played games with Rosie and Moishe for two hours, I've been grinding colors all afternoon — say, I need more mineral oil, can I have another litre? It's a much better pigment vehicle than the vegetable oil."

"Sure. But listen. I have something for you better than that. Little Tel Aviv has got their pulp mill going full time. They sent a truck over yesterday with paper — "

"Paper?"

"Half a ton of it! I took two hundred sheets for you. It's in the office." He was off like a shot, and was into the bundle of paper before she even got there. "Oh, God," he said, holding up a sheet, "beautiful, it's beautiful!" And she thought how often she had heard him say that, "beautiful!" of one drab useful thing or another. He didn't know what beauty was; he'd never seen any. The paper was thick, substantial, greyish, in big sheets, intended to be cut small and used sparingly, of course; but let him have it for his painting. There was little enough else she could give him.

"When you let me out of here," Genya said, hugging the unwieldly bundle with both arms, "I'll go over to Tel Aviv and paint their pulp mill, I'll immortalise their pulp mill!"

"You'd better go lie down."

"No, listen, I promised Moishe I'd beat him at chess. What's wrong with him, anyhow?"

"Rashes, edema."

"He's like me?"

Miriam shrugged. "He was fine till this year. Puberty triggered something. Not unusual with allergic symptoms."

"What is allergy, anyhow?"

"Well, call it a failure of adaptation. Back home, people used to feed babies cows' milk, from bottles. Some of the babies could adapt to it, but some got rashes, breathing trouble, colic. The cow's key didn't fit their metabolic lock. Well, New Zion's protein keys don't fit our locks; so we have to change our metabolism with the metas."

"Would Moishe or I have been an allergic on Earth?"

"I don't know. Prematures often are. Irving, he died, oh, twenty years ago, he was allergic to this terrible list of things on Earth, they should never have let him come, poor thing, he spends his life on Earth half suffocated and comes here and starves to death even on a quadruple dose of metas."

"Aha," said Genya, "you shouldn't have given him metas at all. Just Zion mush."

"Zion mush?" Only one of the native grains yielded enough to be worth harvesting, and it produced a gluey meal which could not be baked.

"I ate three bowls of it for lunch."

"He lies around the hospital all day complaining," Miriam said, "and then stuffs his belly with that slop. How can an artistic soul eat something that tastes like jellied bilge?"

"You feed it to your helpless child patients in your own hospital! I just ate the leftovers."

"Oh, get along with you."

"I am. I want to paint while the sun's still up. On a piece of new paper, a whole piece of new paper. . . . "

It had been a long day at the clinic, but there were no inpatients. She had sent Osip home last night in a cast with a good scolding for being so careless as to tip his tractor over, endangering not only his life but the tractor, which was even harder to replace. And young Moishe had gone back to the children's house, though she didn't like the way his rash kept coming back.

And Rosie was over her asthma, and the Commander's heart was doing as well as could be expected; so the ward was empty, except for her permanent inmate of the past two weeks, Genya.

He was sprawled out on his bed under the window, so lax and still that she had a moment of alarm; but his color was good, he breathed evenly, he was simply asleep, deeply asleep, the way people slept after a hard day in the fields, exhausted.

He had been painting. He had cleaned up the rags and brushes, he always cleaned up promptly and thoroughly, but the picture stood on his makeshift easel. Usually these days he was secretive about his paintings, hid them, since people had stopped admiring them. The Commander had murmured to her, "What ugly stuff, poor boy!" But she had heard young Moishe, watching Genya paint, say, "How do you do it, Genya, how do you make it so pretty?" and Genya answer, "Beauty's in the eye, Moishe."

Well, that was true, and she went closer to look at the painting in the dull afternoon light. Genya had painted the view out the big window of the ward. Nothing vague and half created this time: realistic, all too realistic. Hideously recognisable. There was the flat ridge of Ararat, the mud-colored trees and fields, the hazy sky, the storage barn and a corner of the school building in the foreground. Her eyes went from the painted scene to the real one. To spend hours, days, painting that! What a waste, what a waste.

It was hard on Genya, it was sad, the way he hid his paintings now, knowing that nobody would want to see them, except maybe a child like Moishe fascinated with the mere skill of the hand, the craftsman's dexterity.

That night as Genya helped her straighten up the injection cabinets — he was a good deal of help around the infirmary these days — she said, "I like the picture you painted today."

"I finished it today," he corrected her. "Damn thing took all week. I'm just beginning to learn to see."

"Can I put it up in the Living Room?"

He looked at her across a tray of hypodermic needles, his eyes quiet and a little quizzical. "In the Living Room? But that's all pictures of Home."

"It's time maybe we had some pictures of our new home there."

"A moral gesture, eh? Sure. If you like it."

"I like it very much," she lied blandly.

"It isn't bad," he said. "I'll do better, though, when I've learned how to fit myself to the pattern."

"What pattern?"

"Well, you know, you have to look until you *see* the pattern, till it makes sense, and then you have to get that into your hand, too." He made large, vague, shaping gestures with a bottle of absolute alcohol.

"Anybody who asks a painter a question in words deserves what they get, I guess," said Miriam. "Babble, babble. You take the picture over tomorrow and put it up. Artists are so temperamental about where they get their pictures hung, and the lighting. Besides, it's time you were getting out. A little. An hour or two a day. No more."

"Can I eat dinner in the dining hall, then?"

"All right. It'll keep Tina from coming here to keep you from being lonely and eating up all the infirmary rations. That girl eats like a vacuum pump. Listen, if you go out in the middle of the day, will you kindly take the trouble to wear a hat?"

"You think I'm right, then."

"Right?"

"That it was sunstroke."

"That was *my* diagnosis, if you will recall."

"All right: but my addition was that I do better without metas."

"I have no idea. You've got along fine before for weeks, and then poof, down again. Nothing whatever has been proved."

"But a pattern has been established! I've lived a month without metas, and gained six pounds."

"And edema of the head, Mr. Know It All?"

She saw him the next day sitting with Rachel, just before
dinnertime, on the slope below the storage barn. Rachel had not
come to see him in the infirmary. They sat side by side, very
close together, motionless, not talking.

Miriam went on to the Living Room. A half hour there
before dinner had become a habit with her lately. It seemed to
rest her from the weariness of the day. But the room was less
peaceful than usual this evening; the Commander was awake,
and talking with Reine and Avram. "Well, where did it come
from then?" he was saying in his heavy Italian accent — he
had not learned Hebrew till he was forty, in the Transit Camp.
"Who put it there?" Then seeing Miriam he greeted her as always with a grand cordiality of voice and gesture. "Ah, Doctor!
Please, join us, come, solve our mystery for us. You know each
picture in this room as well as I do. Where, do you think, and
when did we acquire the new one? You see?"

It's Genya's, Miriam was about to say, when she saw the
new picture. It wasn't Genya's. It was a painting, all right, a
landscape, but a landscape of the Earth: a wide valley, the fields
green and green-gold, orchards coming into flower, the sweeping
slope of a mountain in the distance, a tower, perhaps a castle or
medieval farm building, in the foreground, and over all the pure,
subtle, sunlit sky. It was a complex and happy painting, a celebration of the spring, an act of praise.

"How beautiful," she said, her voice catching. "Didn't you
put it up, Avram?"

"Me? I can photograph, I can't paint. Look at it, it's no
reproduction. Some kind of tempera or oils, see?"

"Somebody brought it from Home. Had it in their bag-
gage," Reine suggested.

"For twenty-five years?" said the Commander. "Why?
And who? We all know what all the others have!"

"No. I think" — Miriam was confused, and stammered

— "I think it's something Genya did. I asked him to put up one of his paintings here. Not this one. How did he do this?"

"Copied from a photograph," Avram suggested.

"No no no no, impossible," old Marca said, outraged. "That is a painting, not a copy! That is a work of art, that was seen, seen with the eyes and the heart!"

With the eyes and the heart.

Miriam looked, and she saw. She saw what the light of NSC 641 had hidden from her, what the artificial Earth daylight of the room revealed to her. She saw what Genya saw: the beauty of the world.

"I think it must be in Central France, the Auvergne," Reine was saying wistfully, and the Commander, "Oh no no no, it's near Lake Como, I am certain," and Avram, "Well it looks to me like where I grew up in the Caucasus," when they all turned to look at Miriam. She had made a strange noise, a gasp or laugh or sob. "It's here," she said. "Here. That's Ararat. The mountain. That's the fields, our fields, our trees. That's the corner of the school, that tower. See it? It's here. Zion. It's how Genya sees it. With the eyes and the heart."

"But look, the trees are green, look at the colors, Miriam. It's Earth — "

"Yes! It is Earth. Genya's Earth!"

"But he can't — "

"How do we know? How do we know what a child of Zion sees? We can see the picture in this light that's like Home. Take it outside, into the daylight, and you'll see what we always see, the ugly colors, the ugly planet where we're not at home. But he is at home! He is! It's we," Miriam said, laughing in tears, looking at them all, the anxious, tired, elderly faces, "we who lack the key. We with our — with our — " she stumbled and leapt at the idea like a horse at a high wall, "with our meta pills!"

They all stared at her.

"With our meta pills, we can survive here, just barely, right? But don't you see, he lives here! We were all perfectly adjusted to Earth, too well, we can't fit anywhere else — he wasn't, wouldn't have been; allergic, a misfit — the pattern a little wrong, see? The pattern. But there are many patterns, infinite patterns, he fits this one a little better than we do — "

Avram and the Commander continued to stare. Reine shot an alarmed glance at the picture, but asked gamely, "You're saying that Genya's allergies — "

"Not just Genya! All the sicklies, maybe! For twenty-five years I've been feeding them metas, and they're allergic to *Earth* proteins, the metas just foul them up, they're a different pattern, oh, idiot! Idiot! Oh, my God, he and Rachel can get married. They've got to marry, he should have kids. What about Rachel taking metas while she's pregnant, the foetus. I can work it out, I can work it out. I must call Leonid. And Moishe, thank God! maybe he's another one! Listen, I must go talk to Genya and Rachel, immediately. Excuse me!" She left, a short, grey woman moving like a lightning bolt.

Marca, Avram, and Reine stood staring after her, at each other, and finally back at Genya's painting.

It hung there before them, serene and joyful, full of light.

"I don't understand," said Avram.

"Patterns," Reine said thoughtfully.

"It is very beautiful," said the old Commander of the Exile Fleet. "Only, it makes me homesick."

Mazes

I HAVE TRIED HARD to use my wits and keep up my courage, but I know now that I will not be able to withstand the torture any longer. My perceptions of time are confused, but I think it has been several days since I realised I could no longer keep my emotions under aesthetic control, and now the physical breakdown is also nearly complete. I cannot accomplish any of the greater motions. I cannot speak. Breathing, in this heavy foreign air, grows more difficult. When the paralysis reaches my chest I shall die: probably tonight.

The alien's cruelty is refined, yet irrational. If it intended all along to starve me, why not simply withhold food? But instead of that it gave me plenty of food, mountains of food, all the greenbud leaves I could possibly want. Only they were not fresh. They had been picked; they were dead; the element that makes them digestible to us was gone, and one might as well eat gravel. Yet there they were, with all the scent and shape of greenbud, irresistible to my craving appetite. Not at first, of course. I told myself, I am not a child, to eat picked leaves! But the belly gets the better of the mind. After a while it seemed better to be chewing something, anything, that might still the pain and craving in the gut. So I ate, and ate, and starved. It is a relief, now, to be so weak I cannot eat.

The same elaborately perverse cruelty marks all its behavior. And the worst thing of all is just the one I welcomed with such relief and delight at first: the maze. I was badly disoriented at first, after the trapping, being handled by a giant, being dropped into a prison; and this place around the prison is disorienting, spatially disquieting. The strange, smooth, curved wall-ceiling is of an alien substance and its lines are meaningless to me. So when I was taken up and put down, amidst all this strangeness, in a maze, a recognisable, even familiar maze, it was a moment of strength and hope after great distress. It seemed pretty clear that I had been put in the maze as a kind of test or investigation, that a first approach toward communication was being attempted. I tried to cooperate in every way. But it was not possible to believe for very long that the creature's purpose was to achieve communication.

It is intelligent, highly intelligent, that is clear from a thousand evidences. We are both intelligent creatures, we are both maze-builders: surely it would be quite easy to learn to talk together! If that were what the alien wanted. But it is not. I do not know what kind of mazes it builds for itself. The ones it made for me were instruments of torture.

The mazes were, as I said, of basically familiar types, though the walls were of that foreign material colder and smoother than packed clay. The alien left a pile of picked leaves in one extremity of each maze, I do not know why; it may be a ritual or superstition. The first maze it put me in was babyishly short and simple. Nothing expressive or even interesting could be worked out from it. The second, however, was a kind of simple version of the Ungated Affirmation, quite adequate for the reassuring, outreaching statement I wanted to make. And the last, the long maze, with seven corridors and nineteen connections, lent itself surprisingly well to the Maluvian mode, and indeed to almost all the New Expressionist techniques. Adaptations had to be made to the alien spatial understanding, but a certain quality of creativity arose precisely from the adaptations. I worked hard at the problem of that maze, planning all night long, re-imagining the links and spaces, the feints and pauses, the erratic, unfamiliar, and yet beautiful course of the True Run. Next day when I was placed in the long maze and the alien began to observe, I performed the Eighth Maluvian in its entirety.

It was not a polished performance. I was nervous, and the spatio-temporal parameters were only approximate. But the Eighth Maluvian survives the crudest performance in the poorest maze. The evolutions in the ninth encatenation, where the "cloud" theme recurs so strangely transposed into the ancient spiralling motif, are indestructibly beautiful. I have seen them performed by a very old person, so old and stiff-jointed that he could only suggest the movements, hint at them, a shadow gesture, a dim reflection of the themes: and all who watched were inexpressibly moved. There is no nobler statement of our being. Performing, I myself was carried away by the power of the motions and forgot that I was a prisoner, forgot the alien eyes watching me; I transcended the errors of the maze and my own weakness, and danced the Eighth Maluvian as I have never danced it before.

When it was done, the alien picked me up and set me down in the first maze — the short one, the maze for little children who have not yet learned how to talk.

Was the humiliation deliberate? Now that it is all past, I see that there is no way to know. But it remains very hard to ascribe its behavior to ignorance.

After all, it is not blind. It has eyes, recognisable eyes. They are enough like our eyes that it must see somewhat as we do. It has a mouth, four legs, can move bipedally, has grasping hands, etc.; for all its gigantism and strange looks, it seems less fundamentally different from us, physically, than a fish. And yet, fish school and dance and, in their own stupid way, communicate!

The alien has never once attempted to talk with me. It has been with me, watched me, touched me, handled me, for days: but all its motions have been purposeful, not communicative. It is evidently a solitary creature, totally self-absorbed.

This would go far to explain its cruelty.

I noticed early that from time to time it would move its curious horizontal mouth in a series of fairly delicate, repetitive gestures, a little like someone eating. At first I thought it was jeering at me; then I wondered if it was trying to urge me to eat the indigestible fodder; then I wondered if it could be communicating *labially*. It seemed a limited and unhandy language for one so well provided with hands, feet, limbs, flexible spine, and all; but that would be like the creature's perversity, I thought. I studied its lip motions and tried hard to imitate them. It did not respond. It stared at me briefly and then went away.

In fact, the only indubitable *response* I ever got from it was on a pitifully low level of interpersonal aesthetics. It was tormenting me with knob-pushing, as it did once a day. I had endured this grotesque routine pretty patiently for the first several days. If I pushed one knob I got a nasty sensation in my feet, if I pushed a second I got a nasty pellet of dried-up food, if I pushed a third I got nothing whatever. Obviously, to demonstrate my intelligence I was to push the third knob. But it appeared that my intelligence irritated my captor, because it removed the neutral knob after the second day. I could not imagine what it was trying to establish or accomplish, except the fact that I was its prisoner and a great deal smaller than it. When I tried to leave the knobs, it forced me physically to return. I must sit there pushing knobs for it, receiving punishment from one and mockery from the other. The deliberate outrageousness of the situation, the insufferable heaviness and thickness of this air, the feeling of being forever watched yet never understood, all combined to drive me into a condition for which we have no description at all. The nearest thing I can suggest is the last interlude of the Ten Gate Dream, when all the feintways are closed and the dance narrows in and in until it bursts terribly into the vertical. I cannot say what I felt, but it was a little like that. If I got my feet stung once more, or got pelted once more with a lump of rotten food, I would go vertical forever. . . . I took the knobs off the wall (they came off with a sharp tug, like flower buds), laid them in the middle of the floor, and defecated on them.

The alien took me up at once and returned me to my prison. It had got the message, and had acted on it. But how unbelievably primitive the message had had to be! And the next day, it put me back in the knob room, and there were the knobs as good as new, and I was to choose alternate punishments for its amusement. . . . Until then I had told myself that the creature was alien, therefore incomprehensible and uncomprehending, perhaps not intelligent in the same *manner* as we, and so on. But since then I have known that, though all that may remain true, it is also unmistakably and grossly cruel.

When it put me into the baby maze yesterday, I could not move. The power of speech was all but gone (I am dancing this, of course, in my mind; "the best maze is the mind," the old proverb goes) and I simply crouched there, silent. After a while it took me out again, gently enough. There is the ultimate perversity of its behavior: it has never once touched me cruelly.

It set me down in the prison, locked the gate, and filled up the trough with inedible food. Then it stood two-legged, looking at me for a while.

Its face is very mobile, but if it speaks with its face I cannot understand it, that is too foreign a language. And its body is always covered with bulky, binding mats, like an old widower who has taken the Vow of Silence. But I had become accustomed to its great size, and to the angular character of its limb positions, which at first had seemed to be saying a steady stream of incoherent and mispronounced phrases, a horrible nonsense dance like the motions of an imbecile, until I realised that they were strictly purposive movements. Now I saw something a little beyond that, in its position. There were no words, yet there was

communication. I saw, as it stood watching me, a clear significa-
tion of angry sadness — as clear as the Sembrian Stance.
There was the same lax immobility, the bentness, the assertion
of defeat. Never a word came clear, and yet it told me that it
was filled with resentment, pity, impatience, and frustration. It
told me it was sick of torturing me, and wanted me to help it. I
am sure I understood it. I tried to answer. I tried to say, "What
is it you want of me? Only tell me what it is you want." But I
was too weak to speak clearly, and it did not understand. It has
never understood.

And now I have to die. No doubt it will come in to watch
me die; but it will not understand the dance I dance in dying.

The Pathways of Desire

TAMARA HAD THOUGHT he was off taping, but he was in his hut, lying on the cot, looking thin and cold. "Sorry, Ram! I'm after those photographs of the kids."

"That box." His gesture pointing out which box was so uncharacteristically languid that she asked, guardedly, "You all right?"

"Could be better." From him, the admission was a catalogue of misery; but still she did not drop her guard. She waited; and he said, "Diarrhoea."

"You should have said something."

"Humiliation."

Bob was wrong, then. He did have a sense of humor.

"I'll ask Kara," she said. "They must have something for the trots."

"Anything but hot dogs and milkshakes," Ramchandra said, and she laughed, for the description was apt; the staple foods of the Ndif were boneless poro meat and the mushy sweet fruit of the lamaba tree.

"Keep drinking plenty. I'll refill that. Lomox doesn't help?"

"Nothing left for it to work on." He looked up at her; his

eyes were large, black, and clear. "I wish that I throve here," he said, "like Bob."

That took her off guard. Rebuff and aloofness she expected, trust and candor she did not. She was unready, and her response inadequate. "Oh, he's happy here."

"Are you?"

"I hate it." She dangled the crude clay water jug, and sought exactness. "Not really. It's beautiful. But I . . . get impatient."

"Nothing to chew," Ramchandra said bitterly.

She laughed again, and went to fill his water jug at the spring a few meters away. The brightness of the sunshine, the perfumes of the air, the gorgeous colors of the lamaba trees, purple trunks, blue and green leaves, red and yellow fruits, all were delightful; the little spring welled up holy and innocent in its bed of clean brown sand. But she returned with gratitude to the hut containing one sullen linguist with diarrhoea. "Take it easy, Ram," she said, "and I'll try and get something useful out of Kara and the others."

"Thank you," he said.

Lovely words, she thought, as she went down the path through perfumed light and shadows towards the river; lovely in the man's soft, precise accent. When their team of three had first been put together, at the Base on Ankara, she had been drawn to Ramchandra, a direct, powerful, unmistakable attraction of sex. She had suppressed it, with self-mockery and some shame, for the man was cold, holding himself ostentatiously apart and untouched. And then there was Bob, big beautiful blond Bob, lean tanned tough Bob, perfect hero of male wish fulfilment, irresistible. Why resist? Easier to give the easy pleasure he expected; easy, pleasant, a little depressing, but never mind that. Don't look down into depressions. You might fall in. Live life as it comes, etc. She and Bob would come together inevitably. But they hadn't; for the three of them had come to Yirdo, and met Yirdo's inhabitants, the Ndif.

The Young Women of the Ndif — all females between age twelve and age twenty-two or -three — were sexually available, eager, and adept. They had bright wavy hair of gold or russet, long tilted eyes of green or violet, slender waists and ankles. They wore soft garments of slit pandsu leaves, clinging, modestly parting to reveal the merest glimpse of buttock or nipple. The under fourteens danced the hypnotic saweya dance in long lines, chanting in their soft, light voices, their round faces mischievously serious. From fourteen to eighteen they danced the baliya, leaping naked, one at a time, into the circle of swaying, clapping men, twisting their sinuous bodies into all the postures of practised eroticism, while the girls waiting their turn to dance sang the pulsing chorus, "Ah-weh, weh, ah-weh, weh. . . ." After they were eighteen they no longer danced in public. Tamara left it to Bob to find out what they did in private. After forty-one days on Yirdo he was indubitably an expert in that.

She saw now that though she hadn't wanted him, the promptness, the flatness of his loss of interest in her had hurt. Even last night she had been flirting at him; competing; trying to be a dancing girl, with short wiry hair, shit-brindle eyes that tilted the wrong way, muscular wrists. . . . Stupid, stupid her self-mockery, her self-abasement, her self, self, self, swept away now like veils of cobweb as she followed the forest path downward to the washing place at the river thinking, How beautiful the bridge of Ram's nose is. He can't weigh much more than I do, maybe less; fine-boned. Thank you, he said. "Askiös, Muna! How's the baby? Askiös, Vanna! Askiös, Kara!" How beautiful thy nose, my beloved, like unto a promontory between two wells of water, and the water thereof is exceeding black and cold. Thank you, thank you. "Hot today, no?"

"Hot today, hot today," all the Middle-Aged Women agreed enthusiastically, as they trampled out the village laundry in the shallow, laughing water. "Put your feet in the river, you'll get cool," Vanna encouraged her. Brella patted her shoulder affectionately, murmuring, "Askiös!" as she went by to lay out her portion of the village laundry on a rock to dry.

The Middle-Aged Women were between twenty-three and (forty? data still uncertain), and some of them, in Tamara's opinion, were more beautiful than the Young Women, a beauty which included missing teeth, sagging breasts, and stretchy bellies. The gapped smiles were blithe, the drooping tits held the milk of human kindness, the pregnancy-streaked bellies were full of belly laughs. The Young Women giggled; the Middle-Aged Women laughed. They laughed, Tamara thought watching them now, as if they had been set free.

The Young Men were off hunting poro (the pursuit of the fanged hot dog, she thought, and she too, being a Middle-Aged Woman of twenty-eight, laughed); or they were sitting goggling at the saweya and baliya dancers; or they were sleeping. There were no Middle-Aged Men. Males were Young till about forty, when they stopped hunting, stopped watching the dancers, and became Old. And died.

"Kara," she said to her best informant, while she took off her sandals to put her feet in the cool water as Vanna had suggested, "my friend Ram is sick in the belly."

"Oh me, oh dear, askiös, askiös," the nearby women murmured. Kara, who looked to be pretty nearly an Old Woman, her knotted hair thin and greying, demanded practically, "Is it gwullaggh or kafa-faka?"

Tamara had never heard either word before, but translation was superfluous. "Kafa-faka," she said.

"Puti berries, he needs," said Kara, slapping a loincloth on a wet boulder.

"The food we eat here, he says it's very good, too good."

"Too much fried poro," said Kara, nodding. "When children eat too much and spend all night shitting in the bushes, you feed them puti berries and boiled guo for a week. It tastes all right, with honey. I'll boil Uvana Ram a pot of guo as soon as the washing's done."

"Kara is a beautiful noble person," Tamara said. It was a stock phrase, the usual Ndif way of saying thank you.

"Askiös!" said Kara, grinning. That was a much commoner, and more difficult, expression. Ramchandra had arrived at no set translation for it. Bob had suggested German *bitte*, but it covered even more ground that *bitte*. Please, you're welcome, sorry, wait a minute, never mind, hello, goodbye, yes, no, and maybe, all seemed to fall within the connotations of askiös.

With her questions about kafa-faka and how to wean babies and when you had to stay in the Unclean Huts and what was the best kind of cooking pot, Tamara was always a welcome excuse for a conversation break. They sat around on hot boulders in the cool water and let the river wash the laundry and the sun dry and bleach it, while they talked. With a part of her mind Tamara listened to Heraclitus telling her that you shall not step twice into the same river; with the rest of it she sought information concerning birth control among the Ndif. The subject once opened, the women discussed it leisurely and frankly, but there wasn't much to discuss. There were no devices or systems of birth control at all. Nature provided for the Young Women: for all their single-minded devotion to erotic practice, they did not become fertile till they were over twenty. Tamara was incredulous, but the women were perfectly certain: the dividing line between the Young and the Middle-Aged was, in fact, fertility. Once the line was crossed their only protection against perpetual pregnancy was abstinence, which they admitted was boring. Abortion and infanticide were not mentioned. When Tamara cautiously suggested them, heads were shaken. "*Women* can't kill *babies*," Brella said with horror. Kara observed more dryly, "If they get caught at it, the Men pull out all their hair and send them to the Unclean Huts to stay." — "Nobody in our village would do such a thing," Brella said. "Nobody got caught at it," Kara said.

A group of Juvenile Males (nine to twelve) came whooping down to the river to swim and fish. They ran right over the drying laundry; the laundresses scolded, unauthoritatively; and the conversation ceased, because the ears of Males were not to be polluted with Unclean talk. The woman rescued the laundry and set off back to the village. Tamara looked in on Ramchandra, who was asleep, and went on to take some photographs of Juvenile Males playing bhasto. After supper — communal, cooked and served by the Middle-Aged Women — she saw Kara, Vanna, and old Binira go into Ramchandra's hut, and followed them.

They woke him up and fed him boiled guo, pinkish cereal like sticky tapioca; they rubbed his legs, sat on his shoulders, put heated stones on his stomach, rearranged his cot so that he lay with his head to the north, made him drink a sip of something hot, black, and minty-smelling; Binira sang at him for a while; they left him at last with a fresh hot stone, and went off. He accepted all this with ethnological aplomb or with the satisfaction of the invalid being fussed over. When they had gone he looked comfortable, curled up around the large rock, and half asleep. Tamara was going out when he asked in a remote, tranquil voice, "Did you tape the old lady's song?"

"No. Sorry."

"Askiös, askiös," he whispered. Then, propping himself on his elbow, "I am better. Too bad we didn't tape that. I missed most of the words."

"Is Old Ndif a different language?"

"No. Only much fuller. Complete."

"The Middle-Aged Women seem to have a much bigger vocabulary than the Youngs."

"At Buvuna, the Young Women averaged 700 words; the Young Men 1,100, since they have the hunting vocabulary; I estimate the Middle-Aged Women here to know at least 2,500 words. I can make no estimate of the Old Men and Women yet. These are odd people." Ramchandra lay back and cautiously rearranged himself around the hot stone. His tone, also, was cautious. There was a slight pause.

"Do you want to sleep?"

"To talk," he said.

Tamara sat down on the woven cane stool. Beyond the open doorway the night was growing bright as day had been; Uper, the big gas planet of which Yirdo was a moon, was rising over the forest like a vast striped balloon. Its silver-gilt light pierced every crack in the mud and wattle walls of the hut and pooled incandescent on the ground outside the doorway. The dusk inside the hut was shot through with gleams, shafts, arrows dazzling the eye, a light that revealed nothing, that dissolved bodies and faces into radiant darkness.

"Nothing is real," Tamara said.

"Of course not," said the other shadow, amused, precise.

"They're like actors."

"No."

"Yes. I don't mean consciously acting, deceiving. I mean artificial. Too simple. Beautiful simple people in ever-bountiful paradise."

"Ha," Ramchandra said, and a patch of planet light blazed in his hair as he sat up.

"Why shouldn't there be a South-Sea-Island world?" she argued with herself. "Why does it seem too simple — phony? Am I a Puritan, am I looking for original sin?"

"No, no, of course not, rubbish," he said. "All that is theories. But listen." For a minute he said nothing to listen to, then he said some Ndif words: "Vini. Pandsu. Bhasto. Askiös. — Askiös-bhis iyava oe is-bhassa. — What is that in English?"

"Well — 'please let me get by.'"

"Literal translation!"

"The great teaching tradition of the Brahman caste," Tamara said. "I don't know, the words have so many uses. 'Sorry, I want to go this way'?"

"You don't hear it."

"Hear what?"

"People cannot hear their native language. All right, listen, carefully please!" He was charming when he got excited; the hauteur fell off him like dried mud from a water buffalo. "I'm going to say a sentence in English the way my uncle, who didn't attend World Government School, spoke English. Now. 'Excuse please I have to go by this path.' Repeat!"

"Excuse please I have to go by this path."

"Askiös-bhis iyava oe is-bhassa."

A chill, like a touch of that cold dazzling planet light, proceeded slowly up Tamara's backbone and prickled in the roots of her hair.

"Funny," she said.

"Saweya: sway. Baliya: belly dance, Bali. Fini: ravine, vines. Bhasto: bat, baseball. Bhani: cabin, cabana. Shuwushu: ocean, sea — "

"Onomatopoeia."

"Oe: go. Tunu: return. Itunu: I return; utunu: you return; tunusi: he returns. Padu, to hit, strike. Fatu, to build, make — facere, factus — factory. Say a word in Ndif!"

"Sikka."

"Fishing lines. Wait. No, I can't get that one. Another please."

"Fillisa."

"The Unclean Huts. — Filth, filthy."

"Uvanai."

"Strangers. Visitors. Foreigners . . . singular uvana. You-foreigner."

"Ram, you don't have diarrhoea. You have paranoia."

"No," he said, so harsh and loud that she started. He cleared his throat. She could not see his eyes but she knew him to be looking at her. "I am serious, Tamara," he said. "I am frightened."

"Of what?" she jeered.

"Frightened sick," he said. "Scared shitless. You must take words seriously. They are all we have."

"*What* are you frightened of?"

"We are thirty-one light-years from Earth. No one from Earth ever came to this solar system before us. These people speak English."

"They don't!"

"The structure and vocabulary of Young Ndif is based at least sixty percent upon the structure and vocabulary of Modern English."

His voice shook, as if with fear, or with relief.

Tamara sat solidly, clasping her knees, and held fast to incredulity. A Ndif word went through her mind, and another, and another, each one followed by its English root or shadow, shadows that had been waiting for the light to show them; but it was absurd. She should not have said the word "paranoia." It was true. The man was ill. Weeks of touch-me-not rudeness and now this sudden change to talk, excitement, warmth. A manic change; and paranoid. The Ndif speaking an English-based code, for mysterious purposes, understood by the expert alone. . . . Ono, one. Te, two. Ti, three . . .

"All female names," Ramchandra said morosely, "end in 'a.' That is a cosmic constant established by H. Rider Haggard. Male names never end in 'a.' Never."

His voice, light-timbred, still a little uneven, confused her thoughts. "Listen, Ram."

"Yes."

He was listening, all right. She could not ask him, as she had intended, whether he was playing an elaborate and disagreeable joke on her. His trust must be met in kind. She did not know how to go on; and he broke urgently into her pause —

"I saw this within a week, Tamara. First the syntax — Then I wouldn't see it. Meaningless coincidence, et cetera, et cetera. I said no. But it says yes. It is so. It is English."

"Even the Old language?"

"No, no, that's different," he said, hurried, grateful, "that's not English, that's itself, wherever it's not based on the baby talk. But the —"

"All right, then. The Old language *is* old, the original language, and the Youngs have been influenced, corrupted, by some contact with Space Service people we don't know about, weren't told about."

"How? When? They say we are the first. Why would they lie?"

"The Space Service?"

"Or the Ndif. They both say we are the first!"

"Well, if we are the first, then it's us. *We*'re influencing the Ndif. They talk the way we unconsciously expect people to talk. Telepathy. They're telepaths."

"Telepaths," he said, seizing the idea eagerly; and during the pause that followed he was evidently wrestling with it, trying to make it fit the circumstances, for he said at last, with frustration, "If only we knew anything about telepathy!"

Tamara meanwhile had been going around the problem in another direction, and asked, "Why didn't you say anything about this till now?"

"I thought I was insane," he said, in the controlled precise tone that sounded arrogant because his honesty would not permit him to evade. "I have been insane. Six years ago, after my wife died. There were two episodes. Linguists are often unstable."

After a little while Tamara said almost in a whisper, "Ramchandra is a beautiful noble person. . . ." She spoke in Ndif.

Ah-weh, weh, ah-weh, weh, went the chanting of the baliya dancers off on the dancing grounds at the edge of the village. A baby cried in a nearby hut. The dark-dazzling air was rich with the scent of night-blooming flowers.

"Look," she said. "Doesn't a telepath know what you're thinking? The Ndif don't. I've known people who do. My grandfather, he was Russian, he always knew what people were thinking. It was maddening. I don't know if it was telepathy, or being old, or being Russian, or what. But anyhow, they'd get the *thoughts*, not the *words* — wouldn't they?"

"Who knows? Maybe — You said it's like a stage play, a movie, the island paradise. Maybe they sense what we expect or desire, and act it, perform it."

"What for?"

"Adaptation," he said, triumphant. "So that we like them and therefore don't harm them."

"But I *don't* like them! They're boring! No kinship systems, no social structure except stupid age-grading and detestable male dominance, no real skills, no arts — lousy carved spoons, all right, like a Hawaiian tourist trap — no ideas — once they grow up, *they're* bored. Kara told me yesterday, 'Life's much too long.' If they're trying to produce a facsimile of somebody's heart's desire, it isn't mine!"

"Nor mine," Ramchandra said. "But Bob?"

There was a harshness, a homing-in quality, to the question. Tamara hesitated. "I don't know. At first, sure. But he's been restless, lately. After all he's a myths man. And they don't even tell stories. All they ever talk about is who they slept with last night and how many poro they shot. He says they all talk like Hemingway characters."

"He doesn't talk with the Old Ones." Again that harshness, and Tamara, defensive of Bob, said, "Neither do I, much; do you? They don't participate, they seem so shadowy . . . unimportant."

"That was a healing song old Binira sang."

"Maybe."

"I think so. A ritual song, in the more complex language. If there is high culture, the Old Ones have it. Maybe they lose the telepathic power as they grow older; so then they can withdraw; they're no longer influenced, forced to adapt —"

"Forced by whom to adapt to what? They're the only intelligent species on the planet."

"Other villages, other tribes."

"But then they'd all talk each other's language, all their customs would melt together — "

"Exactly! That explains the homogeneity of the culture! A solution to Babel!"

He sounded so pleased, and it sounded so plausible, that Tamara did her best to accept the hypothesis. The best she could do was admit finally, "The idea makes me queasy, for some reason."

"The Old Ones have developed true language, non-telepathic language. They are the ones to talk with. I will request admission to the Old Men's House tomorrow."

"You'll have to grow some grey hair . . ."

"Easily! Is it still black?"

"You'd better get some sleep."

He was silent a while, but did not lie down. "Tamara," he said, "you are not humoring me, are you?"

"No," she said gruffly, shocked that he was so vulnerable.

"It is so very like a delusional system."

"Then it's *folie à deux*. All this about the language just brings the rest into focus. All six villages we've visited, all the same, the same things missing, the same — improbability — only it's like overprobability — "

"*Projected* telepathy," he said, brooding. "*They* are influencing *us*. Confusing our perceptions, forcing us into subjectivity — "

"Driving us away from the Reality Principle?" she said, defensive, now, of him. "Rubbish." She recognized the quotation, and laughed. "We're talking much too cleverly to be gaga."

"I talked brilliantly in the mental institution," he said. "In several languages. Even Sanskrit." He sounded reassured, however; and she stood up. "I'm going to bed," she said. "A fine night's sleep I'll have now! Do you need a fresh hot rock?"

"No, no. Listen, I'm sorry — "

"Askiös, askiös."

No rest for the wicked. She had just lit her oil lamp and was spitting on her fingers and pinching the wick to keep it from smoking, which it continued to do, when Bob appeared in the doorway of her hut. The light of Uper haloed his thick fair hair; the importance of his return filled the entire biosphere as the bulk of his body filled the doorway. "I just got back," he announced.

"From where?"

"Gunda." The next village downriver.

He came in and sat down on the cane stool, while she swore at the burned poro fat on her fingers. An even more world-shaking announcement than that of his return loomed, imminent, in his scowl. She beat him to the draw. "Ram's sick," she said.

"What with?"

"Delhi belly, you could call it."

"How could anybody get sick here?"

"They have a cure. You sleep with a hot boulder."

"Christ! Sounds like a cure for potency!" Bob said, and they both broke into laughter. While laughing she almost began to tell Bob about Ram's peculiar linguistic discovery, which for a moment seemed equally ridiculous; but she should let Ram do it, even if it was just a joke. Bob had gone serious again, and now emitted his announcement. "I have to fight a duel. Single combat."

"Oh, Lord. When? Why?"

"Well, that girl. Potita, you know, the redhead. One of the Young Men in Gunda has his eye on her. So he challenged me."

"An exogamy arrangement? Has he a claim on her?"

"No, you know they don't have any affiliation patterns, stop hunting for them. All she is is an excuse for a combat."

"I thought you'd get into trouble," Tamara said priggishly, though she had thought no such thing. "You can't sleep with all the native girls and not expect the assegai of a maddened savage in your back — Half the native girls, O.K., but not all of them — "

"Shit," Bob said with discouragement. "I know. Look, I never got mixed up like this before. Sleeping with informants and stuff. I can't seem to keep anything straight here. But they *expect* it. We talked it all out, way back in Buvuna, remember? Ram said he wouldn't. That's O.K., he's forty, he's an old man to them, anyhow he looks alien. But I look just like them, and if I refuse I'm offending local custom. It's practically the only custom they've got. I have no choice — "

A laugh, a deep, Middle-Aged Woman belly laugh, welled up from Tamara. He looked at her a little startled. "All right, all right," he said, and laughed too. "But God damn it! They always talked like these combats were voluntary!"

"They're not?"

Bob shook his head. "I represent Hamo village against Gunda. It's the only kind of war they have. All the Young Men are really worked up. They haven't won a combat with Gunda for half a year, or some such huge historical timespan. It's the World Cup. Tomorrow I get purified."

"A ceremony?" Tamara found Bob's predicament funny but trivial; she leapt from it to the hope of a ceremony, a ritual, anything that would prove some sense and structure in the rudimentary social life of the Ndif.

"Dances. Saweya and baliya. All day."

"Bah."

"Look, I know you'd like some patterns to study, being a configurationist and all, but I have an even more urgent problem. I have to fight a man day after tomorrow. With knives. In front of the entire population of two villages."

"With knives?"

"Right. Hunters wrestle. Sallenzii fight with knives."

"Sallenzii?" — As Bob translated, "Competitors for a girl," she transliterated: "Challengers. . . ."

After a short silence she suggested, "Could you just give him the girl?"

"No. Honor, local pride, all that."

"And she . . . she's content just to be the prize pig?"

Bob nodded.

"The pattern is familiar," she said, and then, abruptly, "Nothing — There is nothing alien about these people. Nothing!"

"What?"

"Never mind. Let me work it out. Ram has an idea. . . . Listen, Bob, I think you ought to get out of this, even if you lose face. We can always move on. It would be better than you killing the fellow! Or getting killed."

"Thanks for the afterthought," Bob said kindly. "Don't worry. I'll cheat."

"Hypodermic?"

"Karate ought to do. I don't mind. It's just that I feel so damned foolish. Public knife fights for a girl. Like a lot of stupid teenagers."

"It's a teenage society, Bob."

"Locker-room aliens!" He scratched his lion's mane of hair and stood up, stretching. He was very beautiful; no wonder the villagers had picked him for their champion. The fact that his physical splendor was informed and animated by an intellectual spirit of no less splendor, a passionate trained mind that sought the stuff of poetry for its own sake — this fact would mean nothing much to the Ndif, or to many people on Earth, for that matter. But Tamara, in that moment, saw the young man as what he was, a king.

"Bob," she said, "say no. Beg off. We can just move on."

"No sweat!" he said, and, grateful for her concern, gave her an affectionate bear hug. "I'll clobber the poor bastard before he knows what hit him. And then give a lecture. Freshman Hygiene: Murder Is Hazardous to Your Health. It'll wow 'em."

"Do you want me there, or not there?"

"There," he said. "Just in case he's a black belt too."

She was down at the laundry beach next afternoon having an interesting discussion of menopause with Kara and Libisa when Ramchandra came out onto the beach from the peacock-colored forest. Watching him from her rock amid the swirling waters, she thought how foreign he looked, how alien, as Bob had said — like the shadow of somebody standing up in the front row against the marvelous flowing colors of a jungle epic on a movie screen: too small, too black, too solid. Kara saw him too and shouted, "How's the belly, Uvana Ram?"

When he was close enough not to have to shout, he replied, "Askiös, Kara, much better. I finished the guo this morning."

"Good, good. Another potful tonight. You're all skin," Kara said, not inaccurately.

"Maybe if he eats enough guo he'll turn people-colored," said Brella, studying him; Kara's mention of skin seemed to have brought Ramchandra's swarthy, dusky complexion to her notice for the first time. The Ndif were remarkably inattentive to details. Brella now compared the two foreigners and said, "You too, Tamara. If you only ate people-colored food, maybe you wouldn't be so ugly and brown."

"I never thought of that," said Tamara.

"Tamara, we are invited to the Old Men's House."

"Both of us? When?"

"Both. Now."

"How did you swing that?" Tamara asked in English, splashing ashore from the boulder she had been sharing with Kara, Libisa, and a lot of freshly washed loincloths.

"I asked."

"I'll come too," Kara announced, splashing after Tamara. "Askiös!"

"Is it right for women to do, Kara?"

"Of course. It's the *Old* Men's House, isn't it?" Kara dusted off her flat little breasts and brought the fold of her sari-like garment neatly across them. "Go on ahead. I'll stop by and pick up Binira. She told me it's worth listening to sometimes in there. I'll see you there."

Tamara, her wet feet rimmed with the silvery river sand, joined Ramchandra and entered the peacock forest with him on the narrow path.

She was intensely aware of his brown shoulder beside hers, his dark, well-knit, and fragile body, the excellent nose in the stern profile. She was aware that she was aware of this, but it was not the important thing just now. "Are they holding a ceremony for us?"

"I don't know. I haven't got some of the key words yet. My request to go there appears to be sufficient reason for a gathering there."

"Is it all right to bring that?" He was carrying a tape recorder.

"Anything goes in Cloud-Cuckoo Land," he said, and the stern profile softened with a laugh.

Two of the withered, shadowy, scarce Old Men of the Ndif preceded them into the House, a large decrepit dugout; six or seven more were sitting around inside. There was much muttering of "askiös" and a strong reek of poro fat. The two foreigners joined the ill-defined circle, sitting on the dirt. No fire was lit. No apparatus or atmosphere of ritual was apparent. Presently Kara and Binira came in and sat down muttering "askiös" and cracking mild jokes with the Old Men. From across the circle — the place was lit only by the smokehole, and it was hard to see faces clearly — somebody asked something of Kara. Tamara did not understand the question. Kara's response was, "I'm getting old enough, aren't I?" There was a general laugh. One more came in, Bro-Kap, said once to have been a famous hunter, still a big man but stooped, wrinkled, and turtle-mouthed from the loss of his teeth. Instead of sitting down he went to the empty firepit under the smokehole and stood there, arms at his sides. Silence grew around him.

He turned slowly till he faced Ramchandra.

"Have you come to learn to dance?"

"If I may," Ramchandra answered clearly.

"Are you old?"

"I am no longer young."

My God, Tamara thought, it's an initiation — can Ram keep it up? And the next question, sure enough, she did not understand at all; there were no Young or Middle Ndif words in it. Ram, however, appeared to understand, and replied promptly, "Not often."

"When did you last bring home the kill?"

"I have never killed an animal."

That brought a hoot, laughs, and some critical discussion. "He must have been born fifty years old!" Binira said, sniggering. "Or else he is terribly lazy," said a youngish Old Man with a simple look, very earnestly.

Two more questions and answers Tamara could not follow, and then Bro-Kap demanded, harshly she thought, "What do you hunt?"

"I hunt peremensoe."

Whatever it was, it was right. Audible and tangible approval, backslaps, relaxation. Bro-Kap nodded once, shortly, wiped his nose with the back of his hand, and sat down in the circle beside Ramchandra. "What do you want to know?" he inquired, in a thoroughly unritualistic and offhand manner.

"I should like to know," Ramchandra said, "how the world began."

"Oh ho ho!" went a couple of geezers across the circle. "Too old for his years, this one! A hundred years old, this fellow!"

"We say this," Bro-Kap replied. "Man made the world."

"I should like to know how he did it."

"In his head, between his ears, how else? Everything is in the head. Nothing is wood, nothing is stone, nothing is water, nothing is blood, nothing is bone; all things are sanisukiarad."

In her frustration at never knowing the key word, Tamara watched Ram's face as if she could interpret from it; and indeed he understood. His eyes shone; he smiled, so that his features rounded out and grew gentle.

"He dances," he said. "He dances."

"Maybe so," Bro-Kap replied. "Maybe Man dances in his head, and that makes sanisukiarad."

Only with this repetition did Tamara hear the name "Man" as a name, a Ndif name or word which happened to coincide in sound with the English word "man" — but she had taken it to coincide in meaning —

Did it?

For a minute everything fell apart into two levels, two over-lapping screens or veils, one of them sounds, one of them mean-ings, neither of them real. Their overlap and interplay, their shift and movement, confused everything, concealed or revealed everything, in that flow there was nothing to take hold of, not even once can you step into the river unless you are the river. The world began and nothing was happening, some wizened old men and women talking nonsense with Lord Shiva in a smelly hut. Talking, merely talking, words, words that meant nothing twice.

The parted veils closed again.

She checked that the tape was running in the recorder, and turned up the gain a little. Replaying all this later, with Ram to interpret and explain, maybe it would make sense.

They did dance, at last. After much talk Binira announced, "That's enough peremenkiarad without music," and Bro-Kap rather ungraciously said, "All right, askiös, go ahead." At which Binira began to sing in a small unearthly creaking voice; and presently one old man, and then another, got up and danced, a slow dance, the feet close to the ground, the torso still and poised, intensity concentrated in the hands, arms, and face. It brought tears to Tamara's eyes, the dance of the shadowy old men. Others joined; now they were all dancing, all but Kara and herself. Sometimes they touched one another, lightly and solemnly, or bowed like cranes. All of them? Yes, Ram was dancing with them. The golden dusty light from the smokehole flowed along his arms; lightly and softly he lifted and set down his bare feet. An old man faced him. "O komeya, O komeya, ama, O, O," sang the creaking cricket trill, and Kara's hands, Tamara's hands patted time on the brown dirt. The old man's hands were lifted as in supplication. Ramchandra reached to him, the flowing arm, the poised and separated fingers; smiling, he touched, and turned, still dancing, and the old man smiled and began to sing, "O komeya, ama, ama, O. . . ."

"Do we have a session on tape for you to listen to!" Tamara said, but she said it mainly to distract Bob from his hangdog mood as they went together down the path towards the clearing where the duel was to be fought. The path was littered with lamaba-fruit rinds, as most of the village had preceded them.

"More love songs?"

"No. Well, yes. Love songs to God. . . . You know what God's name is?"

"Yes," Bob said indifferently. "Old man at Gunda told me. Bik-Kop-Man."

The duel went nearly, but not quite, as planned by both parties. Since it was the one group action by the Young Ndif besides saweya and baliya dancing which seemed to be a genuine ritual or meaning-focussed act, Tamara diligently taped, filmed, and note-took the whole thing, including the redheaded Potita's expression (and here she is, Miss America); the infliction of a knife stab in Bob's thigh by Pit-Wat, the Gunda Challenger; Bob's fine gesture throwing away his long-bladed knife (a glittering arc into the pink-flowered puti bushes); and the karate throw that stretched Pit-Wat flat and apparently lifeless on the ground.

Bob did not stay to deliver his lecture on the unhygienic aspects of murder. His wound was bleeding hard, and Tamara cut off the movie camera and got to work with the first-aid kit. Thus the jubilation of Hamo village and the discomfiture of Gunda were recorded only on sound tape; and the tape recorder was off when Pit-Wat revived, to the discomfiture of both Hamo and Gunda. Slain sallenzii were not supposed to come alive and get up, staggering but undamaged. By this time, however, Bob was on the homeward path to Hamo, white-faced and not unwilling to hold on to Tamara's arm. "Where's Ram?" he asked for the first time, and she explained that she had not even told Ram a duel was to take place.

"Good," Bob said. "I know what he'd say."

"I don't."

"Irresponsible involvement in native lifeways — "

She shook her head. "I didn't tell him because I didn't even see him today, and I thought — " She had in fact forgotten about the duel, it had seemed so silly, so unreal, compared to that dancing in the Old Men's House; it had all been a stupid annoying joke, right up to the moment when she saw the color, the splendid and terrible color of blood in the sunlight; but she could not tell Bob that. "He's made a kind of breakthrough. By getting involved himself — he spent all day in the Old Men's House. I want him to talk with you tonight. Once we get your leg looked after. And he'll want to know what the people in Gunda said about Man. About God, I mean. Look out for that vine. Oh, Lord, here come the football fans." A troupe of Young Women were pursuing them, halfheartedly pelting Bob with puti flowers.

"Where's Potita?" Bob muttered, setting his teeth.

"Not in this lot. Are you really fond of her, Bob?"

"No. It's that my leg hurts. No, it was just fun and games. I just wondered if Pit-Wat got her or I did."

It turned out that Pit-Wat got her, since he stayed on the field of combat and performed the Victory Dance, rather shakily to be sure. Bob was relieved, since Pit-Wat was certainly better suited to Potita by temperament and circumstance; and as for the Victory Dance, a two-minute fit of stomping and posing, they had already got several films of champion wrestlers performing it. "All we needed was a movie of *me* beating my chest," Bob said. "Christ! With my leg spouting. And feeling like a prize ass all round anyhow."

"Ass all round, curious image," Ramchandra said. They had got a fire going in Bob's hut. It was raining — it rained only at night on Yirdo — and Bob had lost enough blood that a little extra warmth and cheer might do him good. The air got smoky, but the ruddy light was pleasant; it made Tamara think of winter, of rain and firelight in winter, a season unknown to Yirdo. Bob lay stretched out on his cot and the other two sat by the hearth, feeding the fire with dried lamaba rinds, which burned with a clear flame and a scent of pineapple.

"Ram, what does peremensoe mean?"

"Thinking. Ideas. Understanding. Talk."

"And peremenkiarad, is that right?"

"About the same. Plus a connotation of . . . illusion, deception, trickery — play."

"Is this Old Ndif?" Bob inquired. "If you're making dictionaries, let me see 'em, Ram. I couldn't understand anything the old boys were telling me in Gunda."

"Except God's name," Tamara said.

Ramchandra raised his eyebrows.

"Bik-Kop-Man made the world with his ears," Bob said. "And that is the Ndif equivalent of Genesis, Book One."

"Between his ears," Ramchandra corrected coldly.

"With them or between them, it's a pretty poor excuse for a Creation myth."

"How do you know, if your vocabulary is inadequate?"

Why did he take that tone with Bob? Supercilious, pedantic, offensive, even the voice high and schoolmarmish. Bob's solid good nature shone by contrast in his reply: "It's taken me weeks to realize that if I'm after myth or history the only people here who may have them are the Old Ones. I should have been checking in with you much earlier."

Ramchandra stared into the fire and said nothing.

"Ram," Tamara said, profoundly irritated with him, "Bob should know about this thing we talked about the other night. The derivation of Young Ndif."

He went on staring into the fire, mute.

"You can explain it better than I can."

After a moment he merely shook his head.

"You've decided it was a mistake?" she demanded, more exasperated than ever, but also with a flash of hope.

"No," he said. "The documentation is in that notebook I gave you."

She fetched the notebook from her hut, lighted the oil lamp, and sat down on the floor by Bob's cot so he could read over her shoulder. For half an hour they went over Ramchandra's orderly and exhaustive proofs of the direct derivation of Young Ndif from Modern Standard English. Bob laughed at first, taking the whole thing as a grand scholarly joke; then he laughed at the sheer lunacy of it. It did not seem to disturb him, as it disturbed Tamara.

"If it's not your hoax, Ram, it's still a hoax — a terrific one."

"By whom? How? Why?" Tamara asked, hopeful again. A mistake made sense; a hoax made sense.

"All right. This language," and he tapped the notebook, "isn't authentic. It's a fake, a construct — invented. Right?"

Ramchandra, who had not said a word all this while, agreed in a remote, unwilling tone: "Invented. By an amateur. The correspondences with English are naïve, unconscious, as in 'speaking in tongues.' — But Old Ndif is an authentic language."

"An older one, an archaic survival — "

"No." Ramchandra said "No" often, flatly, and with satisfaction, Tamara thought. "Old Ndif is alive. It is based upon Young Ndif, has grown out of it, or over it. Like ivy on a telephone pole."

"Spontaneously?"

"As spontaneously as any language, or as deliberately. When words are wanted, needed, people have to make them. It 'happens,' like a bird singing, but it's also 'work,' like Mozart writing music."

"Then you'd say the Old Ones are gradually making a real language out of this fake one?"

"I cannot define the word 'real' and therefore would not use it." Ramchandra shifted his position, reclasping his arms round his knees, but did not look up from the fire. "I would say that the Old Ndif seem to be engaged in creating the world. Human beings do this primarily by means of language, music, and the dance."

Bob stared at him, then at Tamara. "Come again?"

Ramchandra was silent.

"So far," Tamara said, "working in three widely separate localities, we've found the same language, without major dialectical variations, and the same set of very rudimentary social and cultural patterns. Bob hasn't found any legends, any expressions of the archetypes, any developed symbology. I haven't found much more social structure than I'd find in a herd of cattle, about what I might find in a primate troop. Sex and age determine all roles. The Ndif are culturally subhuman; they don't exist fully as human beings. The Old Ndif are beginning to. Is that it, Ram?"

"I don't know," the linguist said, withdrawn.

"That's missionary talk!" Bob said. "Subhuman? Come on. Stagnant, sure. Maybe because there's no environmental challenge. Food falls out of the trees, game's plentiful, and they don't have sexual hangups — "

"That's *in*human," Tamara interjected; Bob ignored her.

"There's no stimulus. O.K. But the Old Ones get shoved

out of the fun and games. They get bored; that's the stimulus. They start playing around with words and ideas. So what rudiments of mythopoetics and ritual they've got are their creation. That's not an unusual situation, the young busy with sex and physical competitions, the old as culture transmitters. The only weird thing is this English-Ndif business. That needs explaining. I just don't buy telepathy, you can't build a scientific explanation on an occultist theory. The only rational explanation is that these people — the whole society — are a plant. A quite recent one."

"Correct," Ramchandra said.

"But listen," Tamara said with fury, "how can a quarter of a million people be 'planted'? What about the ones over thirty? We've only had FTL spaceflight for thirty years! The Exploratory Survey to this system was unmanned, and it was only eight years ago! Your rational explanation is pure nonsense!"

"Correct," Ramchandra said again, his clear, dark, sorrowful gaze on the flickering fire.

"Evidently there's been a manned mission, a colonising mission, to this planet, which the World Government doesn't know about. We have stumbled into something, and it begins to scare me. The So-Hem faction — "

Bob was interrupted by the sudden entrance (the Ndif never knocked) of Bro-Kap, two other Old Men, and two baliya dancers, beautiful half-naked sixteen-year-olds with flowers in their tawny hair. They knelt by Bob's cot and made soft lamenting sounds. Bro-Kap stood as majestically as he could in the now very crowded hut, and gazed down at Bob. He was clearly waiting for the girls to be quiet, but one of them was now chattering cheerfully and the other was drawing circles around Bob's nipples with her long fingernails. "Uvana Bob!" Bro-Kap said at last. "Are you Bik-Kop-Man?"

"Am I — Askiös, Wana! — No. Askiös, Bro-Kap, I don't understand."

"Sometimes Man comes," the old Ndif said. "He has come

to Hamo, and to Farwe. Never to Gunda or to Akko. He is strong and tall, golden-haired and golden-skinned, a great hunter, a great fighter, a great lover. He comes from far away and goes away again. We have thought that you were He. You are not He?"

"No, I am not," Bob said decisively.

Bro-Kap took a breath that heaved his wrinkled chest. "Then you will die," he said.

"Die?" Bob repeated without comprehension.

"Die how? Of what?" Tamara demanded, standing up so that in the press of people in the little hut she was brought face to face with the old man. "What do you mean, Bro-Kap?"

"Gunda challengers use poisoned knives," the old man said. "To find out which ones from Hamo are Bik-Kop-Man. Poison doesn't kill Bik-Kop-Man."

"What poison?"

"That's their secret," Bro-Kap said. "Gunda is full of wicked people. We of Hamo use no poisons."

"For Christ's sake," Bob said in English, and in Ndif, "Why didn't you tell me?"

"The Young Men thought you knew. They thought you were Man. Then when you let Pit-Wat wound you, when you threw away your knife, when you killed him but he came back to life, they weren't sure. They came to the Old Men's House to ask. Because we in the Old Men's house have peremensoe about Man." There was pride in the old man's voice. "Thus I came to you. Askiös, Uvana Bob." Bro-Kap turned and pushed his way out; the other old men followed him.

"Go away," Bob said to the smiling, caressing girls. "Go on now." They left, reluctant, swaying, their pretty faces troubled.

"I'll go to Gunda," Ramchandra said, "see if there's an antidote." And he was off at a run.

Bob's face was dead white.

"Another damned hoax," he said, smiling.

"You bled a lot, Bob. Probably bled out the poison right

away, if there really was any. Let me have a look at it. . . . It looks absolutely clean. No inflammation."

"My breath's been coming short," the young man said. "Most likely shock."

"Yes. Let me get the medical handbook."

The handbook had no recommendations, and Gunda had no antidote. The poison acted on the central nervous system. Paroxysms began two hours after Bro-Kap's visit. They increased quickly in severity and frequency. Some time after midnight, long before dawn, Bob died.

Ramchandra struck the tenth useless blow over the stopped heart, raised his arm to strike again, and did not strike. The dancer's raised arm: creator, destroyer. The clenched, dark fist relaxed; the poised and separated fingers hovered above the white face and the unbreathing chest. "Ah!" Ramchandra cried aloud, and dropping down beside the cot broke into tears, a passion of tears.

Wind gusted the rain against the roof. Time passed and Ramchandra was silent, as silent as Bob, beside whom he crouched, his arms stretched across Bob's body and his head sunk between them; exhausted, he had fallen asleep. The rain thinned and weakened and then beat hard again. Tamara put out the oil lamp, her movements slow and certain, full of the knowledge of what they meant. She added the last of the fuel to the fire and sat down at the little hearth. One must watch with the newly dead, and the sleeping should not sleep unprotected. She sat awake and watched the fire die out, and long afterwards, the grey light reborn.

Ndif funerals were, as she had expected, graceless. There was a burying ground not far off in the forest, which nobody talked about or ever visited except for burials. Gravedigging was the Old Men's task. They had dug a shallow pit. Two of them, plus Kara and Binira, helped carry Bob's body to the grave. The

Ndif used no coffins, dumped their dead naked in the earth; it was too cold that way, too cold, Tamara thought with rage, and she had put Bob's white shirt and trousers on him, left his gold Swiss watch strapped on his wrist since he owned no other treasure, and wrapped the long, silky, bluish leaves of the pandsu carefully about him. She lined the shallow grave with leaves before they laid him in it; the four old men and women watched, expressionless. They laid him on his side, his knees a little bent. Tamara turned for a flower to put by his hand, but the pink and purple blossoms sickened her; she broke the chain around her neck, on which hung a little turquoise her mother had given her, a fragment of the Earth, and put that in the dead man's hand. She had to be quick; the old men were already scraping the dirt back over the grave with their crude wooden shovels. As soon as that was done all four Ndif turned without a word and went off, not looking back.

Ramchandra knelt down by the grave. "I am sorry I was jealous of you," he said. "If we meet reborn, you will be a king again, but I will be the dog at your heel." He bowed down, touching the raw, damp clods of the grave, then slowly stood up. He looked at Tamara. She knew his look, the dark, clear, grieving eyes, but she could not meet them, or speak. It was her turn to cry. He came to her across the grave, as if it was any bit of ground, and put his arms around her, holding her so she could weep. When the first hardest sobbing was done and she could walk, they set off slowly down the narrow, half-overgrown path through the peacock splendors of the forest, back to the village.

"Burning is better," Ramchandra said. "The spirit is freed sooner to go on."

"Earth is best," Tamara said, very low and hoarse.

"Tamara. Do you want to radio Ankara Base to send the launch to us?"

"I don't know."

"There's no hurry to decide."

The gorgeous colors of the lamabas blurred and cleared and

blurred again. She stumbled, though Ramchandra's hand was kind and firm on her arm.

"We might as well go on and finish what we came for."

"The ethnology of dreams."

"Dreams? Oh no. This is real. . . . Much realler than I wish it were."

"So are all dreams."

In three days they put in their regular call to Ankara, the inner planet where the central base for the various research groups in Yirdo's solar system was established; they reported Bob's death, "by misunderstanding — no blame," in the Ethnographic Corps code. They did not request relief.

Life in Hamo village went on as before. The Middle-Aged Women said nothing about Bob's death to Tamara, but several evenings old Binira sat just outside her hut and sang to her, a quiet cricket trill. Once she saw two of the little saweya dancers leaving a flowering branch at the door of Bob's empty hut; she went towards them, but they trotted off, giggling. Soon after, the Young Men set fire to the hut, deliberately or by accident, there was no telling; it burned to ashes and all trace of it was gone within a week. Ramchandra spent his days and nights with the Old Ones of Hamo and Gunda, gathering an increasingly solid bulk of linguistic and mythic data. The long lines of saweya dancers undulated, the baliya dancers thrust their high breasts left and right, the singers chanted "Ah-weh, weh, ah-weh, weh," and the forest glades round the dancing ground at dusk swarmed with coupled bodies. Hunters returned proudly with dead poro, like suckling pigs with blunt, curved fangs, slung on carrying poles. On the twelfth night after Bob's death Ramchandra came to Tamara's hut; she had been trying to read over some notes, but the pages might as well have been empty, her head ached and nothing made sense, nothing meant anything. He came to the doorway, dark, slight, shadowy, and she looked up at him with dull eyes. He said something that meant

nothing about loneliness, and then he said, with the darkness
around him and behind him, "It's like fire. Like burning in a
fire. But the spirit caught too, burning — "
    "Come in," she said.

A few nights later they lay talking, in the dark, the soft
windy rain sighing in the forest and on the thatch of the hut
above them.
    "Since I first saw you," he said. "Truly, since the day we
met, in the canteen at Ankara Base."
    With a laugh, Tamara said, "You scarcely behaved as if . . ."
    "I didn't like it! I refused. I said, No, no, no! — my wife
was enough, this doesn't come twice to a man in one life, I will
remember her."
    "You do," Tamara murmured.
    "Of course. To her in me now I can say, Yes, and to you
with me, Yes, yes. . . . Listen, Tamara, you set me free, your
hands free me. And bind me. Tighter to the wheel, never in this
life now will I get free, never cease to desire you, I don't *want* to
cease. . . ."
    "It's so simple now. What was in our way?"
    "My fear. My jealousy."
    "Jealousy? — Of Bob?"
    "Oh yes," he said, shivering.
    "Oh Ram, never — Right from the beginning, you — "
    "Confusion," he whispered. "Illusion. . . ."
    His warmth against her the length of her body; and cold
Bob, cold in the ground. Fire is better than earth.
    She woke; he was stroking her hair and cheek, soothing her,
whispering, "Sleep again, it's all right, Tamara," his voice heavy
with sleep and tenderness.
    "What — did I — "
    "A bad dream."
    "Dream. Oh, no — it wasn't bad — just queer."
    The rain had ceased and the light of the giant planet,

greyed and filtered by clouds, was like a faint mist in the hut. She could just make out the hook of his nose, the darkness of his hair, in that grey dust of light.

"What was the dream?"

"A boy — a young man — no, a boy, about fifteen. Standing in front of me. Sort of filling everything, taking up all the room, so that I couldn't possibly get past him or around him. But just an ordinary boy, with glasses, I think. And he was staring at me, not threatening, not even really seeing me, but he kept staring and saying 'Bill me, bill me.' And I didn't think he owed me anything, so I said, 'What for?' But he just kept saying, 'Bill me!' And then I woke up."

"Bill me, how funny," Ramchandra said sleepily. "Bill me. . . . Me Bill. . . ."

"Yes. That's it. I'm Bill, that's what he meant."

"Oh," Ramchandra said, a deep exhalation, and she felt his relaxed body go tense. Since Bob's death she had not trusted the Ndif, or rather without distrusting any one of them she had lost trust in their world, she feared harm. She raised her head quickly to see if someone had entered the hut. "What's wrong?"

"Nothing is wrong."

"What is it?"

"Nothing. Go back to sleep. You talked to God."

"The dream?"

"Yes. He told you his name."

"Bill?" she said, and because the alarm was past and she was still sleepy and Ramchandra was laughing, she laughed. "God's name is Bill?"

"Yes, yes. Bill Kopman, or Kopfman, or Cupman."

"Bik-Kop-Man?"

"The 'l' assimilates to the 'k,' as in sikka, the fiber they make fishing lines of — silk."

"What are you babbling about?"

"Bill Kopman, who made this world."

"Who what? Who?"

"Who made this world. *This* world — Yirdo, the poro, the puti bushes, the Ndif. You saw him in your dream. A fifteen-year-old boy, with glasses, probably also acne and weak ankles. You saw him, and so my eyes see for a moment too. A skinny boy, lazy, shy. He reads stories, he daydreams, about the great blond hero who can hunt and fight and make love all day and night. His head is full of the hero, himself, and so it all comes to be."

"Ram, stop it."

"But you talked to him, not I! You asked him, 'What for?' But he couldn't tell you. He doesn't know. He doesn't understand desire. He is entirely caught in it, bound by it, he sees and knows nothing but his own immense desire. And so he makes the world. Only one free of desire is free of the worlds, you know."

Tamara looked, as if over her shoulder, back into her dream. "He speaks English," she said, unwillingly.

Ramchandra nodded. His tranquillity, his acceptant, playful tone, reassured her; it was interesting to lie looking together at the same silly dream.

"He writes it all down," she said, "his fantasies about the Ndif. Maps and everything. A lot of kids do that. And some adults. . . ."

"Perhaps he has a notebook of his invented language. It would be interesting to compare with my notebooks."

"Much easier just to go find him and borrow his."

"Yes, but he doesn't know Old Ndif."

"Ramchandra."

"Beloved."

"You are saying that because a boy writes nonsense in a notebook in — in Topeka, a planet thirty-one light-years away comes into existence, with all its plants and animals and people. And always has been in existence. Because of the boy and the notebook. And what about the boy with a notebook in Schenectady? or New Delhi?"

"Evidently!"

"Your nonsense is much worse than Bill Kopman's."

"Why?"

"Time — And there isn't room — "

"There is room. There is time. All the galaxies. All the universes. That is infinity. The worlds are infinite, the cycles are endless. There is room. Room for all the dreams, all the desires. No end to it. Worlds without end."

His voice now was remote.

"Bill Kopman dreams," he said, "and the God dances. And Bob dies, and we make love."

She saw the boy's blind yearning face before her, filling the world, no way around it, no path.

"You're only joking, Ramchandra," she said; she was shivering, now.

"I'm only joking, Tamara," he said.

"If it weren't a joke I couldn't bear it. Being caught here, stuck in somebody else's dream, dream world, alternate world, whatever it is."

"Why caught? We call Ankara; they send the launch for us; next passage out we can go back to Earth if we like. Nothing has changed."

"But this idea that it's somebody else's world. What if — what if — while we're still here — Bill Kopman woke up?"

"Once in a thousand thousand years does a soul wake up," Ramchandra said, and his voice was sad.

She wondered why that made him sad; she found it comforting. Brooding, she found further comfort. "It wouldn't all depend on him, even if he started it," she said. "All the uninhabited places, they'd just be blanks on his maps, but they're full of life, animals and trees and ferns and little flies. . . . Reality is what works, isn't it? And the old men and women. They aren't, they wouldn't be, part of . . . of Bill's wet dreams. He probably doesn't even know any old people, he isn't interested. So they get free."

"Yes. They begin to imagine their world for themselves. To think, to make words. To tell the story."

"I wonder if he ever thinks of death."

"Can anyone think of death?" Ramchandra asked. "One can only do it. As Bob did it. . . . Can one dream of sleep?"

The soft, dust-grey light was more intense, as the clouds thinned, drifting silent to the east.

"He looked anxious, in the dream," Tamara murmured. "Frightened. As if . . . 'Bill me. . . .' As if Bob paid . . . the debt."

"Tamara, Tamara, you go before me, always before me." His forehead was against her breasts; she touched his hair lightly.

"Ramchandra," she said, "I want to go home, I think. Away from this place. Back to the real world."

"You go before, I follow you."

"Oh, humble you are, liar, hoaxer, dancer, you're so humble, but you don't really care, do you? You're not frightened."

"Not any more," he said, in a breath, barely audible.

"How long have you understood about this place? Since you danced with Bro-Kap and the others, that first time?"

"No, no. Only now, since your dream, this night, now. You saw. All I can do is say. But yes, if you like, I can say it because I have always known it. I speak my native tongue, because you have brought me home. The house under the trees behind the temple of Shiva in a suburb of Calcutta, is that my home? Is this? The world, the real world, which one? What does it matter? Who dreamed the Earth? A greater dreamer than you or I, but we are the dreamer, Shakti, and the worlds will endure as long as our desire."

West

Gwilan's Harp

THE HARP had come to Gwilan from her mother, and so had her mastery of it, people said. "Ah," they said when Gwilan played, "you can tell, that's Diera's touch," just as their parents had said when Diera played, "Ah, that's the true Penlin touch!" Gwilan's mother had had the harp from Penlin, a musician's dying gift to the worthiest of pupils. From a musician's hands Penlin too had received it; never had it been sold or bartered for, nor any value put upon it that can be said in numbers. A princely and most incredible instrument it was for a poor harper to own. The shape of it was perfection, and every part was strong and fine: the wood as hard and smooth as bronze, the fittings of ivory and silver. The grand curves of the frame bore silver mountings chased with long intertwining lines that became waves and the waves became leaves, and the eyes of gods and stags looked out from among the leaves that became waves and the waves became lines again. It was the work of great craftsmen, you could see that at a glance, and the longer you looked the clearer you saw it. But all this beauty was practical, obedient, shaped to the service of sound. The sound of Gwilan's harp was water running and rain and sunlight on the water, waves

breaking and the foam on the brown sands, forests, the leaves
and branches of the forest and the shining eyes of gods and stags
among the leaves when the wind blows in the valleys. It was all
that and none of that. When Gwilan played, the harp made music; and what is music but a little wrinkling of the air?

Play she did, wherever they wanted her. Her singing voice
was true but had no sweetness, so when songs and ballads were
wanted she accompanied the singers. Weak voices were borne up
by her playing, fine voices gained a glory from it; the loudest,
proudest singers might keep still a verse to hear her play alone.
She played along with the flute and reed flute and tambour, and
the music made for the harp to play alone, and the music that
sprang up of itself when her fingers touched the strings. At weddings and festivals it was, "Gwilan will be here to play," and at
music-day competitions, "When will Gwilan play?"

She was young; her hands were iron and her touch was silk;
she could play all night and the next day too. She travelled from
valley to valley, from town to town, stopping here and staying
there and moving on again with other musicians on their wan-
derings. They walked, or a wagon was sent for them, or they got
a lift on a farmer's cart. However they went, Gwilan carried her
harp in its silk and leather case at her back or in her hands.
When she rode she rode with the harp and when she walked she
walked with the harp and when she slept, no, she didn't sleep
with the harp, but it was there where she could reach out and
touch it. She was not jealous of it, and would change instruments with another harper gladly; it was a great pleasure to her
when at last they gave her back her own, saying with sober envy,
"I never played so fine an instrument." She kept it clean, the
mountings polished, and strung it with the harp strings made by
old Uliad, which cost as much apiece as a whole set of common
harp strings. In the heat of summer she carried it in the shade of
her body, in the bitter winter it shared her cloak. In a firelit hall
she did not sit with it very near the fire, nor yet too far away,
for changes of heat and cold would change the voice of it, and

perhaps harm the frame. She did not look after herself with half the care. Indeed she saw no need to. She knew there were other harpers, and would be other harpers; most not as good, some better. But the harp was the best. There had not been and there would not be a better. Delight and service were due and fitting to it. She was not its owner but its player. It was her music, her joy, her life, the noble instrument.

She was young; she travelled from town to town; she played "A Fine Long Life" at weddings, and "The Green Leaves" at festivals. There were funerals, with the burial feast, the singing of elegies, and Gwilan to play the Lament of Orioth, the music that crashes and cries out like the sea and the seabirds, bringing relief and a burst of tears to the grief-dried heart. There were music days, with a rivalry of harpers and a shrilling of fiddlers and a mighty outshouting of tenors. She went from town to town in sun and rain, the harp on her back or in her hands. So she was going one day to the yearly music day at Comin, and the landowner of Torm Vale was giving her a lift, a man who so loved music that he had traded a good cow for a bad horse, since the cow would not take him where he could hear music played. It was he and Gwilan in a rickety cart, and the lean-necked roan stepping out down the steep, sunlit road from Torm.

A bear in the forest by the road, or a bear's ghost, or the shadow of a hawk: the horse shied half across the road. Torm had been discussing music deeply with Gwilan, waving his hands to conduct a choir of voices, and the reins went flipping out of those startled hands. The horse jumped like a cat, and ran. At the sharp curve of the road the cart swung round and smashed against the rocky cutting. A wheel leapt free and rolled, rocking like a top, for a few yards. The roan went plunging and sliding down the road with half the wrecked cart dragging behind, and was gone, and the road lay silent in the sunlight between the forest trees.

Torm had been thrown from the cart, and lay stunned for a minute or two.

Gwilan had clutched the harp to her when the horse shied, but had lost hold of it in the smash. The cart had tipped over and dragged on it. It was in its case of leather and embroidered silk, but when, one-handed, she got the case out from under the wheel and opened it, she did not take out a harp, but a piece of wood, and another piece, and a tangle of strings, and a sliver of ivory, and a twisted shell of silver chased with lines and leaves and eyes, held by a silver nail to a fragment of the frame.

It was six months without playing after that, since her arm had broken at the wrist. The wrist healed well enough, but there was no mending the harp; and by then the landowner of Torm had asked her if she would marry him, and she had said yes. Sometimes she wondered why she had said yes, having never thought much of marriage before, but if she looked steadily into her own mind she saw the reason why. She saw Torm on the road in the sunlight kneeling by the broken harp, his face all blood and dust, and he was weeping. When she looked at that she saw that the time for rambling and roving was over and gone. One day is the day for moving on, and overnight, the next day, there is no more good in moving on, because you have come where you were going to.

Gwilan brought to the marriage a gold piece, which had been the prize last year at Four Valleys music day; she had sewn it to her bodice as a brooch, because where on earth could you spend a gold piece. She also had two silver pieces, five coppers, and a good winter cloak. Torm contributed house and household, fields and forests, four tenant farmers even poorer than himself, twenty hens, five cows, and forty sheep.

They married in the old way, by themselves, over the spring where the stream began, and came back and told the household. Torm had never suggested a wedding, with singing and harp-playing, never a word of all that. He was a man you could trust, Torm was.

What began in pain, in tears, was never free from the fear

of pain. The two of them were gentle to each other. Not that they lived together thirty years without some quarrelling. Two rocks sitting side by side would get sick of each other in thirty years, and who knows what they say now and then when nobody is listening. But if people trust each other they can grumble, and a good bit of grumbling takes the fuel from wrath. Their quarrels went up and burnt out like bits of paper, leaving nothing but a feather of ash, a laugh in bed in the dark. Torm's land never gave more than enough, and there was no money saved. But it was a good house, and the sunlight was sweet on those high stony fields. There were two sons, who grew up into cheerful sensible men. One had a taste for roving, and the other was a farmer born; but neither had any gift of music.

Gwilan never spoke of wanting another harp. But about the time her wrist was healed, old Uliad had a travelling musician bring her one on loan; when he had an offer to buy it at its worth, he sent for it back again. At that time Torm would have it that there was money from selling three good heifers to the landowner of Comin High Farm, and the money should buy a harp, which it did. A year or two later an old friend, a flute player still on his travels and rambles, brought her a harp from the South as a present. The three-heifers harp was a common instrument, plain and heavy; the Southern harp was delicately carved and gilt, but cranky to tune and thin of voice. Gwilan could draw sweeetness from the one and strength from the other. When she picked up a harp, or spoke to a child, it obeyed her.

She played at all festivities and funerals in the neighborhood, and with the musician's fees she bought good strings; not Uliad's strings, though, for Uliad was in his grave before her second child was born. If there was a music day nearby she went to it with Torm. She would not play in the competitions, not for fear of losing, but because she was not a harper now, and if they did not know it, she did. So they had her judge the competitions, which she did well and mercilessly. Often in the early years mu-

sicians would stop by on their travels and stay two or three
nights at Torm; with them she would play the Hunts of Orioth,
the Dances of Cail, the difficult and learned music of the North,
and learn from them the new songs. Even in winter evenings
there was music in the house of Torm: she playing the harp —
usually the three-heifers one, sometimes the fretful Southerner
— and Torm's good tenor voice, and the boys singing, first in
sweet treble, later on in husky unreliable baritone; and one of
the farm's men was a lively fiddler; and the shepherd Keth,
when he was there, played on the pipes, though he never could
tune them to anyone else's note. "It's our own music day tonight," Gwilan would say. "Put another log on the fire, Torm,
and sing 'The Green Leaves' with me, and the boys will take the
descant."

Her wrist that had been broken grew a little stiff as the
years went on; then the arthritis came into her hands. The work
she did in house and farm was not easy work. But then who,
looking at a hand, would say it was made to do easy work? You
can see from the look of it that it is meant to do difficult things,
that it is the noble, willing servant of the heart and mind. But
the best servants get clumsy as the years go on. Gwilan could
still play the harp, but not as well as she had played, and she did
not much like half measures. So the two harps hung on the wall,
though she kept them tuned. About that time the younger son
went wandering off to see what things looked like in the North,
and the elder married and brought his bride to Torm. Old Keth
was found dead up on the mountain in the spring rain, his dog
crouched silent by him and the sheep nearby. And the drouth
came, and the good year, and the poor year, and there was food
to eat and to be cooked and clothes to wear and to be washed,
poor year or good year. In the depth of a winter Torm took ill.
He went from a cough to a high fever to quietness, and died
while Gwilan sat beside him.

Thirty years, how can you say how long that is, and yet no
longer than the saying of it: thirty years. How can you say how

heavy the weight of thirty years is, and yet you can hold all of them together in your hand lighter than a bit of ash, briefer than a laugh in the dark. The thirty years began in pain; they passed in peace, contentment. But they did not end there. They ended where they began.

Gwilan got up from her chair and went into the hearth room. The rest of the household were asleep. In the light of her candle she saw the two harps hung against the wall, the three-heifers harp and the gilded Southern harp, the dull music and the false music. She thought, "I'll take them down at last and smash them on the hearthstone, crush them till they're only bits of wood and tangles of wire, like my harp." But she did not. She could not play them at all any more, her hands were far too stiff. It is silly to smash an instrument you cannot even play.

"There is no instrument left that I can play," Gwilan thought, and the thought hung in her mind for a while like a long chord, till she knew the notes that made it. "I thought my harp was myself. But it was not. It was destroyed, I was not. I thought Torm's wife was myself, but she was not. He is dead, I am not. I have nothing left at all now but myself. The wind blows from the valley, and there's a voice on the wind, a bit of a tune. Then the wind falls, or changes. The work has to be done, and we did the work. It's their turn now for that, the children. There's nothing left for me to do but sing. I never could sing. But you play the instrument you have." So she stood by the cold hearth and sang the melody of Orioth's Lament. The people of the household wakened in their beds and heard her singing, all but Torm; but he knew that tune already. The untuned strings of the harps hung on the wall wakened and answered softly, voice to voice, like eyes that shine among the leaves when the wind is blowing.

Malheur County

"EDWARD," said his mother-in-law, "face the facts. You can't withdraw from your life. People aren't going to let you. You're too useful, too likable, too good-looking even, though you don't seem to be aware of it." She paused for breath, then said in a colder voice, "I used to wonder if Mary was really aware of it."

He sat silent across the hearth from her, huddled up over his long arms and legs.

"You can't withdraw from something you haven't got into! Oh, I'm sorry," she said savagely.

He smiled, but looked a little punch-drunk.

"The Navajo Indians," she said, "I think, don't let mothers-in-law and sons-in-law speak to one another. It's tabu. A very sensible arrangement. We're so damned sophisticated, no tabus, no defenses." She fell grimly silent, a grey-haired, full-figured woman in her sixties sitting erect in an armchair in the firelight. She always sat erect. The cigarette in her left hand and whiskey glass in her right appeared as elements of her rugged femininity. She came from eastern Oregon, from Malheur County, the last, barren frontier, from a decent feckless family that had left a century of failed farms, male suicides, and infant graves across the land from Ohio to the Coast, pushing always unprofitably westward.

"Of course she knew that you were good-looking," she went on thoughtfully, "she was proud of it. But I never saw that she got much pleasure out of it. Not as you took pleasure in her, real joy."

He was only twenty-seven. Leaning forward to toss her cigarette into the fire Harriet Avanti saw, through her shrewdly rambling thoughts and the press of various emotions, his face; and the rest dropped clear away. "I shouldn't think aloud," she said, "I didn't mean to hurt you."

"You don't. You can't." He turned his kind, somber young face to her, reassuring.

"But I do. You're sensitive, and I'm not. You're guilt-ridden, and I don't even know what guilt is."

But again she had touched a nerve; he frowned, and spoke: "No, I'm not guilt-ridden, Harriet. It wasn't my fault. It's not my fault that I survive. Only I don't see the point."

"The point!" She sat erect, moveless. "There is no point."

Staring at the fire he whispered, "I know."

They were silent a good while. Harriet thought of her daughter Mary, the beautiful dissatisfied child. "This is Edward, Mother." And the young man watching the girl with incredulous, delighted passion — oh, it had been he, alone, who had roused Harriet from her long drab grief after her husband's death, who had shown her once again, from the flat plain and barren land, the incredibly high peaks. He had reminded her that after all there is more in life than endurance. For unfortunately, as she knew, endurance was her native style. She would have endured right through life, steady and heavy as a rock, if she hadn't had the luck to meet and marry John Avanti, who taught her joy. He dead, she had fallen back at once upon endurance, and never would have known delight again if her daughter had not marched in one night with the tall radiant boy: "This is Edward, Mother."

"I don't think you do know," she said abruptly. "Pointlessness isn't your line. It's mine. I was intended to lead a pointless life, like my parents and my brothers. By some mistake I got into a highly rewarding life with a point to it. Just the sort of life you were intended for. And then you, of all people, meet up with this, with the drunk on the highway, with waste and senselessness, when you're only twenty-five. Another mistake, no doubt. But it's not essential, Edward. Mary's death is not going to be the essential event in your life. To accept it as essential, to accept pointlessness, would be — for you — an act of cowardice."

"Maybe," he said. "But the fact is, Harriet, that I, lately, that I seem to have about reached my limit."

She was frightened by his anguish, diffident as it was. She did not know much about anguish, only about misery, the endurable unending pain not the destroying one. She tried now to back away from the point of agony, saying, "Well, a limit's always a beginning. . . ." What she feared was his crying. Twice here in this room with her he had broken down and wept, once when he was first home from hospital after the wreck, then again months later. She dreaded his tears, the coping with pain at second hand. It shattered her to pity as to be pitied. When he got up suddenly from the low hearth seat she sat tense. But he said only, "I'd like another shot. You?" He took her glass and went off to the kitchen. As he went the clock behind her on the mantel struck twelve solemnly, taking a long time about it; and now it was November not October. They had lived another month. Here she sat by the fire, there was Edward opening cupboards in the kitchen, both of them warm and full of good bourbon; and then there was Mary, eighteen months dead. Was it because she was a hard woman that she had not really wept for her child's death? If she had died before John, I would have cried for her, Harriet thought.

Edward returned, sat down, stretched out his legs. "I have tried," he said with such serious equanimity that she lost all fear of his breaking down and waited to find out what he meant. He was candid but inarticulate, and his mind, trained to the rigors of chemistry, pursued logic into places where it does not exist. "I've honestly tried," he repeated, lapsed into silence, crossed his ankles, drank thoughtfully, and at last went on, "Technician in the medical department. Elinor Schneider. Fairly good-looking, blond, very intelligent. She's around my age." (Older, thought Harriet.) "Well, so . . ." Edward paused, raised his glass in self-mocking salute. "I tried."

"To?"

"To get interested."

Poor Elinor Schneider, lying awake now perhaps seeing in the dry darkness his face. Pain is self-centered. Harriet sighed a little. "I suppose a laboratory is the place for an experiment. . . ."

"Anyway, it was an effort to reconnect, whatever you want to call it. It didn't work. I can't do it. I don't want to do it. I know you think me weak."

"You? I certainly don't. And if I did, what then? You know yourself best."

"No, I don't, Harriet. You're really the first person who seems to know much about me. To judge me objectively. My parents . . ." He was the child of a divorce, passed back and forth from father and wife to mother and husband, a bone of contention. He let that go, but added, "And Mary and I were rather stupid about each other, in some ways."

"You were very young."

"We had no time," he said, so clear and quiet in his statement of the chance lost that Harriet sat still, outclassed, rejoicing in being outclassed.

"So," he said, pursuing logic, "in you I see the first clear reflection of myself. It looks weak."

"The mirror is old, it warps."

"No; you see people very justly."

"Do you really want to know how I see you?" she demanded, for he had poured her a strong drink and she wasn't used to a second nightcap. He did want to know. "As a bright and fortunate man," she said after seeking the words. "Fortunate, not

lucky. You haven't had much luck. And yet you've been fortunate. You got your freedom early, too early, but then a lot of
people never get it. You've known real passion, real fulfilment,
and no letdown. You never will know the letdown, the dead level. You got into manhood a free man, and you'll go on free,
or — " But the "or" had carried her too far. Had she been
younger, his equal, she could have finished the sentence, "or
you'll kill yourself." But between generations there should not
be talk of death. Of the dead, yes, of dying, yes, of your death,
no. Tabu, Harriet told herself, disgusted at her whole speech.
Edward however seemed pleased or intrigued; he brooded over it
a while. Then he said, "Another thing about Elinor, this girl at
the lab, she likes kids. I always think of Andy."

"Andy's got me, Edward, he'll survive, for mercy's sake.
Nobody's asking you to marry a nursemaid! God forbid!"

He looked relieved, but slowly, through the mists of weariness and whiskey, she perceived that Elinor had turned up
again.

"When I said you'd find that you couldn't withdraw,
couldn't disengage yourself, disconnect yourself, you know, I
was warning you. You're in a very vulnerable position. You
could get caught. I don't want to see you caught." As you were
by Mary, she thought; for she believed her daughter had married less for love than self-assertion, even envy. She knew in
Mary, under the dark soft vivacity and Italian grace, the hard
destructive strain from her side, the fecklessness, the pointless
yen that brought them all in the end to the County of Malheur.
She had never been able to weep much for Mary, she had never
been able to judge her; yet it was very bitter to think, as she had
thought before, that Mary's early death might prove a fortunate
thing for the man who loved her.

"You spoil me, Harriet," said the young man, gravely considering.

"Of course I do. But I don't spoil your son. I discriminate
between incorruptibility and mere innocence." She gave a short

laugh of pleasure at her own multisyllables. "I'm getting verbose, I'm going to bed. Good night."

"Good night," he answered reluctantly as she went to the stairs, so reluctantly he almost held her back. As if he need worry about "reconnecting." He had never, even in the worst of his pain, withdrawn himself, ceased to give to those who needed him. What he had left, the baby and the old woman, he loved with perfect generosity. And there was no denying that the three of them got on pretty happily. At least I'm a good stopgap, she thought with pride.

Since her husband's death four years ago she had not slept well at night. Half the dark hours she waked and read, and was up often before the baby started chirping. So she remembered her mother in old age, in the silent kitchen lit by a kerosene lamp, looking in silence out the window at the huge sky paling above the sagebrush plain. But this night Harriet slept at once, falling into a night-long trap of dreams. They kept coming and telling her that someone was dead, but would not tell her exactly who, or whether he was dying now or dead already; only once, in a summerhouse she had not known was in her garden, she found him lying huddled on the floor, one long arm thrown out, but that was only the empty sleeve of a grey suit. She ran away in terror into an older nightmare, fifty years older, of the blind thing that hunted her over the desert. At last sunlight broke down the walls and horizons of the dreams and woke her, yet it did not illuminate her fear. She denied that her anxiety had been for Edward, but she was rather grim with him at breakfast. All morning she housecleaned, making the baby play by himself, trying to work off that fear before her conscience made her accept it as a rational one.

The baby could not be indefinitely resisted. He was two. He looked like a little chimpanzee; the physical beauty of his parents, mixed, had got lost. His disposition was thoughtful and experimental. "Hat, Hat, Hat," he cried, staggering into the kitchen. "Mulk! Mulk!" — "Not till lunchtime," Harriet told him. He smiled, gazing up with wise eyes like a chimpanzee. "Mulk? Cacky? Appa?" — "Nothing till lunch, you greedy-gut," the grandmother said sternly. "Hat, Hat!" said the baby, madly embracing her leg.

He was a loving child, a very fine child. That afternoon she dropped housework and took him down the hill to the park, the rose garden full of the last roses, lemon-yellow, peach-yellow, gold, bronze, crimson, following him as he trotted and shouted along the paths between the thorny, fragrant bushes in the autumn sun.

Edward Meyer sat in his parked car looking across the lights of Berkeley and across the black, diamond-shackled bay to the Golden Gate, faint fragile center of the great sweep of lights and darknesses. Eucalyptus rustled over the car in a dry wind from the north, the winter wind. He stretched. "Damn," he said.

"Why?" said the woman beside him.

"What's in it for you?"

"All I want."

"Sorry," he muttered, and took her hands. When they touched they both quieted. Her grace was silence. He drank stillness from her as water from a spring. The dark dry wind of January blew, city after city flared below them round the bridge-strung bay.

He lit a cigarette; Elinor murmured, "Not fair." She had recently given up smoking for the fifth or sixth time. She was a woman not very sure of things, biddable and quiet, taking what came. Edward handed her the lighted cigarette. She took it with a small sigh and smoked it.

"This is the right idea," he said.

"For now."

"But why stop halfway?"

"We're not stopping. Only waiting."

"Waiting for what? Till my psyche's patched up, or you're

sure I'm not on the rebound, or something. Meanwhile we make love in my car because you've got a roommate and I've got a mother-in-law and we don't go to motels because we're supposed to be waiting — only we don't. The whole thing's illogical."

At this she suddenly gave a hard, dry sob. His nervous anger turned to alarm, but she drew away from him, refusing comfort. She had never refused him anything before. He tried to apologise, to explain. She said, "Please take me home," and all down the steep streets from Grizzly Peak to South Berkeley she sat silent, a silence turned against him, a defense. She was out of the car before he had it fully stopped in front of her rooming house; she whispered "Good night" and was gone. He sat in the car, blank, anxious, foolish. He started the engine, and with the noise of it his anger rose. When he got home ten minutes later he was very angry. Harriet, looking up from her book by the fireside, seemed startled. "Well!" she said. "Well," he said.

"Excuse me," said Harriet, "I'm finishing a chapter."

He sat down, stretched out his legs, stared at the fire. He was bitterly angry at Elinor's weak obstinacy, her irresolute, indecisive, temporising ways. There sat Harriet, thank God, like a rock, like an oak, finishing her chapter. If the house fell down in an earthquake around Harriet she would fix a bed for the baby, light a fire, and finish her chapter. No wonder Elinor hadn't married before this, there was nothing to her, she had no character. He sat there full of self-vindicating anger and warm with the perfect sexual satisfaction she had given him, ready for more anger, more passion, more fulfilment, and for the first time in two years happy. Harriet finished her chapter. "Nightcap?" he said.

"No, I'm going to bed." She stood up, erect, short, solid; he looked at her with admiration. "You look grand," he said.

"Pooh," she said, "whatever have you been up to? Good night, my dear."

She had a cold. She usually got a cold in April. It went into her chest so that she rumbled like a truck and ached and coughed; at last she got on the phone and asked old Joan to come out and look after Andy. When Edward got home and looked surprised, she snapped, "I'm not up to running after the child today." Then she went back to bed and lay cursing herself for having complained. One must never complain to men. Women at least knew complaint for what it was, part of coping, but he would interpret it, he would take it to mean that the full-time care of a child was too much to ask of a women of sixty-two; and then nothing she said or did would matter; he would have the idea in his head. And the child would be taken from her. Gradually or all at once she would lose him, the son she had always missed and to whom she was a wiser mother than she had been to her own two girls. The little monkey-face, the song at morning, the shirts to iron, the small automobiles and journals of chemistry left lying about, the presence by night and day of the son, of the man, of the man of the house gone, gone, all of it gone.

When he came in she did not turn her face to him. She lay grim, aching in the marrow of her bones.

"Well," he said, "Andy's spilled his milk and thrown his egg on the floor. Hear him yelling for Hat?" There were in fact loud, theatrical cries from below. "If you don't recover in a day or two we'll have to send him to reform school."

"I intend to recover tomorrow," she said, still grim, but lying easier. His kindness was exact: it hit the spot, carelessly it seemed, and healed.

"I detest being sick," she said after a while.

"I know. You aren't very good at it. Look here, I asked those people in Friday night, I'll put them off a week."

"Nonsense, I'll be up day after tomorrow. Is your friend the checkers player coming?"

Edward laughed. "Yes. He wants to be pulverised again." She had heard the young Philadelphian boast that he had never

lost a game of checkers since he was fifteen, had taken him on
and beat him six games running.

"I am a vengeful old woman, Edward," she said, lying
moveless, her short grey hair disordered.

"He doesn't care — he's trying to figure out your game."

"I don't like boasting." That was Malheur County that
spoke in her, the frontier without hope, the end of pushing on.
"We're all fools enough without adding that," she said, unyield-
ing, desolate.

"How about a drink before dinner?"

"Yes, I'd like a whiskey in hot water. But no dinner, I can't
eat with a cold. Bring me a hot toddy, and *Dombey and Son,*
would you? I was just starting it."

"How many times have you read it?"

"Why, I don't know. Every few years since I was twenty.
And put that poor baby to bed, Edward, he isn't used to Joan."

"She scares me too," he said.

"Well she might; you won't get round her with charm and
persuasion. I have an understanding with her," she went on,
driven by a sudden will she did not stop to understand, "that
when you and Andy move out she'll move in with me, if it still
suits her. She isn't doing any regular cleaning any more, and her
husband's dead and her son's in the Marines. And we've always
got on."

He stood silent, taken off guard. She looked up at him, the
tall figure that dominated all the house, vulnerable and kingly,
the young man.

"Don't look so stricken," she said with mild irony, "can't I
provide ahead for the winter? Now do go get my whiskey, Edward, my throat's like sandpaper."

To leave him free, that was her job. And she was good at
her job. That had been her fault as a mother of daughters, she
did not know if a girl should be left free or not, and so had
vacillated; Rose had come out a bit weak, and Mary spoilt. But

with a boy there was no question, he must have courage, and so needed freedom. Perhaps what a girl must have was patience, but she was not sure; in any case she was herself too impatient — not for pleasure and possession, like Mary, but for completion, for the end of things: unhopeful, and impatient.

She enjoyed her night and day in bed, entertained by Dickens, rain on the window, Joan in the kitchen singing long dreadful Methodist hymns. She rose much refreshed on Thursday, washed and ironed all the bedroom curtains, and weeded the iris beds in the fresh wind of April while the baby investigated all the possibilities of fresh wet dirt, and discovered the earthworm. On Friday night Edward's friends came: two married couples, Tom the checkers expert, whom she beat twice and once inadvertently let win, and a little fair woman called Elinor. Elinor, what had she heard, a while ago, about an Elinor? She was pleasant to look at, anyhow, with thick fair hair and a face as quiet as a pool of water. She was looking at Edward. Water in sunlight. O radiance, incredible brightness of the true sun, incredible heights.

"I'm never as good playing the red," Harriet said, an ungraceful loser. "But I'll leave you holding the field, Mr. Harris." And young Tom Harris, appalled at having beaten her, apologised in his Eastern voice till she had to laugh. He so plainly thought her a wonderful old woman, a daughter of the pioneers, if she told him she learned checkers from Chief Joseph he would probably believe it. But all the time her heart's eye was on Elinor.

No beauty. Timid, often defeated, getting on for thirty. Oh, yes, but patient; a patient woman: owning that passionate, intelligent patience that will wait, wait ten years, not for a lucky break but for the known, foreknown, fulfilment. One of the fortunate ones, who know that there is a point. It takes luck too, Harriet cried inwardly: you might have waited all your life, and let it all go by! — But this one was like Edward, one of the fortunate. They did not push on, they were not restless. They took what came, and when they spoke they were answered. They had seen the high peaks, and tragedy served them. Edward had met his match.

Harriet did not go upstairs before she had chatted a while with Elinor. Each felt the other's earnest effort to show good-will, to offer true friendliness; neither could quite accept; yet liking arose. Harriet went upstairs at ten feeling pleased with herself. In her dressing gown she crossed her room to look at the photograph of her husband, a vivid dark face, John Avanti at thirty, when she had first known him. Her heart rose as always to meet the challenge of him. He had changed her utterly, he lived therefore in her; she spoke to him. Well, John, I push on, she said, not aloud. She got into bed, finished *Dombey,* listened to the soft cheerful sound of voices downstairs, and fell asleep.

She woke in the grey light before sunrise and knew what she had lost. They would go now, within a year or so, the child and the man; all grace, all danger, all fulfilment, leaving her, as John dying had not left her, alone. She need not be impatient any longer. Even that wore out in the end. She had done right, she had done her job. But there was no point to it, for her. All she would need from now on was endurance. She was back down to bedrock, she had come in the end where all her people came. She sat up in bed, grey-haired in the grey light, and wept aloud.

The Water Is Wide

"You here?"

"To see you."

After a while he said, "Where's here?" He was lying flat, so could not have much in view but ceiling and the top third of Anna; in any case his eyes looked unfocussed.

"Hospital."

Another pause. He said something like, "Is it me that's here?" The words were slurred. He added clearly enough, "It's not you. You look all right."

"I am. You're here. And I'm here. To see you."

This made him smile. The smile of an adult lying flat on his back resembles the smile of an infant, in that gravity works with it, not against it.

"Can I be told," he said, "or will the knowledge kill me?"

"If knowledge could kill you, you'd have been dead for years."

"Am I sick?"

"Do you feel well?"

He turned his head away, the first bodily movement he had made. "I feel ill." The words were slurred. "Full of drugs, some

kind drugs." The head moved again, restless. "Don't like it," he
said. He looked straight at her now. "I don't feel well," he said.
"Anna, I'm cold. I feel cold." Tears filled the eyes and ran down
from them into the greying hair. This happens in cases of human suffering, when the sufferer is lying face up and is middle-
aged.

Anna said his name and took his hand. Her hand was somewhat smaller than his, several degrees warmer, and very similar
in structure and texture; even the shape of the nails was similar.
She held his hand. He held her hand. After some time his hand
began to relax.

"Kind drugs," he said. The eyes were shut now.

He spoke once more; he said either "Wait," or "Weight."
Anna answered the first, saying, "I will." Then she thought he
had spoken of a weight that lay upon him. She could see the
weight in the way he breathed, asleep.

"It's the drugs," she said, "he's asked every time if you
could stop giving him the drugs. Could you decrease the dose?"

The doctor said, "Chemotherapy," and other words, some
of which were the names of drugs, ending in zil and ine.

"He says that he can't sleep, but he can't wake up either. I
think he needs to sleep. And to wake up."

The doctor said many other words. He said them in so rapid, distinct, and fluent a manner, and with such assurance, that
Anna believed them all for at least three hours.

"Is this a loony bin?" Gideon inquired with perfect clarity.

"Mhm." Anna knitted.

"Thought wards."

"Oh, it's all private rooms here. It's a nice private sort of
place. Rest home. Polite. Expensive."

"Senile, incont . . . incontinent. Can't talk. Anna."

"Mhm?"

"Stroke?"

"No, no." She put her knitting down on her knee. "You got overtired."

"Tumor?"

"No. You're sound as a bell. Only a little cracked. You got tired. You acted funny."

"What'd I do?" he asked, his eyes brightening.

"Made an awful fool of yourself."

"Did?"

"Well, you washed all the blackboards. At the Institute. With soap and water."

"That all?"

"You said it was time to start all over. You made the Dean fetch the soap and buckets." They both jolted softly with laughter at the same time. "Never mind the rest. You had them all quite busy, believe me."

They all understood now that his much publicised New Year's Day letter to the *Times,* which he had defended with uncharacteristic vehemence, had been a symptom. This was a relief to many people, who had uncomfortably been thinking of the letter as a moral statement. Looking back, everyone at the Institute could now see that Gideon had not been himself for some months. Indeed the change could be traced back three years, to the death of his wife Dorothea of leukemia. He had borne his loss well, of course, but had he not remained somewhat withdrawn — increasingly withdrawn? Only no one had noticed it, because he had been so busy. He had ceased to take vacations at the family cabin up at the lake, and had done a good deal of public speaking in connection with the peace organisation of which he was co-chairman. He had been working much too hard. It was all clear now. Unfortunately it had not become clear until the evening in April when he began a public lecture on the Question of Ethics in Science by gazing at the audience in silence for 35 seconds (approx.: one of the mathematical philosophers present in the audience had begun to time the silence at the point when it became painful, though not yet unendurable), and then, in a slow, soft, rough voice which no one who heard it could forget, announced, "The quantification of Death is now the major problem facing theoretical physicists in the latter half of the Western Hemisphere." He had then closed his mouth and stood gazing at them.

Hansen, who had introduced his talk and sat on the speakers' platform, was a large man and a quick-witted one. He had without much trouble induced Gideon to come backstage with him, to one of the seminar rooms. It was there that Gideon had insisted that they wash all the blackboards perfectly clean. He had not become violent, though his behavior had been what Hansen termed "extraordinarily wilful." Later on, in private, Hansen wondered whether Gideon's behavior had not always been wilful, in that it had always been self-directed, and whether he should not have used, instead, the word "irrational." That would have been the expectable word. But its expectability led him to wonder if Gideon's behavior (as a theoretical physicist) had ever been rational; and, in fact, if his own behavior (as a theoretical physicist, or otherwise) had ever been adequately describable by the term "rational." He said nothing, however, of these speculations, and worked very hard for several weekends at building a rock garden at the side of his house.

Though he offered no violence to others or himself, Gideon had attempted escape. At a certain moment he appeared to understand suddenly that medical aid had been summoned. He acted with decision. He told the Dean, Dr. Hansen, Dr. Mehta, and the student Mr. Chew, all of whom were with him (several other members of the audience or of the Institute were busy keeping busybodies and reporters out), "You finish the blackboards in here, I'll do Room 40," and taking up a bucket and a sponge went rapidly across the hall into a vacant classroom, where Chew and Hansen, following him at once, prevented him from opening a window. The room was on the ground floor, and his intention was made clear by his saying, "Let me get out, please, help me get out." Chew and Hansen were compelled to restrain his arms by force. He struggled briefly to free himself; failing, he became silent and apparently thoughtful. Shortly before the medical personnel arrived he suggested in a low voice to Chew, "If we sat down on the floor here they might not see us." When the medical personnel entered the room and came close to him he said loudly, "All right, have it your way," and at once began to yell wordlessly, or scream. The graduate student Chew, a brilliant young biophysicist who had not had much experience of human suffering, let go of his arm and broke into tears. The medical personnel, having had perhaps excessive experience of human suffering, promptly administered a quick-acting sedative or tranquilliser by hypodermic. Within 35 seconds (approx.) the patient fell silent and became tractable, accepting the straitjacket without resistance, and with only a slight expression (facial, not verbal) of bewilderment, or, possibly, curiosity.

"I have to get out of here."

"Oh, Gid, not yet, you need to rest. It's a decent place. They've eased up on the drugs. I can see the difference."

"I have to get out, Anna."

"You're not well yet."

"I am not a patient. I am impatient. Help me get out. Please."

"Why, Gid? What for?"

"They won't let me go where I have to go."

"Where do you have to go?"

"Mad."

Dear Lin,

They continue to let me visit Gideon every afternoon from five to six, because I am his only relative, the widower's widowed sister, and I just sort of barge in. I don't think the doctor approves of my visits, I think he thinks I leave the patient disturbed, but he hasn't the authority to keep me out, I guess, until Gideon is committed. I guess he doesn't really have any authority, in a private rest home like this, but he makes me feel guilty. I never did understand when to obey people. He is supposed to be the best man here for nervous breakdowns. He has been disapproving lately and says Gideon is deteriorating, ceasing to respond, but all he gives him to respond to is drugs. What is he supposed to say to them? He hasn't eaten for four days. He responds to me, when nobody else is there, or anyhow he talks, and I respond. He asked me about you kids yesterday. I told him about Kate's divorce. It made him sad. "Everybody is divorcing everybody else," he said. I was sad too and I said, "Well, we didn't. You and Dorothea, me and Louis. Death us did part. Which is preferable, I wonder?" He said, "It comes out much the same. Fission, fusion. The human race is one great Nuclear Family." I wondered if the doctor would think that's the way an insane person talks. Maybe he would think that's the way two insane people talk.

Later on Gideon told me what the weight is. It is all the people who are dying. A lot of them are children, little, hollow, empty children. Some of them are old people, very light, hollow, old men and women. They don't weigh much separately, but there are so many of them. The old people lie across his legs. The children are in a great heap on his chest, across his breastbone. It makes it hard for him to breathe.

Today he only asked me to help him get out and go where he has to go. When he speaks of that he cries. I always hated for him to cry when we were children, it made me cry too, even when I was thirteen or fourteen. He only cried for real griefs. The doctor says that what he has is an acute depression, and it should be cured with chemicals. But Gideon is not depressed. I think what he has is grief. Why can't he be allowed to grieve? Would it destroy the rest of us, his grief? It's the people who don't grieve who are destroying us, it seems to me.

"Here's your clothes. You'll have to get up and get dressed, Gideon. If you want to come away with me. I didn't get permission. I just can't get through to that doctor, he wants to cure you. If you want to go, you'll have to get up and walk."

"Shall I take up my bed?"

"Don't be silly."

"Bible."

"For God's sake don't go religious now. If you do I'll bring you right back here. Hurry up. Here's your pants."

"Please get off me just for a minute," he said to the dying children and old men and women.

"Oof, how thin you are. Let me button that. All right. Can you manage? Hang on. No! hang onto me. You haven't been eating, you're dizzy."

"Dizzy Giddy."

"Do shut up! Try to look ordinary."

"We are ordinary."

They walked out of the room and down the hall arm in arm, an ordinary middle-aged couple. They walked past the old woman in the wheelchair nursing her doll, and past the room of the young man who stared. They walked past the receptionist's desk. Anna smiled and said in a peculiar voice at the receptionist, "Going out for a walk in the garden." The receptionist smiled and said, "Lovely weather." They walked out onto the brick front path of the rest home, and down it, between lawns, to the iron gate. They walked through the gate and turned left. Anna's car was parked halfway down the block, under elm trees.

"Oh, oh, if I have a heart attack it's all your fault. Wait. I'm so shaky I can't get the key in. You all right?"

"Sure. Where are we going?"

"To the lake."

"He went out with his sister, doctor. For a walk. About half an hour ago."

"A walk, my God," the doctor said. "Where to?"

I am Anna. I am Gideon. I am Gideanna. I am sister's

brother, brother's sister. I am Gideon who am dying, but it is your death I die, not mine. I am Anna who am not mad, but I am your brother, who is mad. Take my hand, brother, from the dark! Reich' mir das Hand, mein Leben, komm' in mein Schloss mit mir. O, but that castle I do not want to enter, brother mine; that is the castle I do not want to enter. It has a dark tower. Who do you think I am, Childe Roland? A Roland to your Oliver? No, look, we know this place, this is the old place, where we were children. Let's dance here, on the lakeshore, by the water. You be the tower, I will be the lake. You will dance in me reflected, I will be full of you, of the wave-broken shimmering stones. Lie lightly on me, tower, brother, see, if you lie lightly we are one. But we have always been one, sisterbrother. We have always danced alone. I am Gideon who dances in your soul, and I am dying. I can't dance any longer. I am borne down, borne down, borne down. I cannot lie, I cannot dance. All the reflections are dissolved. I cannot dance. I cannot breathe. They lie on me, they lie in me. How can the starving be so heavy, Anna?

Gideon, is it our fault? It can't be your fault. You never harmed a living soul.

But I am the fault, you know. The fault in my soul and yours, the fault itself. The line on which the ground moves. So the earthquake comes, and the people die, the little puzzled children, and the young men with guns, and the women pausing shopping bag in hand in the dissolving supermarket, and the old people who crouch down and reach out with wrinkled fingers to the faltering earth. I have betrayed them all. I did not give them enough food to eat.

How could you have? You're not God!

Oh yes I am. We are.

We are?

Yes, we are. Indeed we are. If I weren't God how should I be dying now? God is what dies. God is bereavement. We all die for each other.

If I am God I am the Woman-God, and I shall be reborn. Out of my own body I shall bear my birth.

Surely you will, but only if I die; and I am you. Or do you deny me, at the grave's edge, after fifty years?

No, no, no. I don't deny you, though I've often wanted to. But that's not a grave's edge, my young darkness, my terror, my little brother soul. It's only a lakeshore, see?

There is no other shore.

There must be.

No; all seas have one shore only. How could they have more?

Well, there's only one way to find out.

I'm cold. It's cold, the water's cold.

Look: there they are. So many of them, so many. The children float because they're hollow, swollen up with air. The older people swim, for a while. Look how that old man holds a clod of earth in his hand, the piece of the world he held to when the earthquake came. A little island, not quite big enough. Look how she holds her baby up above the water. I must help her, I must go to her!

If I touch one, they will take hold of me. They will clutch me with the grip of the drowning and drag me down with them. I'm not that good a swimmer. If I touch them, I'll drown.

Look there, I know that face. Isn't that Hansen? He's holding onto a rock, poor soul, a plank would serve him better.

There's Kate. There's Kate's ex-husband. And there's Lin. Lin's a good swimmer, always was, I'm not worried about Lin. But Kate's in trouble. She needs help. Kate! Don't wear yourself out, honey, don't kick so hard. The water's very wide. Save your strength, swim slowly, sweetheart, Kate my child!

There's young Chew. And look there, there's the doctor, in right over his head. And the receptionist. And the old woman with the doll. But there are so many more, so many. If I reach out my hand to one, a hundred will reach for it, a thousand, a thousand million, and pull me down and drown me. I can't save one child, one single child. I can't save myself.

Then let it be so. Take my hand, child! stranger in the darkness, in the deep waters, take my hand. Swim with me, while we can. Let us be drowned together, for it's certain we shall not be saved alone.

It's silent, out here in the deep waters. I can't see the faces any more.

Dorothea, there's someone following us. Don't look back.

I'm not Lot's wife, Louis, I'm Gideon's wife. I can look back, and still not turn to salt. Besides, my blood was never salt enough. It's you who shouldn't look back.

Do you take me for Orpheus? I was a good pianist, but not that good. But I admit, it scares me to look back. I don't really want to.

I just did. There's two of them. A woman and a man.

I was afraid of that.

Do you think it's them?

Who else would follow us?

Yes, it's them, our husband and our wife. Go back! Go back! This is no place for you!

This is the place for everyone, Dorothea.

Yes, but not yet, not yet. O Gideon, go back! He doesn't hear me. I can't speak clearly any more. Louis, you call to them.

Go back! Don't follow us! They can't hear us, Dorothea. Look how they come, as if the sand were water. Don't they know there's no water here?

I don't know what they know, Louis. I have forgotten. Gideon, O Gideon, take my hand!

Anna, take my hand!

Can they hear us? Can they touch us?

I don't know. I have forgotten.

It's cold, I'm cold. It's too deep, too far to go. I have

reached out my hand, and reached out my hand into the darkness, but I couldn't tell what good it did; if I held up some child for a while, or if some shadow hand reached back to me, I don't know. I can't tell the way. Back on the dry land they were right. They told me not to grieve. They told me not to look. They told me to forget. They told me eat my lunch and take my pills that end in zil and ine. And they were right. They told me to be quiet, not to shout, not to cry out aloud. Be quiet now, be good. And they were right. What's the good in shouting? What's the good in shouting Help me, help, I'm drowning! when all the rest of them are drowning too? I heard them crying Help me, help me, please. But now I hear nothing. I hear the sound of the deep waters only. O take my hand, my love, I'm cold, cold, cold.

> *The water is wide, I cannot get over,*
> *And neither have I wings to fly.*
> *Give me a boat that will carry two,*
> *And both shall row, my love and I.*

There is, oh, there is another shore! Look at the light, the light of morning on the rocks, the light on the shores of morning. I am light. The weight's gone. I am light.

But it is the same shore, Gideanna.

Then we have come home. We rowed all night in darkness, in the cold, and we came home: the home where we have never been before, the home we never left. Take my hand, and step ashore with me, my sister life, my brother death. Look: it is the beginning place. Here we begin, here by the flood that parts us.

South

The Wife's Story

HE WAS A good husband, a good father. I don't understand
it. I don't believe in it. I don't believe that it happened. I saw it
happen but it isn't true. It can't be. He was always gentle. If
you'd have seen him playing with the children, anybody who
saw him with the children would have known that there wasn't
any bad in him, not one mean bone. When I first met him he
was still living with his mother, over near Spring Lake, and I
used to see them together, the mother and the sons, and think
that any young fellow that was that nice with his family must be
one worth knowing. Then one time when I was walking in the
woods I met him by himself coming back from a hunting trip.
He hadn't got any game at all, not so much as a field mouse, but
he wasn't cast down about it. He was just larking along enjoying
the morning air. That's one of the things I first loved about him.
He didn't take things hard, he didn't grouch and whine when
things didn't go his way. So we got to talking that day. And I
guess things moved right along after that, because pretty soon
he was over here pretty near all the time. And my sister said —
see, my parents had moved out the year before and gone south,
leaving us the place — my sister said, kind of teasing but seri-

ous, "Well! If he's going to be here every day and half the night, I guess there isn't room for me!" And she moved out — just down the way. We've always been real close, her and me. That's the sort of thing doesn't ever change. I couldn't ever have got through this bad time without my sis.

Well, so he come to live here. And all I can say is, it was the happy year of my life. He was just purely good to me. A hard worker and never lazy, and so big and fine-looking. Everybody looked up to him, you know, young as he was. Lodge Meeting nights, more and more often they had him to lead the singing. He had such a beautiful voice, and he'd lead off strong, and the others following and joining in, high voices and low. It brings the shivers on me now to think of it, hearing it, nights when I'd stayed home from meeting when the children was babies — the singing coming up through the trees there, and the moonlight, summer nights, the full moon shining. I'll never hear anything so beautiful. I'll never know a joy like that again.

It was the moon, that's what they say. It's the moon's fault, and the blood. It was in his father's blood. I never knew his father, and now I wonder what become of him. He was from up Whitewater way, and had no kin around here. I always thought he went back there, but now I don't know. There was some talk about him, tales, that come out after what happened to my husband. It's something runs in the blood, they say, and it may never come out, but if it does, it's the change of the moon that does it. Always it happens in the dark of the moon. When everybody's home and asleep. Something comes over the one that's got the curse in his blood, they say, and he gets up because he can't sleep, and goes out into the glaring sun, and goes off all alone — drawn to find those like him.

And it may be so, because my husband would do that. I'd half rouse and say, "Where you going to?" and he'd say, "Oh, hunting, be back this evening," and it wasn't like him, even his voice was different. But I'd be so sleepy, and not wanting to wake the kids, and he was so good and responsible, it was no call

of mine to go asking "Why?" and "Where?" and all like that.

So it happened that way maybe three times or four. He'd come back late, and worn out, and pretty near cross for one so sweet-tempered — not wanting to talk about it. I figured everybody got to bust out now and then, and nagging never helped anything. But it did begin to worry me. Not so much that he went, but that he come back so tired and strange. Even, he smelled strange. It made my hair stand up on end. I could not endure it and I said, "What is that — those smells on you? All over you!" And he said, "I don't know," real short, and made like he was sleeping. But he went down when he thought I wasn't noticing, and washed and washed himself. But those smells stayed in his hair, and in our bed, for days.

And then the awful thing. I don't find it easy to tell about this. I want to cry when I have to bring it to my mind. Our youngest, the little one, my baby, she turned from her father. Just overnight. He come in and she got scared-looking, stiff, with her eyes wide, and then she begun to cry and try to hide behind me. She didn't yet talk plain but she was saying over and over, "Make it go away! Make it go away!"

The look in his eyes, just for one moment, when he heard that. That's what I don't want ever to remember. That's what I can't forget. The look in his eyes looking at his own child.

I said to the child, "Shame on you, what's got into you!" — scolding, but keeping her right up close to me at the same time, because I was frightened too. Frightened to shaking.

He looked away then and said something like, "Guess she just waked up dreaming," and passed it off that way. Or tried to. And so did I. And I got real mad with my baby when she kept on acting crazy scared of her own dad. But she couldn't help it and I couldn't change it.

He kept away that whole day. Because he knew, I guess. It was just beginning dark of the moon.

It was hot and close inside, and dark, and we'd all been asleep some while, when something woke me up. He wasn't there beside me. I heard a little stir in the passage, when I listened. So I got up, because I could bear it no longer. I went out into the passage, and it was light there, hard sunlight coming in from the door. And I saw him standing just outside, in the tall grass by the entrance. His head was hanging. Presently he sat down, like he felt weary, and looked down at his feet. I held still, inside, and watched — I didn't know what for.

And I saw what he saw. I saw the changing. In his feet, it was, first. They got long, each foot got longer, stretching out, the toes stretching out and the foot getting long, and fleshy, and white. And no hair on them.

The hair begun to come away all over his body. It was like his hair fried away in the sunlight and was gone. He was white all over, then, like a worm's skin. And he turned his face. It was changing while I looked. It got flatter and flatter, the mouth flat and wide, and the teeth grinning flat and dull, and the nose just a knob of flesh with nostril holes, and the ears gone, and the eyes gone blue — blue, with white rims around the blue — staring at me out of that flat, soft, white face.

He stood up then on two legs.

I saw him, I had to see him, my own dear love, turned into the hateful one.

I couldn't move, but as I crouched there in the passage staring out into the day I was trembling and shaking with a growl that burst out into a crazy, awful howling. A grief howl and a terror howl and a calling howl. And the others heard it, even sleeping, and woke up.

It stared and peered, that thing my husband had turned into, and shoved its face up to the entrance of our house. I was still bound by mortal fear, but behind me the children had waked up, and the baby was whimpering. The mother anger come into me then, and I snarled and crept forward.

The man thing looked around. It had no gun, like the ones from the man places do. But it picked up a heavy fallen tree branch in its long white foot, and shoved the end of that down

into our house, at me. I snapped the end of it in my teeth and started to force my way out, because I knew the man would kill our children if it could. But my sister was already coming. I saw her running at the man with her head low and her mane high and her eyes yellow as the winter sun. It turned on her and raised up that branch to hit her. But I come out of the doorway, mad with the mother anger, and the others all were coming answering my call, the whole pack gathering, there in that blind glare and heat of the sun at noon.

The man looked round at us and yelled out loud, and brandished the branch it held. Then it broke and ran, heading for the cleared fields and plowlands, down the mountainside. It ran, on two legs, leaping and weaving, and we followed it.

I was last, because love still bound the anger and the fear in me. I was running when I saw them pull it down. My sister's teeth were in its throat. I got there and it was dead. The others were drawing back from the kill, because of the taste of the blood, and the smell. The younger ones were cowering and some crying, and my sister rubbed her mouth against her forelegs over and over to get rid of the taste. I went up close because I thought if the thing was dead the spell, the curse must be done, and my husband could come back — alive, or even dead, if I could only see him, my true love, in his true form, beautiful. But only the dead man lay there white and bloody. We drew back and back from it, and turned and ran, back up into the hills, back to the woods of the shadows and the twilight and the blessed dark.

Some Approaches to the Problem of the Shortage of Time

The Little Tiny Hole Theory

THE HYPOTHESIS put forward by James Osbold of the Lick Observatory, though magnificently comprehensive, presents certain difficulties to agencies seeking practical solutions to the problem. Divested of its mathematical formulation, Dr. Osbold's theory may be described in very approximate terms as positing the existence of an anomaly in the space-time continuum. The cause of the anomaly is a failure of reality to meet the specifications of the General Theory of Relativity, although only in one minor detail. Its effect on the actual constitution of the universe is a local imperfection or flaw, that is, a hole in the continuum.

The hole, according to Osbold's calculations, is a distinctly spacelike hole. In this spatiality lies its danger, since the imbalance thus constituted in the continuum causes a compensatory influx from the timelike aspect of the cosmos. In other words, time is running out of the hole. This has probably been going on ever since the origin of the universe 12 to 15 billion years ago, but only lately has the leak grown to noticeable proportions.

The propounder of the theory is not pessimistic, remarking that it might be even worse if the anomaly were in the timelike aspect of the continuum, in which case space would be escaping, possibly one dimension at a time, which would cause untold discomfort and confusion; although, Osbold adds, "In that event we might have time enough to do something about it."

Since the theory posits the hole's location somewhere or other, Lick and two Australian observatories have arranged a coordinated search for local variations in the red shift which might aid in pinpointing the point/instant. "It may still be a very small hole," Osbold says. "Quite tiny. It would not need to be very large to do a good deal of damage. But since the effect is so noticeable here on Earth, I feel we have a good chance of finding the thing perhaps no farther away than the Andromeda Galaxy, and then all we'll need is what you might call a Dutch boy."

THE NONBIODEGRADABLE MOMENT

A totally different explanation of the time shortage is offered by a research team of the Interco Development Corporation. Their approach to the problem, as presented by N. T. Chaudhuri, an internationally recognised authority on the ecology and ethology of the internal combustion engine, is chemical rather than cosmological. Chaudhuri has proved that the fumes of incompletely burned petroleum fuel, under certain conditions — diffused anxiety is the major predisposing factor — will form a chemical bond with time, "tying down" instants in the same manner as a nucleating agent "ties down" free atoms into molecules. The process is called chronocrystallisation or (in the case of acute anxiety) chronoprecipitation. The resulting compact arrangement of instants is far more orderly than the preexistent random "nowness," but unfortunately this decrease in

entropy is paid for by a very marked increase in bioinsupporta-
bility. In fact the petroleum/time compound appears to be absolutely incompatible with life in any form, even anaerobic bacte-
ria, of which so much was hoped.

The present danger, then, as described by team member
F. Gonzales Park, is that so much of our free time, or radical
time properly speaking, will be locked into this noxious compound (which she refers to as petropsychotoxin or PPST) that
we will be forced to bring up the vast deposits of PPST which
the U.S. Government has dumped or stored in various caves,
swamps, holes, oceans, and back yards, and deliberately break
down the compound, thus releasing free temporal radicals. Sen-
ator Helms and several Sunbelt Democrats have already protest-
ed. Certainly the process of reclaiming time from PPST is risky,
requiring so much oxygen that we might end up, as O. Heiko, a
third member of the team, puts it, with plenty of free time but
no air.

Feeling that time is running out even faster than the oil
wells, Heiko himself favors an "austerity" approach to the problem, beginning with a ban on aircraft flying in excess of the
speed of sound, and working steadily on down through prop
planes, racing cars, standard cars, ships, motorboats, etc., until,
if necessary, all petroleum-powered vehicles have been eliminat-
ed. Speed serves as the standard of priority, since the higher the
velocity of the petroleum-fueled vehicle, and hence the more
concentrated the conscious or subliminal anxiety of the driver/
passengers, the more complete is the petrolisation of time, and
the more poisonous the resultant PPST. Heiko, believing there is
no "safe level" of contamination, thinks that probably not even
mopeds would eventually escape the ban. As he points out, a
single gas-powered lawnmower moving at less than 3 mph can
petrolise three solid hours of a Sunday afternoon in an area of
one city block.

A ban on gas guzzlers may, however, solve only half the
problem. An attempt by the Islamic League to raise the price of

crude time by $8.50/hr was recently foiled by prompt action by the Organisation of Time Consuming States; but West Germany is already paying $18.75/hr — twice what the American consumer expects to pay for his time.

Bleeding Hearts? The Temporal Conservation Movement

Willing to listen to the cosmological and chemical hypotheses but uncommitted to either is a growing consortium of scientists and laypersons, many of whom have grouped themselves into organisations such as Le Temps Perdu (Brussels), Protestants Concerned at the Waste of Time (Indianapolis), and the driving, widespread Latin-American action group Mañana. A Mañanista spokesperson, Dolores Guzman McIntosh of Buenos Aires, states the group's view: "We have — all of us — almost entirely wasted our time. If we do not save it, we are lost. There is not much time left." The Mañanistas have so far carefully avoided political affiliation, stating bluntly that the time shortfall is the fault of Communist and Capitalist governments equally. A growing number of priests from Mexico to Chile have joined the movement, but the Vatican recently issued an official denunciation of those "who, while they talk of saving time, lose their own souls." In Italy a Communist temporal-conservation group, Eppur Si Muove, was recently splintered by the defection of its president, who after a visit to Moscow stated in print: "Having watched the bureaucracy of the Soviet Union in action I have lost faith in the arousal of class consciousness as the principal means towards our goal."

A group of social scientists in Cambridge, England, continues meanwhile to investigate the as yet unproven link of the time shortage with shortage of temper. "If we could show the connection," says psychologist Derrick Groat, "the temporal conservation groups might be able to act more effectively. As it is they mostly quarrel. Everybody wants to save time before it's gone forever, but nobody really knows how, and so we all get cross. If only there were a substitute, you know, like solar and geothermal for petroleum, it would ease the strain. But evidently we have to make do with what we've got." Groat mentioned the "time stretcher" marketed by General Substances under the trademark Sudokron, withdrawn last year after tests indicated that moderate doses caused laboratory mice to turn into Kleenex. Informed that the Rand Corporation was devoting massive funding to research into a substitute for time, he said, "I wish them luck. But they may have to work longer hours at it!" The British scientist was referring to the fact that the United States has shortened the hour by ten minutes while retaining twenty-four per day, while the EEC countries, foreseeing increasing shortages, have chosen to keep sixty minutes to the hour but allow only twenty hours to the "devalued" European day.

Meantime, the average citizen in Moscow or Chicago, while often complaining about the shortage of time or the deteriorating quality of what remains, seems inclined to scoff at the doomsday prophets, and to put off such extreme measures as rationing as long as possible. Perhaps he feels, along with Ecclesiastes and the President, that when you've seen one day, you've seen 'em all.

Sur

A Summary Report of the *Yelcho* Expedition to the Antarctic, 1909–1910

ALTHOUGH I HAVE no intention of publishing this report, I think it would be nice if a grandchild of mine, or somebody's grandchild, happened to find it some day; so I shall keep it in the leather trunk in the attic, along with Rosita's christening dress and Juanito's silver rattle and my wedding shoes and finneskos.

The first requisite for mounting an expedition — money — is normally the hardest to come by. I grieve that even in a report destined for a trunk in the attic of a house in a very quiet suburb of Lima I dare not write the name of the generous benefactor, the great soul without whose unstinting liberality the *Yelcho* Expedition would never have been more than the idlest excursion into daydream. That our equipment was the best and most modern — that our provisions were plentiful and fine — that a ship of the Chilean Government, with her brave officers and gallant crew, was twice sent halfway round the world for

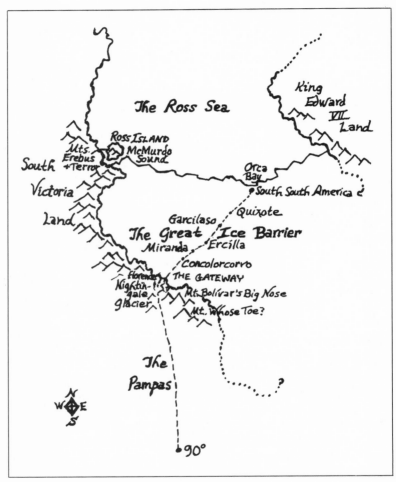

The Map in the Attic

our convenience: all this is due to that benefactor whose name, alas! I must not say, but whose happiest debtor I shall be till death.

When I was little more than a child my imagination was caught by a newspaper account of the voyage of the *Belgica*, which, sailing south from Tierra del Fuego, became beset by ice in the Bellingshausen Sea and drifted a whole year with the floe, the men aboard her suffering a great deal from want of food and from the terror of the unending winter darkness. I read and reread that account, and later followed with excitement the reports of the rescue of Dr. Nordenskjold from the South Shetland Isles by the dashing Captain Irizar of the *Uruguay*, and the adventures of the *Scotia* in the Weddell Sea. But all these exploits were to me but forerunners of the British National Antarctic Expedition of 1902–1904, in the *Discovery*, and the wonderful account of that expedition by Captain Scott. This book, which I ordered from London and reread a thousand times, filled me with longing to see with my own eyes that strange continent, last Thule of the South, which lies on our maps and globes like a white cloud, a void, fringed here and there with scraps of coastline, dubious capes, supposititious islands, headlands that may or may not be there: Antarctica. And the desire was as pure as the polar snows: to go, to see — no more, no less. I deeply respect the scientific accomplishments of Captain Scott's expedition, and have read with passionate interest the findings of physicists, meteorologists, biologists, etc.; but having had no training in any science, nor any opportunity for such training, my ignorance obliged me to forego any thought of adding to the body of scientific knowledge concerning Antarctica; and the same is true for all the members of my expedition. It seems a pity; but there was nothing we could do about it. Our goal was limited to observation and exploration. We hoped to go a little farther, perhaps, and see a little more; if not, simply to go and to see. A simple ambition, I think, and essentially a modest one.

Yet it would have remained less than an ambition, no more

than a longing, but for the support and encouragement of my
dear cousin and friend Juana ———— ———— . (I use no sur-
names, lest this report fall into strangers' hands at last, and em-
barrassment or unpleasant notoriety thus be brought upon un-
suspecting husbands, sons, etc.) I had lent Juana my copy of
The Voyage of the Discovery, and it was she who, as we strolled
beneath our parasols across the Plaza de Armas after Mass one
Sunday in 1908, said, "Well, if Captain Scott can do it, why
can't we?"

It was Juana who proposed that we write Carlota ———— in
Valparaiso. Through Carlota we met our benefactor, and so obtained our money, our ship, and even the plausible pretext of
going on retreat in a Bolivian convent, which some of us were
forced to employ (while the rest of us said we were going to
Paris for the winter season). And it was my Juana who in the
darkest moments remained resolute, unshaken in her determina-
tion to achieve our goal.

And there were dark moments, especially in the early
months of 1909 — times when I did not see how the Expedition
would ever become more than a quarter ton of pemmican gone
to waste and a lifelong regret. It was so very hard to gather our
expeditionary force together! So few of those we asked even
knew what we were talking about — so many thought we were
mad, or wicked, or both! And of those few who shared our folly,
still fewer were able, when it came to the point, to leave their
daily duties and commit themselves to a voyage of at least six
months, attended with not inconsiderable uncertainty and danger. An ailing parent; an anxious husband beset by business
cares; a child at home with only ignorant or incompetent servants to look after it: these are not responsibilities lightly to be
set aside. And those who wished to evade such claims were not
the companions we wanted in hard work, risk, and privation.

But since success crowned our efforts, why dwell on the
setbacks and delays, or the wretched contrivances and down-
right lies that we all had to employ? I look back with regret only

to those friends who wished to come with us but could not, by
any contrivance, get free — those we had to leave behind to a
life without danger, without uncertainty, without hope.

On the seventeenth of August, 1909, in Punta Arenas,
Chile, all the members of the Expedition met for the first time:
Juana and I, the two Peruvians; from Argentina, Zoe, Berta,
and Teresa; and our Chileans, Carlota and her friends Eva, Pepita, and Dolores. At the last moment I had received word that
Maria's husband, in Quito, was ill, and she must stay to nurse
him, so we were nine, not ten. Indeed, we had resigned ourselves
to being but eight, when, just as night fell, the indomitable Zoe
arrived in a tiny pirogue manned by Indians, her yacht having
sprung a leak just as it entered the Strait of Magellan.

That night before we sailed we began to get to know one
another; and we agreed, as we enjoyed our abominable supper in
the abominable seaport inn of Punta Arenas, that if a situation
arose of such urgent danger that one voice must be obeyed without present question, the unenviable honor of speaking with that
voice should fall first upon myself: if I were incapacitated, upon
Carlota: if she, then upon Berta. We three were then toasted as
"Supreme Inca," "La Araucana," and "The Third Mate,"
among a lot of laughter and cheering. As it came out, to my
very great pleasure and relief, my qualities as a "leader" were
never tested; the nine of us worked things out amongst us from
beginning to end without any orders being given by anybody,
and only two or three times with recourse to a vote by voice or
show of hands. To be sure, we argued a good deal. But then, we
had time to argue. And one way or another the arguments always ended up in a decision, upon which action could be taken.
Usually at least one person grumbled about the decision, sometimes bitterly. But what is life without grumbling, and the occa-
sional opportunity to say, "I told you so"? How could one bear
housework, or looking after babies, let alone the rigors of sledge-
hauling in Antarctica, without grumbling? Officers — as we
came to understand aboard the *Yelcho* — are forbidden to

grumble; but we nine were, and are, by birth and upbringing, unequivocally and irrevocably, all crew.

Though our shortest course to the southern continent, and that originally urged upon us by the captain of our good ship, was to the South Shetlands and the Bellingshausen Sea, or else by the South Orkneys into the Weddell Sea, we planned to sail west to the Ross Sea, which Captain Scott had explored and described, and from which the brave Ernest Shackleton had returned only the previous autumn. More was known about this region than any other portion of the coast of Antarctica, and though that more was not much, yet it served as some insurance of the safety of the ship, which we felt we had no right to imperil. Captain Pardo had fully agreed with us after studying the charts and our planned itinerary; and so it was westward that we took our course out of the Strait next morning.

Our journey half round the globe was attended by fortune. The little *Yelcho* steamed cheerily along through gale and gleam, climbing up and down those seas of the Southern Ocean that run unbroken round the world. Juana, who had fought bulls and the far more dangerous cows on her family's *estancia*, called the ship "*la vaca valiente*," because she always returned to the charge. Once we got over being seasick we all enjoyed the sea voyage, though oppressed at times by the kindly but officious protectiveness of the captain and his officers, who felt that we were only "safe" when huddled up in the three tiny cabins which they had chivalrously vacated for our use.

We saw our first iceberg much farther south than we had looked for it, and saluted it with Veuve Clicquot at dinner. The next day we entered the ice pack, the belt of floes and bergs, broken loose from the land ice and winter-frozen seas of Antarctica, which drifts northward in the spring. Fortune still smiled on us: our little steamer, incapable, with her unreinforced metal hull, of forcing a way into the ice, picked her way from lane to lane without hesitation, and on the third day we were through the pack, in which ships have sometimes struggled for weeks and been obliged to turn back at last. Ahead of us now lay the dark grey waters of the Ross Sea, and beyond that, on the horizon, the remote glimmer, the cloud-reflected whiteness of the Great Ice Barrier.

Entering the Ross Sea a little east of Longitude West 160°, we came in sight of the Barrier at the place where Captain Scott's party, finding a bight in the vast wall of ice, had gone ashore and sent up their hydrogen-gas balloon for reconnaissance and photography. The towering face of the Barrier, its sheer cliffs and azure and violet water-worn caves, all were as described, but the location had changed: instead of a narrow bight there was a considerable bay, full of the beautiful and terrific orca whales playing and spouting in the sunshine of that brilliant southern spring.

Evidently masses of ice many acres in extent had broken away from the Barrier (which — at least for most of its vast extent — does not rest on land but floats on water) since the *Discovery's* passage in 1902. This put our plan to set up camp on the Barrier itself in a new light; and while we were discussing alternatives, we asked Captain Pardo to take the ship west along the Barrier face towards Ross Island and McMurdo Sound. As the sea was clear of ice and quite calm, he was happy to do so, and, when we sighted the smoke plume of Mount Erebus, to share in our celebration — another half case of Veuve Clicquot.

The *Yelcho* anchored in Arrival Bay, and we went ashore in the ship's boat. I cannot describe my emotions when I set foot on the earth, on that earth, the barren, cold gravel at the foot of the long volcanic slope. I felt elation, impatience, gratitude, awe, familiarity. I felt that I was home at last. Eight Adélie penguins immediately came to greet us with many exclamations of interest not unmixed with disapproval. "Where on earth have you been? What took you so long? The Hut is around this way. Please come this way. Mind the rocks!" They insisted on our going to visit Hut Point, where the large structure built by Captain Scott's party stood, looking just as in the photographs and drawings that illustrate his book. The area about it, however, was disgusting — a kind of graveyard of seal skins, seal bones, penguin bones, and rubbish, presided over by the mad, screaming skua gulls. Our escorts waddled past the slaughterhouse in all tranquillity, and one showed me personally to the door, though it would not go in.

The interior of the hut was less offensive, but very dreary. Boxes of supplies had been stacked up into a kind of room within the room; it did not look as I had imagined it when the *Discovery* party put on their melodramas and minstrel shows in the long winter night. (Much later, we learned that Sir Ernest had rearranged it a good deal when he was there just a year before us.) It was dirty, and had about it a mean disorder. A pound tin of tea was standing open. Empty meat tins lay about; biscuits were spilled on the floor; a lot of dog turds were underfoot — frozen, of course, but not a great deal improved by that. No doubt the last occupants had had to leave in a hurry, perhaps even in a blizzard. All the same, they could have closed the tea tin. But housekeeping, the art of the infinite, is no game for amateurs.

Teresa proposed that we use the hut as our camp. Zoe counterproposed that we set fire to it. We finally shut the door and left it as we had found it. The penguins appeared to approve, and cheered us all the way to the boat.

McMurdo Sound was free of ice, and Captain Pardo now proposed to take us off Ross Island and across to Victoria Land, where we might camp at the foot of the Western Mountains, on dry and solid earth. But those mountains, with their storm-darkened peaks and hanging cirques and glaciers, looked as awful as Captain Scott had found them on his western journey, and none of us felt much inclined to seek shelter among them.

Aboard the ship that night we decided to go back and set up our base as we had originally planned, on the Barrier itself. For all available reports indicated that the clear way south was across the level Barrier surface until one could ascend one of the confluent glaciers to the high plateau which appears to form the whole interior of the continent. Captain Pardo argued strongly against this plan, asking what would become of us if the Barrier "calved" — if our particular acre of ice broke away and started to drift northward. "Well," said Zoe, "then you won't have to come so far to meet us." But he was so persuasive on this theme that he persuaded himself into leaving one of the *Yelcho*'s boats with us when we camped, as a means of escape. We found it useful for fishing, later on.

My first steps on Antarctic soil, my only visit to Ross Island, had not been pleasure unalloyed. I thought of the words of the English poet:

> *Though every prospect pleases,*
> *And only Man is vile.*

But then, the backside of heroism is often rather sad; women and servants know that. They know also that the heroism may be no less real for that. But achievement is smaller than men think. What is large is the sky, the earth, the sea, the soul. I looked back as the ship sailed east again that evening. We were well into September now, with ten hours or more of daylight. The spring sunset lingered on the twelve-thousand-foot peak of Erebus and shone rosy gold on her long plume of steam. The steam from our own small funnel faded blue on the twilit water as we crept along under the towering pale wall of ice.

On our return to "Orca Bay" — Sir Ernest, we learned years later, had named it the Bay of Whales — we found a sheltered nook where the Barrier edge was low enough to provide fairly easy access from the ship. The *Yelcho* put out her ice anchor, and the next long, hard days were spent in unloading our supplies and setting up our camp on the ice, a half kilometer in from the edge: a task in which the *Yelcho*'s crew lent us invaluable aid and interminable advice. We took all the aid gratefully, and most of the advice with salt.

The weather so far had been extraordinarily mild for spring

in this latitude; the temperature had not yet gone below −20° Fahrenheit, and there was only one blizzard while we were setting up camp. But Captain Scott had spoken feelingly of the bitter south winds on the Barrier, and we had planned accordingly. Exposed as our camp was to every wind, we built no rigid structures above ground. We set up tents to shelter in while we dug out a series of cubicles in the ice itself, lined them with hay insulation and pine boarding, and roofed them with canvas over bamboo poles, covered with snow for weight and insulation. The big central room was instantly named Buenos Aires by our Argentineans, to whom the center, wherever one is, is always Buenos Aires. The heating and cooking stove was in Buenos Aires. The storage tunnels and the privy (called Punta Arenas) got some back heat from the stove. The sleeping cubicles opened off Buenos Aires, and were very small, mere tubes into which one crawled feet first; they were lined deeply with hay and soon warmed by one's body warmth. The sailors called them "coffins" and "wormholes," and looked with horror on our burrows in the ice. But our little warren or prairie-dog village served us well, permitting us as much warmth and privacy as one could reasonably expect under the circumstances. If the *Yelcho* was unable to get through the ice in February, and we had to spend the winter in Antarctica, we certainly could do so, though on very limited rations. For this coming summer, our base — Sudamérica del Sur, South South America, but we generally called it the Base — was intended merely as a place to sleep, to store our provisions, and to give shelter from blizzards.

To Berta and Eva, however, it was more than that. They were its chief architect-designers, its most ingenious builder-excavators, and its most diligent and contented occupants, forever inventing an improvement in ventilation, or learning how to make skylights, or revealing to us a new addition to our suite of rooms, dug in the living ice. It was thanks to them that our stores were stowed so handily, that our stove drew and heated so efficiently, and that Buenos Aires, where nine people cooked, ate, worked, conversed, argued, grumbled, painted, played the guitar and banjo, and kept the Expedition's library of books and maps, was a marvel of comfort and convenience. We lived there in real amity; and if you simply had to be alone for a while, you crawled into your sleeping hole head first.

Berta went a little farther. When she had done all she could to make South South America livable, she dug out one more cell just under the ice surface, leaving a nearly transparent sheet of ice like a greenhouse roof; and there, alone, she worked at sculptures. They were beautiful forms, some like a blending of the reclining human figure with the subtle curves and volumes of the Weddell seal, others like the fantastic shapes of ice cornices and ice caves. Perhaps they are there still, under the snow, in the bubble in the Great Barrier. There where she made them they might last as long as stone. But she could not bring them north. That is the penalty for carving in water.

Captain Pardo was reluctant to leave us, but his orders did not permit him to hang about the Ross Sea indefinitely, and so at last, with many earnest injunctions to us to stay put — make no journeys — take no risks — beware of frostbite — don't use edge tools — look out for cracks in the ice — and a heart-felt promise to return to Orca Bay on the twentieth of February, or as near that date as wind and ice would permit, the good man bade us farewell, and his crew shouted us a great goodbye cheer as they weighed anchor. That evening, in the long orange twilight of October, we saw the topmast of the *Yelcho* go down the north horizon, over the edge of the world, leaving us to ice, and silence, and the Pole.

That night we began to plan the Southern Journey.

The ensuing month passed in short practice trips and depot-laying. The life we had led at home, though in its own way strenuous, had not fitted any of us for the kind of strain met with in sledge-hauling at ten or twenty degrees below freezing. We all needed as much working-out as possible before we dared undertake a long haul.

My longest exploratory trip, made with Dolores and Carlota, was southwest towards Mount Markham, and it was a nightmare — blizzards and pressure ice all the way out, crevasses and no view of the mountains when we got there, and white weather and sastrugi all the way back. The trip was useful, however, in that we could begin to estimate our capacities; and also in that we had started out with a very heavy load of provisions, which we depoted at 100 and 130 miles SSW of Base. Thereafter other parties pushed on farther, till we had a line of snow cairns and depots right down to Latitude 83° 43', where Juana and Zoe, on an exploring trip, had found a kind of stone gateway opening on a great glacier leading south. We established these depots to avoid, if possible, the hunger that had bedevilled Captain Scott's Southern Party, and the consequent misery and weakness. And we also established to our own satisfaction — intense satisfaction — that we were sledgehaulers at least as good as Captain Scott's husky dogs. Of course we could not have expected to pull as much or as fast as his men. That we did so was because we were favored by much better weather than Captain Scott's party ever met on the Barrier; and also the quantity and quality of our food made a very considerable difference. I am sure that the fifteen percent of dried fruits in our pemmican helped prevent scurvy; and the potatoes, frozen and dried according to an ancient Andean Indian method, were very nourishing yet very light and compact — perfect sledging rations. In any case, it was with considerable confidence in our capacities that we made ready at last for the Southern Journey.

The Southern Party consisted of two sledge teams: Juana, Dolores, and myself; Carlota, Pepita, and Zoe. The support team of Berta, Eva, and Teresa set out before us with a heavy load of supplies, going right up onto the glacier to prospect routes and leave depots of supplies for our return journey. We followed five days behind them, and met them returning between Depot Ercilla and Depot Miranda (see map). That "night" — of course there was no real darkness — we were all

nine together in the heart of the level plain of ice. It was the
fifteenth of November, Dolores's birthday. We celebrated by
putting eight ounces of pisco in the hot chocolate, and became
very merry. We sang. It is strange now to remember how thin
our voices sounded in that great silence. It was overcast, white
weather, without shadows and without visible horizon or any
feature to break the level; there was nothing to see at all. We
had come to that white place on the map, that void, and there
we flew and sang like sparrows.

After sleep and a good breakfast the Base Party continued
north, and the Southern Party sledged on. The sky cleared presently. High up, thin clouds passed over very rapidly from southwest to northeast, but down on the Barrier it was calm and just
cold enough, five or ten degrees below freezing, to give a firm
surface for hauling.

On the level ice we never pulled less than eleven miles, sev-
enteen kilometers, a day, and generally fifteen or sixteen miles,
twenty-five kilometers. (Our instruments, being British made,
were calibrated in feet, miles, degrees Fahrenheit, etc., but we
often converted miles to kilometers because the larger numbers
sounded more encouraging.) At the time we left South America,
we knew only that Mr. Shackleton had mounted another expedition to the Antarctic in 1908, had tried to attain the Pole but
failed, and had returned to England in June of the current year,
1909. No coherent report of his explorations had yet reached
South America when we left; we did not know what route he
had gone, or how far he had got. But we were not altogether
taken by surprise when, far across the featureless white plain,
tiny beneath the mountain peaks and the strange silent flight of
the rainbow-fringed cloud wisps, we saw a fluttering dot of
black. We turned west from our course to visit it: a snow heap
nearly buried by the winter's storms — a flag on a bamboo
pole, a mere shred of threadbare cloth — an empty oilcan —
and a few footprints standing some inches above the ice. In some
conditions of weather the snow compressed under one's weight

remains when the surrounding soft snow melts or is scoured away by the wind; and so these reversed footprints had been left standing all these months, like rows of cobbler's lasts — a queer sight.

We met no other such traces on our way. In general I believe our course was somewhat east of Mr. Shackleton's. Juana, our surveyor, had trained herself well and was faithful and methodical in her sightings and readings, but our equipment was minimal — a theodolite on tripod legs, a sextant with artificial horizon, two compasses, and chronometers. We had only the wheel meter on the sledge to give distance actually travelled.

In any case, it was the day after passing Mr. Shackleton's waymark that I first saw clearly the great glacier among the mountains to the southwest, which was to give us a pathway from the sea level of the Barrier up to the altiplano, ten thousand feet above. The approach was magnificent: a gateway formed by immense vertical domes and pillars of rock. Zoe and Juana had called the vast ice river that flowed through that gateway the Florence Nightingale Glacier, wishing to honor the British, who had been the inspiration and guide of our expedition; that very brave and very peculiar lady seemed to represent so much that is best, and strangest, in the island race. On maps, of course, this glacier bears the name Mr. Shackleton gave it, the Beardmore.

The ascent of the Nightingale was not easy. The way was open at first, and well marked by our support party, but after some days we came among terrible crevasses, a maze of hidden cracks, from a foot to thirty feet wide and from thirty to a thousand feet deep. Step by step we went, and step by step, and the way always upward now. We were fifteen days on the glacier. At first the weather was hot, up to 20° F., and the hot nights without darkness were wretchedly uncomfortable in our small tents. And all of us suffered more or less from snowblindness just at the time when we wanted clear eyesight to pick our way among the ridges and crevasses of the tortured ice, and to see the wonders about and before us. For at every day's advance more great, nameless peaks came into view in the west and southwest, summit beyond summit, range beyond range, stark rock and snow in the unending noon.

We gave names to these peaks, not very seriously, since we did not expect our discoveries to come to the attention of geographers. Zoe had a gift for naming, and it is thanks to her that certain sketch maps in various suburban South American attics bear such curious features as "Bolívar's Big Nose," "I Am General Rosas," "The Cloudmaker," "Whose Toe?" and "Throne of Our Lady of the Southern Cross." And when at last we got up onto the altiplano, the great interior plateau, it was Zoe who called it the pampa, and maintained that we walked there among vast herds of invisible cattle, transparent cattle pastured on the spindrift snow, their gauchos the restless, merciless winds. We were by then all a little crazy with exhaustion and the great altitude — twelve thousand feet — and the cold and the wind blowing and the luminous circles and crosses surrounding the suns, for often there were three or four suns in the sky, up there.

That is not a place where people have any business to be. We should have turned back; but since we had worked so hard to get there, it seemed that we should go on, at least for a while.

A blizzard came with very low temperatures, so we had to stay in the tents, in our sleeping bags, for thirty hours, a rest we all needed; though it was warmth we needed most, and there was no warmth on that terrible plain anywhere at all but in our veins. We huddled close together all that time. The ice we lay on is two miles thick.

It cleared suddenly and became, for the plateau, good weather: twelve below zero and the wind not very strong. We three crawled out of our tent and met the others crawling out of theirs. Carlota told us then that her group wished to turn back. Pepita had been feeling very ill; even after the rest during the blizzard, her temperature would not rise above 94°. Carlota was

having trouble breathing. Zoe was perfectly fit, but much preferred staying with her friends and lending them a hand in difficulties to pushing on towards the Pole. So we put the four
ounces of pisco which we had been keeping for Christmas into
the breakfast cocoa, and dug out our tents, and loaded our
sledges, and parted there in the white daylight on the bitter
plain.

Our sledge was fairly light by now. We pulled on to the
south. Juana calculated our position daily. On the twenty-second
of December, 1909, we reached the South Pole. The weather
was, as always, very cruel. Nothing of any kind marked the
dreary whiteness. We discussed leaving some kind of mark or
monument, a snow cairn, a tent pole and flag; but there seemed
no particular reason to do so. Anything we could do, anything
we were, was insignificant, in that awful place. We put up the
tent for shelter for an hour and made a cup of tea, and then
struck "90° Camp." Dolores, standing patient as ever in her
sledging harness, looked at the snow; it was so hard frozen that
it showed no trace of our footprints coming, and she said,
"Which way?"

"North," said Juana.

It was a joke, because at that particular place there is no
other direction. But we did not laugh. Our lips were cracked
with frostbite and hurt too much to let us laugh. So we started
back, and the wind at our backs pushed us along, and dulled the
knife edges of the waves of frozen snow.

All that week the blizzard wind pursued us like a pack of
mad dogs. I cannot describe it. I wished we had not gone to the
Pole. I think I wish it even now. But I was glad even then that
we had left no sign there, for some man longing to be first might
come some day, and find it, and know then what a fool he had
been, and break his heart.

We talked, when we could talk, of catching up to Carlota's
party, since they might be going slower than we. In fact they
had used their tent as a sail to catch the following wind and had

got far ahead of us. But in many places they had built snow cairns or left some sign for us; once Zoe had written on the lee side of a ten-foot sastrugi, just as children write on the sand of the beach at Miraflores, "This Way Out!" The wind blowing over the frozen ridge had left the words perfectly distinct.

In the very hour that we began to descend the glacier, the weather turned warmer, and the mad dogs were left to howl forever tethered to the Pole. The distance that had taken us fifteen days going up we covered in only eight days going down. But the good weather that had aided us descending the Nightingale became a curse down on the Barrier ice, where we had looked forward to a kind of royal progress from depot to depot, eating our fill and taking our time for the last three hundred-odd miles. In a tight place on the glacier I lost my goggles — I was swinging from my harness at the time in a crevasse — and then Juana had broken hers when we had to do some rock climbing coming down to the Gateway. After two days in bright sunlight with only one pair of snow goggles to pass amongst us, we were all suffering badly from snowblindness. It became acutely painful to keep lookout for landmarks or depot flags, to take sightings, even to study the compass, which had to be laid down on the snow to steady the needle. At Concolorcorvo Depot, where there was a particularly good supply of food and fuel, we gave up, crawled into our sleeping bags with bandaged eyes, and slowly boiled alive like lobsters in the tent exposed to the relentless sun. The voices of Berta and Zoe were the sweetest sound I ever heard. A little concerned about us, they had skied south to meet us. They led us home to Base.

We recovered quite swiftly, but the altiplano left its mark. When she was very little, Rosita asked if a dog "had bitted Mama's toes." I told her Yes, a great, white, mad dog named Blizzard! My Rosita and my Juanito heard many stories when they were little, about that fearful dog and how it howled, and the transparent cattle of the invisible gauchos, and a river of ice eight thousand feet high called Nightingale, and how Cousin

Juana drank a cup of tea standing on the bottom of the world under seven suns, and other fairy tales.

We were in for one severe shock when we reached Base at last. Teresa was pregnant. I must admit that my first response to the poor girl's big belly and sheepish look was anger — rage — fury. That one of us should have concealed anything, and such a thing, from the others! But Teresa had done nothing of the sort. Only those who had concealed from her what she most needed to know were to blame. Brought up by servants, with four years' schooling in a convent, and married at sixteen, the poor girl was still so ignorant at twenty years of age that she had thought it was "the cold weather" that made her miss her periods. Even this was not entirely stupid, for all of us on the Southern Journey had seen our periods change or stop altogether as we experienced increasing cold, hunger, and fatigue. Teresa's appetite had begun to draw general attention; and then she had begun, as she said pathetically, "to get fat." The others were worried at the thought of all the sledge-hauling she had done, but she flourished, and the only problem was her positively insatiable appetite. As well as could be determined from her shy references to her last night on the hacienda with her husband, the baby was due at just about the same time as the *Yelcho,* the twentieth of February. But we had not been back from the Southern Journey two weeks when, on February 14, she went into labor.

Several of us had borne children and had helped with deliveries, and anyhow most of what needs to be done is fairly self-evident; but a first labor can be long and trying, and we were all anxious, while Teresa was frightened out of her wits. She kept calling for her José till she was as hoarse as a skua. Zoe lost all patience at last and said, "By God, Teresa, if you say 'José!' once more I hope you have a penguin!" But what she had, after twenty long hours, was a pretty little red-faced girl.

Many were the suggestions for that child's name from her eight proud midwife-aunts: Polita, Penguina, McMurdo, Victoria. . . . But Teresa announced, after she had had a good sleep and a large serving of pemmican, "I shall name her Rosa — Rosa del Sur," Rose of the South. That night we drank the last two bottles of Veuve Clicquot (having finished the pisco at 88° 30' South) in toasts to our little Rose.

On the nineteenth of February, a day early, my Juana came down into Buenos Aires in a hurry. "The ship," she said, "the ship has come," and she burst into tears — she who had never wept in all our weeks of pain and weariness on the long haul.

Of the return voyage there is nothing to tell. We came back safe.

In 1912 all the world learned that the brave Norwegian Amundsen had reached the South Pole; and then, much later, came the accounts of how Captain Scott and his men had come there after him, but did not come home again.

Just this year, Juana and I wrote to the captain of the *Yelcho,* for the newspapers have been full of the story of his gallant dash to rescue Sir Ernest Shackleton's men from Elephant Island, and we wished to congratulate him, and once more to thank him. Never one word has he breathed of our secret. He is a man of honor, Luis Pardo.

I add this last note in 1929. Over the years we have lost touch with one another. It is very difficult for women to meet, when they live so far apart as we do. Since Juana died, I have seen none of my old sledge-mates, though sometimes we write. Our little Rosa del Sur died of the scarlet fever when she was five years old. Teresa had many other children. Carlota took the veil in Santiago ten years ago. We are old women now, with old husbands, and grown children, and grandchildren who might some day like to read about the Expedition. Even if they are rather ashamed of having such a crazy grandmother, they may enjoy sharing in the secret. But they must not let Mr. Amundsen know! He would be terribly embarrassed and disappointed. There is no need for him or anyone else outside the family to know. We left no footprints, even.

Acknowledgments

"The Author of the Acacia Seeds" first appeared in *Fellowship of the Stars*, edited by Terry Carr (Simon & Schuster, Inc.), 1974. "The New Atlantis" first appeared in *The New Atlantis*, edited by Robert Silverberg (Hawthorn Books, Inc.), 1975. "Schrödinger's Cat" first appeared in *Universe 5* edited by Terry Carr (Random House, Inc.), 1974. "Two Delays on the Northern Line" first appeared in *The New Yorker*, 1979. "SQ" first appeared in *Cassandra Rising*, edited by Alice Laurance (Doubleday & Company, Inc.), 1978. "Small Change" first appeared in *Tor zu den Sternen*, edited by Peter Wilfert (Goldmann Verlag), 1981. "The First Report of the Shipwrecked Foreigner" first appeared in *Antaeus*, 1978. "The Diary of the Rose" first appeared in *Future Power*, edited by Gardner Dozois and Jack Dann (Random House, Inc.), 1976. "The White Donkey" first appeared in *TriQuarterly*, 1980. "The Phoenix" appears for the first time in this volume. "Intracom" first appeared in *Stopwatch*, edited by George Hay (New English Library), 1974. "The Eye Altering" first appeared in *The Altered I*, edited by Lee Harding (Norstrilia Press), 1974. "Mazes" first appeared in *Epoch*, edited by Roger Elwood and Robert Silverberg (Berkeley Publishing Corporation), 1975. "The Pathways of Desire" first appeared in *New Dimensions Science Fiction, Number 9*, edited by Robert Silverberg (Harper & Row, Publishing, Inc.), 1979. "Gwilan's Harp" first appeared in *Redbook*, 1977. "Malheur County" first appeared in *Kenyon Review*, 1979. "The Water Is Wide" first appeared as a chapbook published by Pendragon Press, 1976. "The Wife's Story" appears for the first time in this volume. "Some Approaches to the Problem of the Shortage of Time" first appeared under the title "Where Does the Time Go?" in *Omni*, 1979. "Sur" first appeared in *The New Yorker*, 1982.